PLAY NICE

PLAY NICE

MICHAEL GUILLEBEAU

FIVE STAR
A part of Gale, Cengage Learning

GALE
CENGAGE Learning·

Farmington Hills, Mich • San Francisco • New York • Waterville, Maine
Meriden, Conn • Mason, Ohio • Chicago

LIBRARY OF CONGRESS CATALOGING-IN-PUBLICATION DATA

Names: Guillebeau, Michael, author.
Title: Play nice / Michael Guillebeau.
Description: First Edition. | Waterville, Maine : Five Star, a part of Cengage Learning, Inc. 2016.
Identifiers: LCCN 2016001559| ISBN 9781432831660 (hardback) | ISBN 1432831666 (hardcover) | ISBN 9781432831639 (ebook) | ISBN 1432831631 (ebook)
Subjects: | BISAC: FICTION / Mystery & Detective / General. | GSAFD: Suspense fiction | Mystery fiction
Classification: LCC PS3607.U4853 P58 2016 | DDC 813/.6—dc23
LC record available at http://lccn.loc.gov/2016001559

First Edition. First Printing: June 2016
Find us on Facebook– https://www.facebook.com/FiveStarCengage
Visit our website– http://www.gale.cengage.com/fivestar/
Contact Five Star™ Publishing at FiveStar@cengage.com

Printed in the United States of America
1 2 3 4 5 6 7 20 19 18 17 16

We tend to take advantage of women in our society, and maybe in our world. And then we cripple them by demanding that they play nice. This book is dedicated to the women who fight back, and particularly to the ones who find ways to fight back and win while still holding on to the best of themselves.

ACKNOWLEDGMENTS

This book has been helped along by so many people that I can hardly name them all. Jeremy Bronaugh and Cheryl Rydbom, particularly, have hung in through many drafts and a lot of soul searching. Thank you both so very much.

And, of course, the magic folks at Five Star deserve as much credit as the writers who are lucky enough to work with them. Deni Dietz, Tiffany Schofield, and Gordon Aalborg have supported me through three books now, and I hope to work with them for many more.

Last, and most important, as always, is Pat Leary Guillebeau. Stephen King once credited the longevity of his writing career, partly, to staying married. I think he missed the part about marrying the right person: Someone who gives you both support and inspiration. If I ever need a model for a character who's tough and beautiful, funny and sexy, all I have to do is look across the living room. I look across the room a lot.

CHAPTER 1

Detective Stevens leaned across the empty metal table into Cassie's face, and the table groaned under his weight. Cassie's nose burned from the bleach in the Jericho Police Department interrogation room and she could feel the sweat starting to crawl down her back.

"Three strikes, Cassie. You're not very good at this." He ground every word into her face. "This time, it's going to get ugly."

Stevens was sloppy-big and intimidating and ugly himself and comfortable with all of it. Cassie planted her elbows into the table like two spears and leaned into Stevens, their faces an angry inch apart, her tangled blonde hair hanging into his face, determined to show him she was as big and as bad as he was. Between them, the battered metal table cowered like a tiny prop from an elementary-school play.

"You think I can't handle ugly? Particularly, your kind of ugly?"

He opened his mouth and tried to say something but she talked over him.

"Trust me. I can handle all the ugly you can bring."

She kept her face hard but inside she said, *Shit, girl. Don't piss off the monsters.* She knew she had a mouth, worked hard to control it, but without much luck.

Stevens leaned back and laughed and Cassie relaxed a little

and leaned back herself, opening up breathing room between them.

Stevens said, "That attitude used to work for you, didn't it? Back when you were on top of the world? Six-foot-two WNBA player and sometime model? Not so much now that you're a piss-poor drug dealer looking at her third strike." He paused and let that sink in. "But I'm about to give you a chance to do something you might be good at. You need my help."

Cassie put on a big theatrical smile and twanged up her southern accent. "I have always relied on the kindness of strangers, sir. And, I'd like to thank all the kind strangers: Jericho Police Department for ruining my life with trumped-up charges, Detective Stevens who seems to think he's the director of my life . . ." Then she snorted, "Only thing I need from JPD is to leave me alone and let me get on with my real life."

Stevens raised his eyebrows and picked up the paper on his left.

"You want JPD to leave you alone with your real life of selling drugs? Let's look at these trumped-up charges. First drug bust, they let you off light because you were a golden girl. Judge remembered you from your glory days as an All-American basketballer at Jericho University here, saw you on TV playing in the WNBA."

Stevens waited for Cassie to argue but she didn't.

He said, "And because you said you didn't put that bag of drugs in that trash can at the airport, coming back to the Jericho from LA."

She leaned back in at him. "I didn't."

"So you were innocent?"

She looked away.

"But they kept the conviction on the books just the same," Stevens said. "Fired you from your WNBA gig in LA, took away the modeling contracts. Put that ugly red scar down the left side of your face when you tried to escape and left you with nowhere to go but back home here. Dropped you back into your old hometown full of ogres like me."

He waited and Cassie said nothing.

"Second time, I caught you selling," he said. "No doubt about that one. You got probation again, but still a conviction."

Cassie said, "You ever try to get an honest job after a drug conviction? I've got qualifications, but no company in town will touch me. You know I've got to make money."

She slumped down in the chair. "Why the hell are we doing this? I don't need a goddamned history lesson."

Stevens ignored her. "Huh," he said. He read something on the sheet twice. "Pee tests all negative. Never used your own stuff."

He waited for her to talk and got nothing.

He smiled a full, toothy, now-I've-got-you smile at her. "But now, a third time arrest for dealing means you go away for a long time. You've never been to prison yet, have you? See how tough a sweet, middle-class, white girl like you will be there, people lining up to kick the shit out of you just for fun."

They sat there in silence while he waited on her.

He gave up. "And you said it yourself: You need to be out on the street making money."

Cassie pulled her hands away from the metal table and hoped Stevens didn't see the sweat trail she left behind. She forced a cold smile to match his and tried to keep her voice calm.

"Bet there's something you need from me that can make all this go away."

"Don't know how you could think we work that way here. This ain't no pawn shop." He paused and his smile grew. " 'Course, while I'm deciding exactly what charges to file on your ass, I could tell you a story."

"I love stories."

Stevens leaned back and laced his hands on top of his mountain of a stomach.

"The CEO of QBot, company that makes those little quad-helicopter drones for the Army and Homeland, got killed last night, axed to death in his own home. The guy that did it was found passed out from drugs. Lying there, right on top of his victim."

"Sounds like an easy case," Cassie said. "Even you ought to be able to close this one. Legitimately."

"We do everything legitimately here. But city hall wants this closed fast, with no complications."

Cassie laughed. "Sounds like just the kind of story city hall likes: another case of a poor man killing a rich man for no good reason other than drugs. Run it on the news twice, the city fathers will take even more cops out of the poor neighborhoods and put them in fancy neighborhoods to protect the rich from the unwashed masses. That's Jericho, these days."

Stevens smiled, a real smile this time. "You got a cynical streak, you know it?"

Cassie said, "And JPD's starting to use some of those drones to monitor intersections and write tickets. If I were cynical, I'd say that seeing the guy who makes those killed must piss JPD off even more."

"I'd shoot the damned things down, if it was up to me. Hate machine cops. The turd in the punch bowl here is that the killer says he doesn't know how he got there. Says he's got an alibi. Says he kicked the habit, and can prove it. He's trying to turn this thing into some kind of big conspiracy. The city fathers don't want a conspiracy story. Don't want anything scaring away new high-tech businesses looking for a clean city to relocate to."

Cassie made a noise like a snort. "You know a clean city like that?"

"Papers say Jericho is it. One of the top places in the country for high-tech businesses. The city that put man on the moon, back when. Second tech boom now. Shiny new buildings, high-tech jobs—"

"Homeless veterans living under bridges, cops beating up kids who get out of line. Trumping up charges on young girls."

Stevens said, "Have it your way, long as nobody reads those stories. And the chamber of commerce and the mayor don't want to read about this one."

"The mayor can read?"

Stevens leaned hard on the table again and the tired metal bitched a groan back. "The killer's Ron Lyle. Cokehead. Customer of yours. If you were to come forward, good citizen that you are, and testify that you sold him a little blow last night about two A.M., somewhere down in that end of town . . . mention that he was pretty strung out and needed money to buy more . . ."

"I haven't sold to Ron in three months." She paused and added, "If I sold."

Stevens shrugged. "So he's buying from someone else. Can't help it if you can't hold on to your customers."

He leaned back again. "Well, if you were to come forward, that might make this one of those happy-ending stories where the cops have a slam-dunk case and no one listens to the ravings of a coke-mad killer. And this," he held up the sheet with the hand-written arrest report on it, "might just disappear." He laughed. "Think of it as community service to your beloved hometown."

"Huh," snorted Cassie. It was a short, ugly sound.

"You know," said Stevens, "some people don't like that sound that you make all the time, think it sounds like you think you're smarter than them—don't even have to give them a whole word."

Cassie waved him away. "And if my story doesn't check out

and they add perjury charges on top, you'll be there to protect me?"

"No."

"You got a hundred other ways to frame people, 'specially on an easy case like this. You don't need me. This doesn't add up."

Stevens leaned in and smiled. "Like throwing away a charmed life by smuggling drugs you don't even use doesn't add up." He leaned back. "It's a gift, Cassie. Take it." He held up the paper. "Or take door number two."

Cassie looked up at the ceiling like she was thinking about it but they both knew there was nothing to think about.

"You're sure Ron Lyle did this?" she said. Stevens nodded and Cassie laughed at him. "Like JPD was sure I was guilty on that first bust?"

"Like I was sure on the second bust," said Stevens.

Cassie looked away. Stevens paused and studied her, sad and sure, like a father catching a favorite daughter lying again. She looked back, caught his eyes, and Stevens turned his eyes cold and went on. "We both were. And you still haven't thanked me for dropping the assaulting-an-officer charge on that one."

Cassie met his eyes for a moment and then looked away at the wall.

"I want to talk to Ron, see if there's anything there to trip me up."

"Knock yourself out. Tomorrow's Sunday. Come back to me then so I can have this wrapped up by Monday or I'm coming looking for you with this." He waved the arrest report at her and stood up and opened the door.

"You can't run from me, Cassie. I'm the biggest and the baddest around. And we both know you're going nowhere."

She glared up at him from her chair, Stevens towering over her.

"You ever remember, Stevens, how you got into this business

to be the good guy?"

He still smiled, but his eyes were dark. "Trying to do the right thing can get you in bad, can't it?"

"I don't remember."

Stevens stepped back and stood in the doorway. Cassie stood up, feeling unsteady, but made the effort to saunter up to him, push into his space, and stand eye to eye with him.

"Tomorrow," she said.

Stevens still stood in the door.

"Get the fuck out of my way," she said.

Stevens laughed, shifted just enough, and Cassie brushed by him like he was nothing. She marched down the hall with her head up and her eyes hard like she was large and in charge. She passed a rookie patrolman and glared at him until the rookie looked down to see if he had something undone.

Cassie got in her old, white, postal-service truck and drove down the street to the parking lot of a long-closed motel with fearful eyes peering out from the holes where doors and windows had been. She cried until the shaking stopped and she could clean herself up enough to go back.

She felt ashamed of herself for crying and didn't know why.

"Not in Kansas anymore, little girl," she said to the mirror, like her college coach used to tell her when he needed more out of her. "Man up."

Clicked her heels three times but nothing changed.

CHAPTER 2

Tears dried, makeup fixed, Cassie returned to the public safety complex. The visitors' room at the jail was a plain, windowless, concrete shell divided in half by a row of six-foot-high clear Plexiglas booths open at the top, designed to give inmates and visitors the illusion of privacy while delivering none. Cassie paced back and forth in front of one of the booths.

She flashed back to the last time she was on the other side of the glass: the guard pulling her out of her cell, his hand clamped on her arm, grinning and humming Bob Dylan's "Like a Rolling Stone." He had leaned into Cassie and sung the chorus, "How does it feel?" into her ear before shoving her into a booth.

But today Cassie was a visitor, invited by the police.

"I need you to sit down and wait for the resident, miss," said the matron behind her.

Cassie laughed, and the matron gave her that blank look that underlings or clerks are forced to give their betters that says, "I don't know what's funny, sir or ma'am, but I'm sure it is."

"Residents?" said Cassie. "Like you put a mint on their pillows before you tuck them in at night?"

The matron showed no expression. "That's what they tell us to call them when we're talking to voters." She pointed back at the stool and Cassie sat down. Sat down but the energy wouldn't leave her alone so she balanced on the stool, tapping one foot and finger-combing a tangle out of her hair.

They led Ron Lyle in from the other side wearing shackles.

He shuffled in front of the glass trying to look tough until he saw it was Cassie.

He picked up the phone on his side. "Man, Cassie, thanks for coming for me," he said, grinning. The guard behind Ron slammed him down hard on the stool and backed away.

Cassie looked at him and wondered why he would thank her for coming down. Wondered what to say and finally settled on just, "Yeah."

Ron straddled the plastic stool across the glass from Cassie, cut his eyes at her crossways, and tapped his outside foot in time with Cassie. He was a small, young dude, thin, nervous, with dirty, brown hair falling over half his face.

"Knew you'd come," he said into the phone. "All of us count on you, Cassie."

"Yeah," Cassie thought of the little bags of white powder that were the only thing most people counted on her for these days. Ron seemed to be reading her mind.

"No, not just that," he said. "You still got connections from the old days, know how to work the system. People say, you got a problem, go to Cassie."

Cassie gave a harsh laugh. "Who says that, Ron? Nobody I know. Can't even help myself these days. Don't even remember the last time I helped anybody else."

"No, really. Everybody says Cassie will help."

"They remember the old days."

They paused, both waiting for the other to talk, both tapping their feet and trying not to show any expression.

Finally, Ron said, "So how're you going to get me out? Got some clever scam they'll never see coming until we're walking out the door?"

"No, Ron. Listen . . . No, never mind. Just tell me what happened."

"They framed me, Cassie. They know it and I know it and

you know it."

She looked at him. "So they didn't find you on top of a dead body?"

"Well, yeah, that part. But they slipped me something and put me there."

Cassie just watched him.

Ron said, "Ask my mom. She can tell you. I haven't done anything but beer and Jack since I last bought from you. That was years ago. And she knows I was down at the Red Rock last night."

Cassie thought, more like months since you've bought from me. Even with that, Cassie could see the courtroom scene playing out in her head: Ron would say, "My mom can tell you that I don't do drugs no more and I just happened to fall asleep on that dead man. If you don't believe her, ask my drug dealer."

Ron brightened. "With all that, Cassie, you'll come up with something. I mean, this is an obvious frame. They gave me something."

"How?"

"I don't know. I went out for a beer; next thing I know a cop's shaking me awake and I've got blood all over me."

Another believable line for the courtroom. Cassie stared at him for a long second.

"Ron, I don't know."

His bright look turned dark. "What the hell you mean, you don't know? What you doing here if you ain't got some kind of plan up your sleeve to get me out of here? How come they let you in here anyways?"

"Stevens told them to let me see you."

"Stevens? Stevens?! Hell, Cassie, he's one of them. Jericho used to be an honest town, but all that fighting over money for them big, high-tech government contracts turned this town dirty. There's bad shit going on, Cassie, but as long as they keep all that government business coming in, rockets and Army helicopters and genetics and miracle stuff for the six o'clock news and money for rich folks' pockets, nobody cares that all the little guys are getting squashed. And Stevens is the dirtiest of them all and you know it."

"No argument. The biggest and the baddest."

"And, Cassie, you know I couldn't have done it. I ain't never hurt nobody in my life. My only busts have been for small robberies that were really misunderstandings, and, of course, drugs, but we both know drugs ought to be legal anyways. Really, Cassie, everybody knows who I am. I'm the little wimpy guy that everybody beats up. Not the one that beats people up. Sure as hell not a stone-cold killer."

"Yeah," said Cassie. "You're more of a puppy dog than a hound. Nobody fears you." She paused. "No offense."

Ron brightened again. "That's what you're going to do. You're going to tell them I couldn't have done it, had to have been set up by Stevens and his pals."

"Ron, nobody's going to believe that."

"Sure they will, if you tell it. Tell them you was at a secret meeting, them inviting you because you used to be a big princess of the Jericho and all. Heard the mayor say, we need to take this business guy's money, set up Ron Lyle to take the fall for killing him. They'll listen to you, Cassie."

They will, she thought, but not with that story. Tell the story Stevens's way, just a druggie doing what druggies do, and her testimony would cut the legs off Ron's crazy stories and put the nail in his coffin.

She stared at Ron a long time and the thought came into her mind unbidden: *Stupid, pointless murders were one of the things druggies do every day. Even little wimpy druggies. Stevens was probably right. Ron did this. Lying would just be community service.*

She had what she needed here. She stood up.

Ron said, "You can do it, Cassie. Just tell them what they need to hear."

She didn't say anything.

"What?" Ron said, standing up, too. "That's it? Just come down here to laugh at me?"

"Ron, I'm sorry."

Ron tried to hide the disappointment with a pleading smile. "You'll help me. You got to."

"Jesus, Ron, I can't even help myself these days."

"Sure you can, Cassie, everybody remembers you." Then he brightened again. "Hey, you bring me what I need to get through today? Slip a little bag of something white across when the guard's not looking? They's a crack in the edge of the booth, you can just slide a little packet through it. I've done it before."

"Jesus, Ron, no. I didn't bring anything like that into the jail. Think I'm that dumb? Besides, you told me you quit."

"Just a little, Cassie. Just for today. Help me get through this."

"Ron, they ain't too understanding of that kind of thing in here."

"Yeah. They don't understand us here, do they, Cassie?"

Cassie felt her face harden. "Ron, you're the one who's got to understand. Sometimes people have to do what they have to do. If I were trying to get you out—which I'm not, and I don't even have the juice to get you out if I were—you haven't given me any damned reason to believe you're innocent."

"You know you can trust me, Cassie. I'm innocent."

"Yeah. You're innocent. Like you haven't bought from me in years. Like you're not using now."

Ron fidgeted. "That's it, Cassie. You know when I'm bullshitting you." He leaned into the glass as close to her as he could get.

"And you know I'm telling the truth when I say I did not kill anybody."

She hesitated long enough for Ron to see it. His hopeful grin came back. "You know I didn't do this. And I know you know, no matter what you say. And we both know you're going to get me out of here because you won't stand for this."

He pumped his fist and gave Cassie the cheer the crowd used to yell for her on the basketball court.

"Give 'em hell, Cassie."

CHAPTER 3

Cassie could no longer stand the feeling of being slimed-on and being slimy herself that she always got in the Jericho public safety complex. She slipped out with her head down, trying not to look anybody in the eye. In her old postal-delivery truck, she slammed the sliding door shut and tied it closed with a piece of rope. She gripped the steering wheel hard and put her head down and said, "He is guilty. He is a dirty little dweeb and you know he is guilty and this is just one more dirty little thing you have got to do." She sat up, choked off a sob, and cranked the truck.

She cut through Jericho University and got stuck in construction traffic at a new building that looked like a piece of white crystal rising triumphant from the earth. Genetics was the hot new job market: the new genetics building would crank out fresh-faced workers for Jericho's tech industries.

Two years, thought Cassie.

Two years ago she had been another of the shiny, happy students strolling along the campus toward a shiny, happy life. She'd already been drafted by the LA Sparks—first round—and had received offers to model. On her way to the top. She'd even been the student rep from the genetics department on the committee designing this building.

A lilting female voice called out, "Cassie."

A blonde jogged over to her truck and Cassie recognized her. Kaitlin Blackshear, a freshman on the basketball team when

Cassie was a senior. She had followed Cassie around everywhere back then, and her father was still the CTO of one of the emerging genetics companies out in Research Park. Cassie had pestered Kaitlin's dad for jobs—unsuccessfully—more times than she could remember.

Here comes the put-down. Hell, I know I screwed up. Don't need the whole goddamned world to tell me.

She roared away before Kaitlin could get to her.

Cassie drove to what had once been an upper-class neighborhood, sliding down now with age and neglect, and parked in front of a faded, yellow frame house, on the street so she wouldn't interfere with the kids playing basketball in the driveway. Cassie's niece sat in a wheelchair on the edge of the makeshift court. Belva looked younger than the high-school boys banging away under the rim and working hard to ignore her.

"Hey, Rico," the girl yelled. "Learn to play or give me the rock. Better yet, give me the rock and pay me for the lesson."

Rico, dribbling out where the foul line would have been, deliberately looked away from her.

"Yeah, Rico," said the boy guarding him. "Give it up. You picked Belva."

"Didn't pick her. It's her house. Only court on the block."

"C'mon, Rico," Belva yelled. "Give me the rock. You know you can't hit worth shit."

Rico caught the ball off the dribble and slammed it at her hard enough to knock her over. She caught it like it was an easy pass and pushed it at the rim in a flat, hard throw. It was a low-percentage line-drive, but it rattled in. The other boys hooted at Rico.

Rico scooped the ball up from the dirt. "Ugly damn shot, bitch."

Belva grinned. "By any means necessary, amigo. By any

means necessary."

Cassie thought about showing Belva a better shot. She remembered her father's advice: Get the form down, do things right, and good things will happen.

Thought about how that turned out for her and gave Belva a high five instead.

"My arms are still strong, Cassie," she said.

"You're always strong, Belva," Cassie said. "Always strong. Your mom in the house?"

"You hear the TV?"

"Of course."

"Then you know where she is."

Cassie walked up the plywood ramp and opened the screen door into a dirty room with a dirty woman sprawled on a dirty couch. The only brightness came from the TV, which had two people yelling about whose baby had which father.

Cassie wasn't sure her sister was awake. "Jill?"

"You got it?" Jill said without looking away from the TV.

"Well, a warm hello to you, too, big sister."

"Yeah, yeah. Give me the money. Bitch that runs Belva's rehab keeps demanding money. If it was up to me, we wouldn't pay it."

Cassie pulled a roll of bills from her jacket pocket and dumped it on the cluttered coffee table. "That ought to cover it."

Jill stirred, unsteady, an effort to reach over and pick up the roll. She counted the bills. "Enough for her. Not much left over for me."

"Hey, you got it all, except for what I got to have today for rent. Maybe you could get off your ass and do a little more."

Jill yawned. "Whatever. You just don't know how much all this costs. There's still doctors and trips and expensive shit and nobody says it's going to fix things."

"They say it might," said Cassie. "Gotta believe. Have faith in something other than the damned TV."

"Might, maybe. Belva's spine was damaged. Spines don't get better. That's why insurance won't pay for this experimental rehab program you love so much. The only people who believe she'll get better are you and the people down there draining our money."

"Belva believes. Long as Belva fights, we fight," said Cassie.

"Just saying, this costs a lot of money we don't have."

Cassie wanted to explode, remind Jill what this fight had cost her and was still costing her, remind her where the money was coming from. But that fight was old and predictable and pointless.

Instead, Cassie said, "Yeah. I know. I'll get you money, as long as you keep her in the program. I do what I can. You do what you can. Belva's going to have a good life someday."

"The Luna family team. Yay team." Jill looked at the wall and sulked. "Bitch-girl deserves a bullet to the brain."

Cassie felt the rage rising in her and choked it back.

"She's your damned daughter. You broke her body with your damned drunk driving," she said, as calmly as she could. "Keep talking like that, you're going to break her soul."

Jill laughed, a dirty laugh with no joy. "Are you Little Miss Sunshine now, come back home to fix everything? The girl who used to have the big smile, preaching that a little more love solves everything? Haven't seen that preachy attitude in you for a while. Sweetness and light don't work so good now that you're not a princess."

"Belva's got a good heart. I'm not going to let you make her mean." She needed to change the conversation. She jerked her head toward a crater in a wall. "That hole new?"

"A guy came over last night, punched the wall."

"He drunk or high?"

Jill looked at Cassie and laughed. "Didn't ask which." She looked back at the TV. "Whole house is going to shit."

"House looked pretty good when Mom and Dad lived here."

"Yeah, well, they had more time. Since they died, I'm too busy to do much housework."

There was a pause where Cassie intentionally didn't say what she was thinking. Finally, she said, "I'll get somebody over here to fix it."

"You do that."

Cassie turned and put her hand on the door.

Jill rose up on one elbow and said, "Think you could get me a check next time? People look at me funny when I pay everything with cash."

Cassie laughed a harsh laugh. "Yeah. I'll tell my customers, no more of that nasty old cash. Certified checks or American Express only."

She slammed the door on her way out. Belva turned away from the game and looked up at Cassie.

Cassie bent down to Belva's wheelchair. "That wheel looks loose."

"Mom says we don't have money to fix it. Told me that when I was cleaning up the empty bottles of Jack she'd bought for her new Romeo."

"Don't talk about your mother that way."

"Yeah."

Cassie stood up, still looking at the wheelchair wheel. "How much would it cost to fix it?"

Belva said, "Guy at rehab said he can get me a used wheel for a hundred."

Cassie reached into her pocket and handed Belva the hundred. Wondered if her landlord could wait a day. Or two. Or take half. At two hundred a month, it was already the cheapest apartment in Jericho.

"Thanks, Cassie," said Belva. "I'm going to pay you back someday for all of this."

Cassie smiled. "You just might. Stay strong."

Cassie sat in her truck and knew she didn't want to be there but didn't know where she wanted to be. No, she did know where she wanted to be: living in her own house somewhere, maybe raising her own daughter. Working at a job she could brag about instead of selling drugs for money she couldn't keep.

She looked back at the steps peeking out from beneath the ramp. The first two were still shiny from the last time her father painted them a few years ago. The third and final step was crumbling.

She thought of the life she had believed was laid out for her when she was her daddy's little girl, living in the bright yellow house with a bright future ahead.

And wondered where it had all gone.

She felt the rage rise up in her like it did every time she asked herself that question, or thought about the answer. She laughed harshly and kicked herself for whining. There were choices that had been made and choices yet to make, and they all belonged to her.

She breathed in and out and calmed herself. Realized that she hadn't set her intention for the day ahead. Thought about what she wanted. Needed to say it out loud to lock it in to her brain and her soul and maybe make it real.

She tilted the mirror and looked herself in the eye.

"Do some good for somebody today," she said. "Big-girl time."

Time to put away her little-girl dreams, go back to the public safety complex and give Stevens the crap he wants. Do a bad thing to somebody so she could continue to do some good for somebody else and keep her commitment to Belva and move

27

on. The return to princess world would have to wait for another day.

One of the boys yelled at Belva to watch her mouth before she got herself into trouble. Cassie braced herself to go to Belva's rescue.

But Belva shot the boy a bird. "Then at least I'd be somewhere. Better than you and the nowhere boys."

The boys laughed and the game went on.

Cassie cranked up the old postal truck and pulled away. Time to go somewhere, even if it wasn't where she wanted to be.

Chapter 4

Cassie found Stevens in the JPD detectives' break room eating a doughnut, powdered sugar trailing down his shirt, holding his favorite oversized coffee mug with "Bad to the Bone" in big letters.

"You're a fucking cliché, you know it?" she said.

He smiled at her with sugar in his teeth. "And you're a valuable cog in the wheels of justice."

"Fuck you. You'll have your story."

"Want to do it now?"

"Tomorrow. I'll give you a Sunday-morning lie. Going home now and brush my teeth for an hour to get the taste of dealing with you out. May get blitzed tonight just so I can come in with the bad hangover I'll deserve tomorrow."

Stevens smiled bigger and more sugar showed on his teeth.

"Cassie Luna with a hangover and a bad mood. May have to sell tickets to that."

"This is your idea of funny? Take some poor soul's life away? Don't know if he's a killer or not, but hey, let's get a conviction before this thing becomes embarrassing to the power structure? I'll lie for you and be your valuable cog. Just don't tell me it's funny."

"Funny?" Stevens slammed his cup down on the counter, coffee sloshing everywhere. The other men milling around the room stopped their conversations and looked at Stevens and Cassie while pretending to be bored.

"You think this is a joke? I'll show you funny." He grabbed Cassie's arm and tried to jerk Cassie out of the room. Cassie planted her feet and refused to be moved. Stevens jerked her arm again, used to throwing people around like rag dolls. Cassie didn't budge.

Stevens ground his teeth. "Please," he muttered. Cassie tossed her hair back and walked by him, surfing out of the room on a wave of Stevens's growling while the other cops snickered.

Stevens caught up and got ahead of her as they marched back to his desk, Stevens pretending he was leading, Cassie pretending she didn't care.

He walked around to his side of the desk and opened a manila envelope and shook out a stack of photos.

"Here, look at this, you want to see something funny." He rifled the stack and pushed one over at Cassie.

Cassie looked at the body of a middle-aged man lying on a Brazilian hardwood floor. The whole picture was layered in blood so red it looked fake: blood covering his face and the floor and his clothes, so much blood it looked like it would drown the world. Cassie felt behind herself for the chair and sat down, sick to her stomach and unsteady. She tried to look away.

"No, goddamn it," said Stevens. "Don't you look away and pretend this is just some goddamn bloodless TV show. This man died, and someone is damned well going to pay."

Cassie looked back. The man's head was almost off his body. His neck and shoulder were an open mess of meat and bones from a single vicious slash at the base of his neck on the left side. She glanced away, then looked back when she noticed something.

"Huh." She looked up at Stevens and saw that he was almost smiling at her, approving of her noticing.

"Axe?" she said.

"Actually, hatchet," said Stevens. "Like Lizzie Borden. We're

CHAPTER 5

Cassie had to get away and find somewhere safe to think about what she saw in Stevens's pictures.

The old Stowe Mill building had been rescued to make the Haunted Castle arts center for artists and hipsters. Even in the bright North Alabama summer sun, it loomed over the poor neighborhood like a background for a horror movie: crumbling brick with dark dirty streaks like tears and massive, rusting iron windows.

Cassie loved it.

She walked up to the coffee wagon sitting in front of what had once been the loading docks. A young woman with blue and red tat sleeves and a nose ring handed her a plastic cup of water.

"Cassie's usual," she said.

"You know it, Shel."

"Can't handle the hard stuff like coffee or tea?"

Cassie said, "Today, I feel like I need a double espresso to clear my head. Maybe with a big shot of Jack to cloud it up at the same time."

"Not your way, Cassie."

"Not sure, today, what my way is."

Shel reached through the window and put her hand on Cassie's arm. "Hey, whatever it is, people around here still like you. Look up to you."

Cassie snorted. "Tell them to stop it."

"Ain't going to happen. People around here say͏ sie. She's the one who won't put up with things wrong.' "

Another snort. "I've just got a bad temper I c͏ Got used to not letting anybody push me around or͏ court."

Shel patted Cassie's arm and pulled back in͏ thing," she said, picking up a rag and going back t͏ glanced back at Cassie and said, "Namaste."

"Yeah," said Cassie. "Namaste."

Cassie took the water and sat down at a picnic t͏ the sun warm her. She scattered Stevens's photos͏ arrange them, looking for something. Turned the p͏ vin's body lying on the ground, rotated it like he w͏ up and lined him up against the paint spatters. Trie͏ Ron Lyle in the picture and couldn't.

"Huh." She sat there looking at the pictures, won͏ they meant, and what they meant for her.

A noise in the parking lot broke her out of her t͏ guy in paint-spattered coveralls and an old dashiki͏ gling to load a couch-sized painting into the back͏ truck. Cassie swept up Stevens's pictures in one͏ walked over and steadied the painting with her free͏ face blocked by the canvas.

"Thanks, man," the artist said. The painting slid in͏ and Cassie popped her face out from behind.

"Oh, sorry," he said. "Didn't know it was you, Cas͏

"Not the first time I've been called a guy. How͏ Jenks?"

"Doing good—Jesus." He looked at the crime-sce͏ still in Cassie's hand. "What have you got yourself int͏

Cassie turned the photos away. "Nothing."

Jenks started to say something, decided to drop it.͏

calling it an axe for the press, keep a detail back."

"One man," she said, "one whack, did all this?"

"Yeah." Stevens shoved the rest of the pile toward her. "Here. Look at them all."

The next was a close-up of the wound. Cassie felt bile rising in her throat and looked around for a trash can in case she couldn't keep from throwing up.

She looked away and Stevens shoved another at her.

"Look."

It was a shot of the wall, with the body at the bottom of the shot and a patrolman holding a tall measuring stick against the wall. Behind the officer's bland expression, the wall was splattered red around his shoulders and head like a monstrous halo.

"Huh," she said again. She glanced up and caught Stevens searching her face.

"Seen enough?" he said.

Cassie's mind was off somewhere. "Oh, yeah," she finally said.

"Another thing," said Stevens. "Don't you accuse me of suborning perjury in front of everybody else like you did back there. Walls have ears around here."

Cassie shook herself away from what had distracted her. "You mean an honest cop might hear you?"

"Yeah," Stevens said. "That's it."

They sat there for a minute, Cassie looking away and Stevens looking at Cassie.

"So," he finally said. "Tomorrow morning?"

"Yeah," she said. "I guess."

Stevens started to say something but Cassie jumped up and grabbed the photos off his desk.

"Taking these," she said, marching out the door with an untidy stack of photos.

CHAPTER 5

Cassie had to get away and find somewhere safe to think about what she saw in Stevens's pictures.

The old Stowe Mill building had been rescued to make the Haunted Castle arts center for artists and hipsters. Even in the bright North Alabama summer sun, it loomed over the poor neighborhood like a background for a horror movie: crumbling brick with dark dirty streaks like tears and massive, rusting iron windows.

Cassie loved it.

She walked up to the coffee wagon sitting in front of what had once been the loading docks. A young woman with blue and red tat sleeves and a nose ring handed her a plastic cup of water.

"Cassie's usual," she said.

"You know it, Shel."

"Can't handle the hard stuff like coffee or tea?"

Cassie said, "Today, I feel like I need a double espresso to clear my head. Maybe with a big shot of Jack to cloud it up at the same time."

"Not your way, Cassie."

"Not sure, today, what my way is."

Shel reached through the window and put her hand on Cassie's arm. "Hey, whatever it is, people around here still like you. Look up to you."

Cassie snorted. "Tell them to stop it."

"Ain't going to happen. People around here say, 'Go to Cassie. She's the one who won't put up with things when they're wrong.' "

Another snort. "I've just got a bad temper I can't control. Got used to not letting anybody push me around on a basketball court."

Shel patted Cassie's arm and pulled back inside. "Same thing," she said, picking up a rag and going back to work. Shel glanced back at Cassie and said, "Namaste."

"Yeah," said Cassie. "Namaste."

Cassie took the water and sat down at a picnic table and let the sun warm her. She scattered Stevens's photos and tried to arrange them, looking for something. Turned the picture of Irvin's body lying on the ground, rotated it like he was standing up and lined him up against the paint spatters. Tried to imagine Ron Lyle in the picture and couldn't.

"Huh." She sat there looking at the pictures, wondering what they meant, and what they meant for her.

A noise in the parking lot broke her out of her thoughts. A guy in paint-spattered coveralls and an old dashiki was struggling to load a couch-sized painting into the back of a pickup truck. Cassie swept up Stevens's pictures in one hand and walked over and steadied the painting with her free hand, her face blocked by the canvas.

"Thanks, man," the artist said. The painting slid into the bed and Cassie popped her face out from behind.

"Oh, sorry," he said. "Didn't know it was you, Cassie."

"Not the first time I've been called a guy. How you been, Jenks?"

"Doing good—Jesus." He looked at the crime-scene photos still in Cassie's hand. "What have you got yourself into?"

Cassie turned the photos away. "Nothing."

Jenks started to say something, decided to drop it. "Hey, ah, you know I haven't been around to see you lately."

"That's OK."

"Just didn't want you to think I was buying coke from somebody else. I gave it up; found I worked better without it."

"Work is better than coke," she said. "Stick with it." She looked at the painting, a flowing, impressionist view of the Tennessee River in the fall with the gigantic Saturn rocket test stand crumbling in the center. The long-retired test stand, a concrete-and-steel reminder of the glory years when Jericho built the rockets that put men on the moon, stood rusting while the surrounding trees dropped flame-colored leaves at its base.

"That's beautiful," she said. "We need more of that. Remind us of who we were."

"Sold this one to the new bank downtown," said Jenks. "I'm starting to make money doing something I can sign my name to."

"Yeah," said Cassie. "Go with that. Do something good."

"Lot of money flowing in from all that tech work out there."

Cassie laughed, "Yeah, I heard. 'Jericho: The sky is not the limit.' "

"So the chamber of commerce says," said Jenks.

Cassie straightened up.

"Hey, Jenks," she said. "How tall are you?"

He shuffled. "I dunno. Maybe five-six."

More like five-four, thought Cassie.

"You mind helping me out with something?"

"Sure."

She dug in a box of tools in Jenks's truck and pulled out a paint brush and handed it to him. She tapped the side of her neck.

"Hit me here with it."

"You mean like I'm trying to knight you or something?"

"No, like it's a long knife or something and you're trying to cut off my head."

Jenks stared up at her. "Really?"

"Yeah, just try it."

He reached up, tentative, and tapped her with the brush. She felt the brush tickle the front quarter of her neck, as high as he could reach.

"Thanks," she said.

"You're welcome, I guess."

Cassie started to explain but a JPD black-and-white rolled up beside them and a little squirrel of a cop got out and grinned at Cassie with his buck teeth.

"Cassandra Luna?" he said.

"Jesus Fucking Christ," said Cassie. "What the hell is this about?"

"Got a warrant for your arrest, girl. Assume the pose for me."

Cassie's language got worse, but she turned around and put her hands on the truck. The cop came up behind Cassie, hooked a foot into one leg, and shoved her facedown onto the asphalt.

"No, man, stop," muttered Jenks. But he stayed back.

Squirrel jumped on Cassie's back and grabbed her hair and turned her head so the scar was shoved into the pavement.

"Still good looking, from this side," he breathed into her ear. "Have to remember that."

"Son-of-a-bitch Stevens," Cassie said into the pavement.

"Oh, yeah." Squirrel got off her and stood up and laughed. "You can get up."

Cassie pulled herself up and brushed a sharp piece of gravel out of her scar.

Squirrel stood there smiling with his legs apart and his arms folded over his shrunken chest. "Stevens said to let you know we're here, ready to bring you in if we need to. Thought I'd have a little fun while I was at it." He laughed at her. "Don't tell Stevens about our little fun." He reached out and patted her cheek. "Just relax and enjoy it, babe."

Cassie spat in his face.

Squirrel turned ugly and red and his left hand came up and slapped her across the face.

Cassie felt the rage rise in her and saw her leg come off the ground and kick the squirrel hard and fast between the legs, so hard he flew up in the air like a rag doll.

Saw it in her mind but stood there with her head hung down and her hands shaking with shame and untapped adrenaline.

Squirrel punched her in the stomach twice, quick and hard.

"I can do this all day, bitch. Stevens is going to be mad about the black eye, but no one's going to care about hurting you where it doesn't show."

Cassie was bent double, grunting and clenching her teeth to keep from throwing up.

He laughed again, the same nasty laugh that Cassie was getting used to hearing from people. "Black eye looks good, bitch. Matches your scar."

CHAPTER 6

Cassie was driving her old truck away from the Haunted Castle as hard as she could, hunched over the steering wheel and listening for sirens and checking the rearview mirror for flashing lights.

Driving and crying, with a fresh black eye she could feel blooming. She had to have something to give Stevens now.

She took her cell out of her bag and called Belva.

"Belva?"

"Yeah—hey, Cassie, you all right?"

"Fine, just fine. Look, are you at your computer?"

Belva said, "Of course."

"I need you to do something for me. There was a guy killed last night named Irvin. Need you to find his address for me."

"Oh, yeah, let me try deadman.com."

"Less attitude, young lady."

There was a little bit of muttering and key clattering, then Belva said, "Got it. He's up on Pill Hill." She gave Cassie the address.

"Thanks."

"No prob. Cassie, you sure you're all right?"

"Peachy."

Pill Hill was nicknamed that because of the doctors' houses crowding the streets. Irvin's house was at the top in every sense of the word: twice the size of the other McMansions, looking down on all of them.

There was a burning smell coming from under Cassie's truck as she tried to climb the steep hill. She parked halfway up and hoped her truck would look like just another service vehicle. She took her foot off the brake and heard the parking brake squeal as it turned loose and the truck slid back down the hill. She stomped on the brake, stopped, cranked up the engine again, and backed the truck into the curb to hold it steady.

Cassie reached over and fished in her big beach bag until she found the secret pouch. She teased out a quart-sized freezer bag holding small bags of white powder, and put the bag in a little cardboard box taped under the driver's seat. As she latched the compartment closed, her hand brushed the rusty pistol that had come with the old truck when she took it from a customer who couldn't pay for his product. She dried her eyes and looked in the mirror and hardened her face. *Man up.*

Cassie got out and pulled a padlock from her bag. Slamming the door shut, she put the lock on a latch she had taken off a junked garden gate to give her a way to lock up the truck. She snapped the lock shut and walked up the hill huffing and puffing and appalled at how much her conditioning had disappeared in one year away from being a professional athlete. She looked around at the perfect houses and the perfect lawns and felt perfectly out of place and perfectly envious.

Her gaze caught a plastic wrapper blown against a crepe myrtle, looking out of place and a little ugly. She stopped and glared at it, then stomped away, muttering, "I am not the goddamned litter police. I don't have to pick up every piece of trash in the world."

She stopped after two steps and came back.

"C'mon, little fellow." She pulled it free. "You don't belong here either." She shoved it into her bag.

She walked up to the house with the yellow crime-scene tape. The tape was clear: "Do Not Cross." She tried the doorknob, the door opened in her hand, and she ducked under it and into the house.

There was a heavy coppery smell of blood from down a hall. Cassie followed it.

Something moved in a doorway beside her and she threw an elbow by reflex and knocked a man across the room. He started to get up and she grabbed a table lamp and snatched its plug out of the wall. She stood over the man and said, "Move, and you get this." She took out her cell with her left hand and punched in 9-1-1, trying to watch the man and the phone at the same time.

"I've captured a killer," she said. "I need the police."

The man on the floor said, "I am the police."

The woman on the phone said, "What is the nature of your emergency?"

Cassie thought about it. The man opened his jacket gingerly and took out a badge.

"Never mind," said Cassie. She dropped the phone back in her bag.

"You think," the man said, "you could put that down?"

"Oh." Cassie put the lamp back on the table. Saw the cord dangling, went to plug it in, and saw she had ripped the plug off the end of it.

"Sorry," she said.

"Yeah," the man said. "Wouldn't want to hurt the lamp."

He stood up, taller than Cassie. He had styled, strawberry-blond hair and tiny blue eyes, an expensive black suit, and black shirt with no tie. Cassie looked at him and thought he was trying to look like the crime-scene technician from TV, the one who always thought he was more important than the cops. *Arrogant.* Still, looking like a Hollywood star wasn't all bad.

"Hey," he said, speaking in a hoarse, theatrical whisper. "Thought you were Cassandra Luna. Sure of it now. Saw enough of those elbows when you were playing at JU."

"Oh," she said.

"So," he said. "What brings a basketball star to a crime scene?"

"I'm—uh—working with Detective Stevens."

"Stevens? Surprised he's paying for an outside consultant on this. They barely paid for me to process the scene." He put out his hand and put on a big smile. "David Carmello, part-time crime-scene technician and full-time law student."

She took his hand and he held her hand and his smile a moment extra.

"Recognized you from the hair" he said, "you know, from the poster you did back that one year, when you were in the pros and modeling, when the women's league had your poster up everywhere trying to get a little publicity. Back before . . ." He paused, looking for the right words.

"Yeah, I know," Cassie said and felt her mouth tighten. "Got a big red scar from my left eye to my mouth." She touched her eye. "And a fresh black eye. Nobody does posters of me anymore."

"No, I was going to say back before your troubles."

Troubles, she thought. What a kind word.

Cassie said, "Nice of you to remember the old days."

"Remember?" he laughed. "I was at JU when you were. I read an interview where you said you would only date guys at least six-four, taller than you. I sat in the stands at every game with a sign that said, 'I'm six-four.' "

Cassie smiled. It had been a long time since she'd met a fan. "Sorry I never noticed."

"I was a skinny science geek back then, big, black glasses, bushy hair, and everything."

"You appear to have filled out."

They stood there, awkward and quiet. He was still smiling at her.

He tried the hoarse, sexy voice again. "So you're working with Stevens now. Cool. I'm a civilian employee of the department, too. Means we'll probably be working together."

"Oh, yeah."

"Well," he whispered, "let's get to it." He led her deeper into the house.

They rounded the corner and Cassie stopped short. Everything ahead was blocked off by yellow crime-scene tape with just a narrow walkway left open. The floors and the wall behind the tape looked like a large-scale abstract painting filled with angry, red slashes and splatters.

Cassie looked at the wall and got a feeling of sickness at a life ripped away, falling helplessly into a hell of hideous, red slashes in one horrible moment. Someone dying alone and voiceless with no one there to stand between them and the monsters of the world.

She tried to look cold and professional. "So," she said. "He was standing there, with his back to the wall?"

"Yeah." David stepped over the tape and put his finger almost to the wall at a spot at shoulder height.

"Right there," he said. "The hatchet actually took a chunk out of the wall."

"Right there?" she said.

"Yeah."

"So he wasn't sitting down or bending over or anything when it happened?"

"No. Couldn't have been."

"How tall was Mr. Irvin?"

David rummaged through some papers. "Six-one." He shot a grin at Cassie. "Smaller than the two of us."

Cassie said, "The hatchet. It didn't have a long handle or

41

anything, more like an axe?"

"No, it's over here. The handle's about a foot long."

David held up a hatchet in a plastic bag with the blood still shiny and wet.

"Looks new," she said.

David squinted. "Yeah. Sticker still on it. Home Depot."

"Prints?" she said.

"No prints. Wiped down, or maybe just smeared."

"Still, this ought to be pretty easy," she said. "Has to be DNA scattered around, unless the drug-addled killer wore gloves and took them off before he passed out. Get the DNA off the handle, match it to the killer, and you're done."

"Could be done that way, if Stevens wanted to. Right now, the Alabama state lab is backed up with a two-year wait on DNA testing, costs extra to get the test expedited. And the department doesn't like to spend money when it doesn't have to. Stevens said, don't bother. I mean, they've already got the guy. Again, really surprised Stevens is paying you to check this out."

Cassie snorted. "Stevens? Paying?"

"Yeah. I don't get much, either."

Cassie said, "Let me ask you something, just a what-if. If you didn't know anything about the killer, and you just had these pictures and the evidence here, what would you deduce?"

David beamed. "Nobody ever asks me to do any thinking. On TV, the cops respect the crime-scene techs. In real life, not so much."

"Well, I respect you."

David studied the photos and looked at the wall.

"The killer was strong, a real badass. One cut with a small hatchet, almost took the guy's head off."

"Anything else?"

He studied the photos some more, brightened when he found

another nugget to impress Cassie with.

"Tall," he said. "The killer was tall."

"You're sure?"

"Yeah. Look at this." He stepped up to the wall and made a chopping motion. "He cut down. Had to be at least as tall as the victim. Maybe taller. Any shorter and the blow would have hit him more in the front."

"Maybe the victim bent down."

"No. The hatchet wouldn't have hit the wall the way it did unless the victim was pressed against the wall. No, the killer is big. Bad, too. One hack and he almost took the guy's head off."

Cassie said, "Big and bad."

David said, "The biggest, and the baddest."

Cassie was in a hurry to get back to her truck. She slid the door shut with a bang and dug into her bag, hoping she had seen what she thought she had seen. She pulled the plastic wrap she had picked up out of the bag and read the label: Home Depot 12″ Hatchet.

CHAPTER 7

Moonie's Bar was never really open and Moonie's Bar was never really closed. Cassie parked her truck on the far side of the gravel parking lot and stretched, tired and headachy from the things she knew she had to do to get Stevens off her back and Belva back on her feet. Still, a girl had to eat. She looked at the two old pickups and the one bright red Ferrari that were always there. Charles's Ferrari. She walked up to the plywood door in the cinderblock building, ignored the "Closed" sign and pushed the door open.

Anytime, day or night, the inside of Moonie's was the same: Charles sitting at the short bar away from the door, eyes half-closed while an old TV showed wildlife movies in front of him. Two thugs, one black and one white, sat at a table by the door. They would have looked like guards if they looked sober or awake.

"What held you up?" Charles said, voice in a slurred monotone, eyes watching hyenas rip some kind of African deer apart. No emotion or interest in his eyes, just watching.

"Life," said Cassie. "You ought to try it sometime."

"Nah. Too much work."

Cassie said, "So you just fucking well sit here all the time, being fucking mean and those two being fucking stupid."

"Sometimes," Charles said, "we change it up. I'm stupid and they're mean."

"Funny."

"You ever notice," Charles said to the TV, "when she comes in here saying 'fuck' all the time and trying to act tough, means she's got no money?"

White Thug, a big guy with razor stubble on the side of his head and a dyed blond strip down the middle, laughed a loose, rattling laugh then put his head back down like an animatronic dummy awakened for his one line.

"Oh come on," Cassie said. "You know I'm good for it. When have you not made money off me?"

Charles jerked his chin just a little. Black Thug pulled a revolver out of his waistband and sat it on the table, slowly spinning the cylinder: click, click, click.

"Never," said Charles. "Why you're still alive."

"Yeah. And I'm why you're still in business, if you call this being in business. Half of your sales come from me in the bars downtown. Nobody there would buy from guys like you. Nobody there would buy from anybody but me."

"That's why we don't let you buy from nobody but me," said Charles. "Never. I own you." The TV now had a cute family of meerkats playing in the desert. He was watching them with the same interest he had showed the deer mutilations.

He jerked his chin again and Black Thug stood up and put a quart-sized freezer bag filled with small bags of white powder on the counter next to Charles.

"And why you pay extra for your Saturday night supplies. No sweat off my balls if you want to do this the hard way. If you ever get enough scratch to pay me up front, I'll charge you less and I won't care if you sell or not. But if I front you supplies, you bring me money by Friday, or they come looking for you."

She started to say something but he kept on.

"Going to happen one day, the way you keep crashing and burning," he said. "Seen it before. Rich girl spending all your profits on partying yourself. One day you'll run dry, won't make it back on Friday. They'll come for you."

"Oh yeah," said Cassie. "All my money goes to partying. That's why I'm broke now and have to come back for more product to sell to get eating money." She reached for the bag and Charles put his hand on it.

"A little advice, sweetheart. Save something for a rainy day. Sun ain't going to shine on your pretty ass every day."

She snatched the bag away.

"Fuck off," she said.

CHAPTER 8

Cassie parked in front of Ron Lyle's mother's house and wondered how to approach her. She thought of the advice she got in grade school: Every job works better with a smile.

The neighborhood was working class, most of it poorly kept up. But the Lyle house was so gleamingly clean she felt like she needed to take her shoes off as she stepped onto the porch.

The porch light blazed to life and the door opened and a latch snapped shut on the screen door. An old, faded woman in a cotton dress stood behind the screen, face blurred like a priest behind a confessional.

Cassie put on a big smile.

"Mrs. Lyle, I'm—"

"I know who you are."

Cassie said, "Oh. It's so nice to finally meet you—"

"You're the drug dealer that ruined my boy Ron's life."

Cassie thought about all the lines and rationale she could give. Finally just said, "Yes, ma'am."

The face behind the screen hissed, "Don't you 'yes' me like that. Ron was a fine boy until you got your hooks in him."

"He came up to me, ma'am, first time. Every time," Cassie said.

"Of course he did. My Ron is a fine Christian boy but weak. What's he supposed to do? You know he's still got that poster of yours up in his room? All of them boys around here do. So now the big star falls to earth. Ron thinks, I can meet her for myself.

Maybe even get into those sexy pants of hers. All he has to do is go up to her at a bar and say hi and the big girl will smile and talk to him. Talk to him, and sell him drugs. Then, after a time or two, the coke itself becomes the glamor. You did it to him."

"Yes, ma'am," said Cassie. "Maybe. But I'm here to help now. Maybe."

"I told you not to 'yes' me. And he doesn't need your help."

"No, ma'am."

"He quit, did you know? Hasn't been around your way in months. Or that's what he says. He goes down to the Red Rock for a couple of beers, but that's all. He doesn't need you, or what you bring."

"Ma'am." Cassie stepped forward and put out a hand to the screen. Ms. Lyle stepped back and snarled and Cassie dropped her hand.

"I'm trying to help. Really. I just need a lock of Ron's hair. Maybe a hairbrush or something. Could you give me something like that? I'll just wait out here, don't even need to come in."

"You need what? What's wrong with you, girl? Why you need Ron's hair?"

"It's hard to explain. I've got something that will prove whether Ron did it or not. Might prove it. If he's innocent, I may be his only chance."

"And what if he's not? You think he was just a-laying on that body for fun? He was sleeping off drugs that somebody—maybe you—give to him."

"Ma'am," said Cassie, "it's really Ron's only chance."

There was silence for a minute.

"Says who? You? That Detective Stevens?"

Cassie hesitated too long before answering.

Ms. Lyle said, "You think any of you give him a chance? Ron was an innocent boy before he met you. Maybe he's as innocent, now. He says Stevens and all the crooked drug dealers and all the crooked cops in this city are framing him. Maybe you turned him into a murderer."

"Ma'am, I'm trying to do the right thing. I really am. Just a little bit of Ron's hair can prove he's innocent, maybe, I might be able to—"

"And what if he's not? You going to fix the damage you done, turning my sweet boy into a killer? No, you're going to shrug your shoulders and help Stevens put him away?"

Ms. Lyle stood there, the dark screen blurring her features but not the anger or the tears shining in her eyes.

"I don't know what Ron is any more, but Ron was an innocent boy before he met you. I sure as Hades ain't going to trust you."

Cassie started to answer but Ms. Lyle yelled out through the screen.

"Get out of here. You're a murderer of children."

The door slammed and Cassie stood on the porch as the light went out. She turned and walked back to the truck and stood there looking up at the early evening stars for an answer. The polite girl in her wanted to get in the truck and drive away, respect the woman and leave her house and family alone.

But her only chance—maybe Ron's only chance, she told herself—lay inside the house. She crouched down as small as she could and slipped to the side of the house and ducked behind an azalea trying to come into bloom. She looked down at the small bush and felt like a cartoon elephant cowering behind a mouse with pink flowers.

She took two quick steps to the chain-link fence surrounding the back yard and vaulted it. She crept to the first window and peeked into a bathroom. Saw one toothbrush, so the bathroom was probably used by Ron or Ms. Lyle, but not both. There was a brush and comb by the sink. If she broke in and stole the hairbrush, she might have Ron's DNA, or she might have Ron's mother's.

She peeked again, as fast as she could. Ducked down, and realized there was a woman's robe hanging on the door. She smiled to herself. She was getting good at this.

She duck-walked to the next window and did a quick peek. The light was off and she didn't see as much as she needed. Peeked again and still didn't see anything. She got brave and kept her head up until her eyes adjusted to the dim light in the room.

There was a man's jacket on the bed. Ron's room. Magazines in a pile on the floor, a TV and an old computer on the desk. On the chair was a wool cap.

She lowered herself out of sight and reached up so that just her hands showed in the window. Pushed on the sill and felt it give, the window moving. Pushed harder and the window slid open. She stood up and pushed her upper body into the window. Just slide in now, grab the cap and go. This detective business was pretty easy.

The back door flew open and spotlights came on in the back yard. Cassie heard Ms. Lyle yell, "Sic 'em, Sarah Palin." She watched a pit bull come running and snarling at her. Cassie scrambled to get out of the window and landed back on the ground. The dog latched onto her calf and started shaking her.

Cassie screamed and hit the dog on the head and hopped, with the dog holding on, to the fence and pulled herself over, shaking the dog loose and landing on the ground with the dog's muzzle an inch from her face. The dog snarled and snapped but the fence was between them now. Cassie pulled herself up and hobbled back to the truck and drove away.

Maybe smiling wasn't going to work.

CHAPTER 9

The matron at the jail said to Cassie, "Twice in one day? Wouldn't have picked you to be the kind to have a jailhouse crush, 'specially on that one."

Cassie said a line from a country song from the radio. "Whatever it takes, darlin'."

The matron laughed. "None of my business. But you might want to run a comb through your hair. And your leg's bleeding." She paused. "Darlin'."

Ron came dragging in, eyes darting around the room, pretending not to look at Cassie. He threw himself down on his stool and said to the floor, "You're still out there. I'm still in here. What's wrong?"

"Jesus, Ron, it's been what, like four hours? And I'm not your savior. And you're in here for murder. Murder! Do you not comprehend the deep shit you're in?"

"Not my fault." He curled up into a little ball on the stool, arms around his knees, eyes pointed at the floor but focused on nowhere.

Cassie said, "Yeah, well, it's sure as hell not mine. This is not my problem. Don't care how many of you blame me, this is not my problem. I shouldn't be doing half the things I'm doing for you. Feel like I need to tell the whole world that same damned thing: This is not my problem."

Ron shot a little half-grin out of his gloom. "Tell me how that works out for you, Cassie. They get your balls—or, I guess,

51

whatever it is you have—in a vise, you tell them, 'not my problem.' Hope it works out better for you than it has for me."

"Yeah. Yeah. Neither of us with much choice about what we've got to do. But I'm telling you this, Ron: you've got just one chance. It's with me, and it's not a good one, and it's right now. But I've got to know: did you kill that guy?"

"Cassie, I don't even know the guy. Couldn't find his house again if I had to. Read my lips: I ain't never killed nobody."

Cassie leaned into the Plexiglas and locked eyes with Ron, trying the old-fashioned lie detector. "Really?"

Ron said, "Really," but looked away, tapping his foot.

So much for the lie detector.

"Ron," she said, "I've got to know."

More foot tapping.

Cassie said, "I need something from you, and I don't want to attract the attention of the guard. I need you to reach up like you're scratching your head and pull out some hair. When she's not looking, slide your hair through the crack to me."

"Hair? Why the hell you want my hair? You going to make a Ron-wig, use it in some fancy scheme to bust me out of here?"

"No. I mean, of course not."

"You guarantee it's going to help me?"

A long pause, and Cassie said, "Maybe."

"Well, then," Ron drew himself up as much as he could. "The joke's on you, Missy. My momma just called me and said you was trying to steal something personal of mine, probably make some kind of voodoo thing. Says you're working with Stevens." He leaned at the Plexiglas. "Working against me. And I caught you." He folded his arms across his chest. "What you think of that now, missy?"

Cassie sat there, turning things over in her head to say and finding nothing.

"Then I can't help you, Ron. I'm going to wash my hands of

you and just walk away from you like any sensible person. Whatever happens is on you."

"Fine with me. Don't trust you anyway."

"It's all your own fault. This is not my problem."

Ron crossed his arms and tried to stare down his nose at her.

Cassie jumped straight up, one motion, shot her arm across the partition top and grabbed the top of Ron's head and yanked as much hair out as she could get.

The matron scrambled up from her seat.

Ron yelled, "She's stealing my hair!"

Cassie marched past the matron.

"Lovers' quarrel," she said.

CHAPTER 10

Cassie pulled into the parking lot of the white marble Alpha Center on the edge of Research Park. A Black Hawk helicopter went whock-whock-whocking low over her head, outbound from the army base and low enough for Cassie to see the pilot in the night sky. Cassie watched the dark helicopter rise over the steel-and-glass tech cubes scattered across the former cotton fields like glittering dice.

"Hey, Lou," she said to the Alpha Center's guard.

"Hey, Cassie. Going to see Mr. Blackshear?"

She nodded and he pointed to the elevator and pulled out his logbook to mark her down. She took the elevator to the fifth floor, and burst into Randy Blackshear's glass corner office.

Blackshear looked up, startled, then shook his head slowly when he saw who it was. He threw up his hands.

"Cassie, I still can't help you. No matter how many times you blow in here with another brilliant idea of how to game the system and get a job." He paused. "Besides," he motioned to a man standing leaning back on the glass and staring at Cassie. "I'm in the middle of an argument." He paused again. "With an asshole."

The asshole was staring at Cassie. Cassie glanced back at a short, young man with a gymnast's body and spiky, red hair. The man broke off the stare after an awkward pause and said to Blackshear, "Mr. Asshole, to you, since I've got my own company now."

54

" 'Your own company' is a rat hole of a warehouse out in the country with old equipment practically donated by my company and a couple of others. And you're still an asshole. A poor asshole."

"Poor asshole with an idea that will rock the world. Amazing things coming."

"You can't do what you're talking about."

"Watch me."

Blackshear said, "Cassie, this is Gene Lee, boy genius, if you believe his professors, asshole if you actually know him. Look, Cassie, I'm sorry, but I still can't help you."

He stood up and came around the desk to Cassie.

"I don't mean to be blunt, but so what if you came out of JU with a great background in software and bio-tech?" he said. "Companies with government contracts can't hire anybody with your record. And every company in Jericho—including mine—has some kind of government contract."

Cassie said, "Yes, sir, I get it. I mean, I'm sorry to interrupt you, Mr. Blackshear, particularly here at your work on a Saturday night . . ."

Blackshear waved her away. "Hey, you don't know what a dogfight it is in Jericho these days hustling for all this government work. Take a weekend off? Lucky if you get out of this business with your ass in one piece." He took a breath. "Look, Cassie, you played basketball with my daughter, and I've written more letters of recommendation for you than I can count. That's all I can do."

He stood up and went to the window and swept his hand at the other buildings spread across Research Park.

"The chamber of commerce will tell you that what you're looking for is out there, Cassie. Jericho is the city that put men on the moon and built the space station; doing even bigger things now. You've got the brains and the drive and the training but Cassie," he turned and looked at her, "you won't be a part of it. Sorry to say it, but you need to hear it."

"Got it. No, sir, I've got to ask you for a different favor and I really need it."

"Name it."

Cassie pulled a plastic sandwich bag full of hair out of her purse and put it on Blackshear's desk. He looked at her and pushed his eyebrows together into a question. She reached back into her bag, pulled out another bag with the hatchet wrapping inside.

Blackshear looked at her.

"What have you got yourself into this time?"

Cassie shook her head. "Don't ask. I mean, really, don't ask. Look, I know you don't do DNA matching here, but I know the genetic testing lab you've got has equipment that's years ahead of anybody else's. If you sequenced these samples and got someone to write the software to match the components you could do a DNA test here fast. Can you see if these match? Please. It's really important."

Blackshear narrowed his eyes at Cassie.

"And I've got to have it by tomorrow morning," she said.

Blackshear laughed. "Oh, well, that makes it even easier. Even if I could get techs to come in for free, stay up all night . . ."

"Please. I mean, I'm sorry to bother you, Mr. Blackshear. It's really, really important."

"We're a business here. We don't do stuff that doesn't make us money. Cassie, I can't."

Cassie bit her lip and nodded and started to turn away.

"I can," said the asshole at the window.

CHAPTER 11

"Jake, I screwed up," said Cassie.

"Again?" said Jake.

Jake's bar was jumping on a hot Saturday night, but Cassie's business was not. So she sat at the back bar where Jake worked and talked to him while she waited for one of her regulars to come ask her for "party supplies."

"Keep up that attitude, mister," she said, "and I'm going to find another place to buy all my club soda."

"Could buy something more, you know," Jake said. "The sign says we sell a variety of fine adult beverages. You know, stuff you actually have to pay for."

Cassie fidgeted on her barstool. "Hey, I used to buy plenty in here, back when I had money and friends."

Jake was scanning the dance floor keeping an eye on things. He brushed his short, gray hair back and looked at her with tired eyes.

"And you didn't have cops on your tail and weren't trying to make a living doing things that could put you in jail."

Cassie said, "Yeah. Better stick to club soda when I'm working, save my drinking for off-duty. Besides, this day's been so long I'd probably fall asleep on the bar from one beer. I'd buy from you if you'd sell me a case of beer I could take home. Preferably at half-price."

"Don't have a take-out license," said Jake. "I'll let you do the illegal selling around here. I'm too old to go to jail."

"Good plan." Cassie rolled her glass around like she was eyeing something stronger than club soda.

"I may be going back to jail, Jake."

Jake pulled his eyes from the room and focused a sad and pissed look on Cassie.

Cassie said, "Or worse."

"Jesus, Cassie. What the hell's that supposed to mean?"

"If I do what I have to do to stay out of jail, I'm going to hell. I mean, more than I've already gone to hell lately."

Jake studied the front window. "Did we change the name of this place to 'Hell'?"

"Look, you know what I mean."

He studied her and nodded slowly. "Yeah, I do."

"But I mean, with all the shit I've done. Am doing. Still, I've never ruined someone's life before."

Jake held her eyes and waited for her to say it herself.

"Well, except for . . ." She patted the big bag next to her.

They sat there a few seconds. Jake polished a glass, stared out the window, and pretended not to be watching her.

"But it feels like a line I don't want to cross, you know?" she said. "Another line. I've already crossed too many."

Jake stood there polishing the glass.

"So maybe it's just another line in hell somewhere, but I still don't want to cross it, go from this part of hell to that part."

She leaned over toward Jake. "So—unless a long shot I'm trying pays off—that's the choice I've got tomorrow. Maybe even then."

She set the glass down and held out one hand, palm up. "Go to jail. And if I go to jail, nobody looks after my niece."

She held up the other beside it. "Or go to hell."

Waved her hands up and down as if weighing whether to have the steak or the chicken for dinner.

There was a laugh, loud like a race car ripping through the

bar. Jake and Cassie looked over at a table. A good-looking woman and a good-looking man were appreciating each other's good-looking-ness. The woman's laugh was trailing off. The man was leaning back, proud of whatever he had said or done and anticipating where things were going. The woman reached out, slow and deliberate, and laid her hand on his forearm. He smiled back.

Cassie looked at Jake and he was smiling.

"What are you smiling at?" she said.

"Happy couple. Happy for them."

"Huh," she said. "Doesn't know what she's getting into."

"Maybe." Jake put the glass up. "Maybe it'll be something good. Maybe if you hadn't insisted on dating Mr. Hot Actor in Hollywood, you'd have something good now."

"Ric?" She laughed. "Yeah. He was hot. Hot, tall, and well-dressed. All the things I want in a man. 'Course he also ran like a scalded dog when my 'troubles' came. Said his publicist didn't want him 'romantically linked' with me anymore."

Jake said, "You ever think about what things would have been like if you'd have ignored your list, found somebody to stand beside you when things got tough? I'm sure glad my wife ignored whatever her magic list would have been thirty years ago and married me and kept me straight. I'd just be a drifting barfly without her."

"No." She leaned forward, excited to be lecturing. "You got it wrong, Jake. Make a plan and then go get it." She held up one finger and counted it off with her other hand. "One. Well-dressed, because that shows he cares about himself and can care about me." Added a finger. "Two. Tall, because I don't want to feel like a Sasquatch when I'm out with him." Third finger. "And hot, well—figure that one out for yourself. Know what you want, go get it, and don't hesitate."

"Till life gets in your way. Your plan's working out good for you so far."

The crowd parted and David, the crime-scene tech, walked through, still in his black suit. Still tall and hot. A young woman, cute and busty, looked up at him as he came through and brushed up against him. He ignored her and walked over to Cassie.

"Hey," he said.

"Hey yourself," she said. She licked her lips.

"Imagine accidentally bumping into you here," he said. "Only had to go to three other bars, ask about a million questions, for this accident to happen."

He smiled, just a little inviting smile.

Cassie smiled back. Invitation accepted.

"So," he said. "Do you want a drink?"

"No," she ran her hand up his forearm. "You want to save a lady from hell for a night?"

CHAPTER 12

Cassie pulled her truck into the back yard of a crumbling house on the edge of the historic Old Town part of Jericho. The house had been the home of a general after the Civil War, but now it was chopped into four awkward apartments, with peeling paint and untrimmed bushes that loomed like monsters in the dark.

Tonight, she didn't care. She hummed a happy little song, feeling her body alive and tingling and anticipating. Go inside, take a long, hot shower, put on the cute little nothing she hadn't worn in a long time, and wait for the knock at the door. Put Belva and Stevens and drug-dealing all out of her mind for a few hours.

She got out of the truck carrying her bag and shoved the sliding door. The door shrieked and stuck half-open. She cursed and leaned on the warped door to get the latch to engage, clicked the padlock closed, and skipped across the dark patch of mud that served as a parking lot.

The bush by the front door shook and Cassie froze. She thought of the gun under the seat of the truck, thought about how long it would take to scoot back, unlock the truck and . . . be dead before she got that far.

So it was just Cassie and nerve against the monster. She picked up the biggest rock she saw, hurled it into the bush as hard as she could.

"Get the fuck out here!" she shouted. She opened her bag and stuck her hand inside. "Got a piece here. Gonna empty it into that bush unless I see some hands come out empty and slow."

What came out were giggles.

"Hey, don't shoot, Marshal Dillon, don't shoot." Belva rolled out from behind the bush with her hands up. "It's just a poor, old, crippled lady from a ranch on the other side of Dodge City."

"What the hell?" said Cassie. "Do you know what time it is?"

Belva's smile faded to the point where she had to work to hold it up. "I just thought I'd come over here and spend the night with my favorite aunt."

Cassie said, "How did you get here?"

"I told Courtney's mother that I had to get to the hospital and that Jill was in no shape to take me. She dropped me at the hospital door, and I kept going on my own."

"You got yourself all the way over here by yourself? What's that—two, three miles?"

Belva shrugged. "Wasn't too bad."

"In the middle of the night? Through a neighborhood most people wouldn't drive in after dark?"

Belva grinned. "Hey, I'm Cassie's niece. The bad guys are scared of me out there. I might have a rocket launcher, stolen from one of the super-secret military contractors around town, built into this thing for all they know."

"Whatever. OK, come on, let's get you inside and call your mother."

"Oh, man, no. Why you want to do that?" Belva wheeled up fast to Cassie, then forced a grin. "Oh, I know. You got a party going on tonight, think I be in the way. Probably got a good-looking, young stud coming in behind you right now."

Belva winked at Cassie.

"You know," said Cassie, "you get stressed, you talk just like your mother."

"Pardon, madam. Could I request the favor of having you unstress me so I can speak the King's English like my beloved Aunt Cassie again? Please, ma'am? For the poor little crippled girl?"

Cassie smiled, and Belva smiled back.

"Oh, give me a break. All right. Just for a few minutes."

She stepped away and pulled out her cell.

"Hey," said David, in his throaty whisper. "You said give you thirty minutes for a shower. Decide you couldn't wait that long?"

"No. Well, maybe. Something's come up here. We can't do this tonight. Rain check?"

The tone was cold. "Sure." He hung up.

Cassie glared at her phone.

Belva said, "Cassie, I didn't mean to mess things up. Really, I'm used to parties going on around me. I can just stay out in the living room, keep the TV low, you and your friend won't even know I'm there."

Cassie unlocked the door and shooed Belva in. "Yeah, let's see if you can handle all the wildness in here."

There was barely enough room for Belva to maneuver her wheelchair in the tiny living room/kitchen combo, but she lit up like it was a palace.

"Man, this is fantastic. I'll be fine here." She reached back and popped her backpack off the wheelchair onto the floor.

"Uptown? Two rooms hacked out of an old house? With a drainpipe from the upstairs running right through the middle of my living room-slash-kitchen-slash-whatever?"

Belva wheeled over to the pipe and put a hand on it. "We're going to decorate this like a Christmas tree. Our place is going to be beautiful, Cassie."

Cassie said, "Don't get too comfortable, missy. Your mom's going to be here in ten minutes." She pulled her cell out of her pocket.

Belva rolled over and snatched it out of her hands.

"What's wrong with you, young lady?" said Cassie. "You don't take my cell. I'm calling your mother, and that's final."

Cassie reached for the cell. Belva hid it behind her back, reached under Cassie's ribs and tickled her. Cassie jumped back laughing.

"No fair. You know I can't stand that."

"Then stay over there. Leave me and the phone alone and we'll leave you alone."

"Can't." Cassie stepped up and they wrestled, Cassie giggling and Belva saying, "Don't call Mom" over and over. Cassie got the phone and jumped back.

"Really," said Belva, laughter turning to tears in an instant. "Don't call Mom."

Cassie waited for her to say more.

"I don't want to be around her new old man." She paused and waited but Cassie said nothing. "Just let me stay here tonight; give them a little time to get used to each other. Leave me out of it for just one night."

Cassie held the phone and looked at Belva.

"Cassie, you know she won't miss me. Probably don't even know I'm gone, unless her boyfriend notices. Just tonight. Don't make me go back there tonight."

Cassie put the phone in her pocket. "Belva, what's going on?"

"Nothing. I just don't like the guy." She looked at Cassie. "Please don't call DHR either. You know they did nothing last time but put me in a foster home. And then the folks in the foster home threatened to put me in jail."

"Belva, they threatened to put you in the detention home, not jail. Besides, you know you shouldn't have done what you did to them."

"Maybe. But if you call DHR, I'll run away."

Cassie looked at Belva a long time.

"Really, Cassie, all I need is one night. Give them a little time to get used to each other and we'll be one happy family."

"One night," Cassie said. "One night. Then your mother and I are going to have a long talk when I take you back in the morning."

"Thank you, thank you," said Belva. "I'll sleep here on the couch. You'll see—I won't be any trouble."

"I'll sleep on the couch. You'll sleep on the bed. And we're both going to do that now."

Cassie lay on the little couch with her legs hanging off the end until feelings of helplessness turned to dreams of more helplessness. She was in a scary, screwed-up world of monsters and ogres, running as hard as she could from them and going nowhere, when a pounding on the door a foot away from her head snatched her out of the dream and brought her upright with her heart pounding.

"Open the fuck up." She heard Jill's voice.

She jumped up and pulled the door open. Jill was leaning against the door frame with a dirty little man with big glasses behind her.

"Come for Godzilla on Wheels," Jill said. She was talking in a slurred singsong.

Cassie eyed them. Jill could barely stand up. The dirty little man had a glazed look and seemed to be held up only by the strength of his stare at Cassie's breasts in her thin tee shirt.

"Which one of you drove here?" said Cassie.

"What the hell do you care?" Jill pushed past Cassie and into the house.

"Little bitch," she called. "Come on out. We're going home."

Belva rolled out of the bedroom.

"Staying here," Belva said. "Ask Cassie."

Jill smiled and gave a nasty little laugh.

"Ask her yourself." She stepped up to Cassie but talked to Belva. "Ask your auntie here what happens if I make one little phone call. DHR will come and put your ass in a foster home and then they'll put you in jail soon as you screw up. Should take about a day." Jill smiled coldly at Belva. "After that, I'll be rid of you and your goddamned wheelchair and all the goddamned three-times-a-week rehab for good and I can find a man without having to apologize for the cripple in the back room. Cops will also probably search this place and put your dear auntie in jail. Maybe you two can share a cell."

Jill smiled a nasty smile up at Cassie and pointed at her black eye. "Looks like you had your fun."

She cackled, then put her face up at Cassie. "You think I need you, but you need your big sister more than I need you. Tell the little bitch. I'm the one that keeps her at home and you out of jail."

Cassie turned to Belva.

"You have to go home."

Belva's jaws locked and she spun the chair backwards into the bedroom and slammed the door.

Cassie looked at Jill and the man. "But you aren't driving."

Jill smiled again and said, "Your problem, not mine. I ain't paying for no cab ride."

"I know a cabbie who owes me a favor."

They sat on the back stoop and waited for the cab, Belva nervously rolling her wheels back and forth, the man sitting between Jill and Cassie. Cassie felt the man's hand rub her ass a couple of times. She swatted it away and Jill giggled.

"Maybe we'll just drive ourselves," said Jill. "Getting tired of waiting. Starting to sober up."

Cassie stood up and went inside and found a half-full bottle of Jack that she was saving for a special occasion. She sat back down on the stoop and handed it to Jill.

"Might as well have some fun while we wait. See if you can drink as much as your baby sister," said Cassie.

Jill took the bottle and turned it up, the dark liquid bubbling away like water. Handed what was left back to Cassie. Cassie turned it up and held it there, pretending to drink. She let one tiny taste slide down and coat her throat with a luxury she knew she wouldn't be able to afford for a long time.

She handed it back to Jill. Jill emptied the bottle and waved it at Cassie with a cackle.

"Hell, yeah."

Jill threw the bottle into the darkness. It crashed tingling against a tree and Cassie thought, *one more thing to clean up.* Jill leaned against the dirty man and fell asleep.

The cab arrived a few minutes later and the young driver smiled up at Cassie. They loaded a sullen Belva up front and her wheelchair in the trunk. Cassie picked up Jill and shoved her, snoring, into the back. The dirty little man started to climb in next to Jill. Cassie put a hand on his arm and pulled him back.

"You're staying with me," she said.

He started to argue and then leered up at her.

Cassie leaned into the driver's window.

"Sam, I . . ."

"We're square, Cassie. The way you helped me out, back when you were on top, paid for a lot of free rides."

Cassie smiled. "No, it didn't. But I will pay you back someday."

The cab pulled away and it was just Cassie and the little man staring at her chest. She grabbed him by the shoulders and turned him to the road.

"Go four blocks that way. Turn left on Jackson Way. 'Bout half a mile, you'll come to a church shelter. They'll tell you they're closed, but they'll let you sleep there for the night anyway."

The grin fell and the man pumped himself up to argue. Cassie grabbed him by the biceps and squeezed until he could feel the pain in his arms and see the rage in her shaking face. She put her face in his and growled, "Go. If I hear you're back around Jill or Belva, I'll come for you."

His eyes got wide and she watched him stumble away down the street, rocking back and forth like the little tramp in the old Charlie Chaplin movies. Cassie pulled a box out of the dumpster and went to clean up the pieces of the Jack bottle, thinking about the benefits of life in an all-women's prison.

CHAPTER 13

Belva and Jill were gone, but Cassie was too wired to sleep now. There was a strong wind coming up, the trees twitching and whispering in the night. She sat on the back stoop and listened, but there was no magic advice in the wind.

She couldn't leave Belva to Jill. Or to the system. That meant, even if the DNA test on Ron came back negative, she had to give Stevens what he wanted and put Ron in jail. As usual these days, she'd done a bunch of half-thought-out things that accomplished nothing good for nobody. Probably. Maybe. Shitty world.

She didn't want to do this sober. She checked her pocket, found a wadded-up twenty, and walked up to Five Points. The guy in the beverage store said, "Take this shit home, Cassie. I ain't going to have you passed out on the sidewalk out front again."

Cassie hoisted the case of generic beer on her shoulder like a stevedore and walked home.

She sat at her kitchen table watching a rat-sized roach scurry out from behind the refrigerator. She looked at the growing line of empties standing in a half-circle before her like an audience.

"They're coming for me, friend," she said to the roach. "I've got two chances tomorrow morning." She pulled out two cans and lined them up. "Either I get a match tomorrow and feel better about committing perjury and sending a man to death row." She pulled one can forward. "Or I get no match and send

69

a man I know is innocent to death row." Pulled the other can forward and knocked them both down. "Either way, everybody is screwed."

She giggled. "Except me. I can't even get screwed."

She considered that for a long moment and picked up her phone.

"Hey, David," she said. There was a long pause. "Too late?"

CHAPTER 14

Cassie's cell buzzed a little before five in the morning. She rolled over in bed, naked, the sheets a mess, and picked it up without looking at the caller ID.

"Coming back for more?" she said, half awake.

"Wasn't planning on it. This is Gene Lee, Randy's friend."

She sat up in the bed, covers falling to her waist. Pulled the covers back up as if the man on the phone could see her.

"I thought you were—oh, never mind. Do you know what time it is? On a Sunday morning?"

"You said you wanted results, early. I get results, early. I've got two things for you."

"Oh—yeah. Thanks, Gene. I mean, thanks Mr. Lee. Okay, I'm awake now. What'd you come up with?"

"You're wrong," he said. "Wrong twice. First, my name is Gene, not Mr. Lee. But the second is the biggie: the DNA samples don't match."

"Shit. Maybe. I guess. I don't know. It's good news, just . . . not for me."

"So you were trying to prove that the guy with the hair shops at Home Depot? Now you have to see if maybe he shops at Lowe's or Ace? Doesn't seem like that big a deal."

Cassie ignored him. "You sure you did that right?"

There was a long, icy pause.

He said, "I think I'm going to hang up now."

"No, wait. I just . . . I don't know. It is better, really. I guess.

Just makes things harder for me. Did you ever have one of those days where you've got to make a really tough choice?"

Gene said, "Like when I graduated from school last year and had a couple of big job offers but they wouldn't let me work on what I thought was really important, so I started my own one-man company with a couple of thousand dollars left over from my college fund? My folks still think I'm wasting my life."

"Yeah, but no, not like that. Something where you've got to decide between one hard thing or another, somebody's going to get hurt either way, you're not even sure which one is the right one? God, I don't even know why I'm talking to you like this."

"Maybe because I'm listening. Maybe just because it's five in the morning and you're too sleepy to have your guard up. In any case, I used to read a bunch of detective stories about a guy who lived on a boat. One of his friends always said, 'When you're faced with two moral choices, the more difficult one is usually the right one.' "

Cassie said, "I was hoping for advice that said, 'Just run away to a foreign country, hide out on a beach somewhere.' "

Gene said, "Don't think you could do that. Not just your looks, and the fact that you'd stand out anywhere, but the way you're wired. Girl who bursts into the office of a company president and demands that he do something impossible because she thinks it's right isn't the kind of person to run away from a fight."

Cassie said, "I could learn."

"I doubt it."

"It's just," she stretched, feeling the sheets slide on her skin, smelling the leftover love smells, "that easy things feel so good and difficult things are so . . . difficult."

"Yeah. Well, I said I had two things. The other thing's a good thing for you. Well, maybe it's a good thing. I don't know. It would be up to you."

Cassie pulled the sheets up and started to tell him that she didn't date short men. Particularly not short, arrogant, awkward men.

But he spoke first. "Look, I need some help in my lab. Well, maybe I need some help. I haven't made up my mind. If you want to come to my lab about noon, I can show you around and we can talk."

"Oh. Yes! Yes! Wait—what about all the government regulations and my record?"

"Fuck the government. This is my company. You interested?"

"Yes, yes, hell yes. Can I come there now?"

"No. After staying up all night doing your work, I'm going to get some sleep. If you want to talk, come to my lab at noon and we'll talk work."

Cassie said, "I'll be there at 11:45."

"Then you'll wait on the sidewalk till twelve. I mean it. When it comes to work, I'm an arrogant SOB who does things when and how he thinks he should."

"Won't be the first time I've sat on the sidewalk hoping for a job."

"Long as you don't get your hopes up too high," he said. "Look, a couple of things. First, this may not be that big an opportunity for you. Second—"

"I'll take any opportunity. All I want is a shot."

"Well, that's all this probably is for you, just a shot at proving yourself so that maybe you can get a real job someday. Second, Randy said you were a real math/genetics geek. My experience is that, most of the time, when people say somebody's smart, they're just being polite and that person's only medium-smart. I really am smart, and I'm trying to do something really hard, and I don't have time for anybody who can't keep up or isn't dedicated. So both of us should expect that you'll probably get a polite tour of my lab, a few polite questions, and then a polite handshake goodbye. And, uh, even if things work out, Randy told me about some . . . other things. I don't care about all that, as long as anything with the police is in the past."

"It is. I promise."

Gene said, "Noon," and hung up.

Cassie sat on the bed and looked at her reflection in the window: tangled hair, crooked lipstick, and raccoon eyes from smeared makeup.

"May be a shitty world," she said to herself. "But I don't have to look like shit."

After she showered and brushed out her hair and put on makeup, she stood fidgeting before the mirror. She breathed in and out slowly.

"I will be calm," she said slowly.

"I will choose to be positive," she said, remembering the mantra from yoga class. She looked out the window for the sun but the sky was still dark.

No point in waiting for the sun to catch up before she started her day. She faced the bright spot in the dark sky where the light would soon break through.

"Morning intentions, Sunday," she said. "I will be kind. I will take care of Stevens today, and I will get that job. And I will be grateful . . ." she paused and slowed her breathing down. "I will be grateful for opportunities."

CHAPTER 15

Stevens looked up as Cassie walked into the detectives' bay in mid-morning. One of the young detectives turned and stared as she went by.

"What's this, glamour day?" Stevens said. Then he nodded, a gleam in his eye. "Got it. You finally figured out how the real world works. Trying to impress the people that own you by dressing up and putting on makeup. Even combed your hair like a big girl."

Cassie leaned over Stevens's desk and flashed a big, fake Hollywood smile back at him. Held it for a second, then turned it to a scowl.

"Not for you," she said. She looked back over her shoulder at the other men staring at her and pretending not to. "Not for any of you."

She stood up. "It's because I'm proud of myself. I'm going to get you off of my back today and go back to taking care of my niece."

"And selling drugs to make money?"

Cassie thought about the job interview and smiled. *Maybe not.* Stevens looked at her like he wanted an explanation but she wasn't going to give him one.

Finally he said, "OK, let's go find an interrogation room and get your statement and complete your transformation into a co-operative, upstanding citizen of the Jericho."

"Stevens," said Cassie, "remember the old Stones' song, the

one about how you can't always get what you want, but you can get what you need?"

"What the hell's that supposed to mean?"

"Just keep that in mind while we talk." She turned and started to march away, but stopped when she realized that she didn't know where she was going.

Stevens swept a recorder off of his desk and marched past Cassie toward the door. He stopped when he realized Cassie wasn't following.

"C'mon," he said. When she didn't budge, he added, "Please."

"I thought you'd never ask." Cassie followed him as he rolled his eyes.

They walked down the hall to the same cold room as yesterday. Cassie sat upright in her chair, hands folded neatly in her lap like she had done for press conferences in LA. Stevens noted the posture, grunted, put the recorder on the table between them, and flicked it on.

"Now, let's be sure we do this right," he said.

"That's all I want to do."

Stevens studied her for a minute without saying anything.

"OK, state your name for the record."

"Cassandra Luna."

"Full name."

"You don't need my middle name," said Cassie.

"Full name."

"Beatrice. There, are you happy? Cassandra Beatrice Luna."

"And you swear that the statement you are about to give is the truth, the whole truth, and nothing but the truth?"

She beamed. "I really, really do."

Stevens looked at her again.

"All right," he said slowly. "Let's have your statement."

Cassie cleared her throat.

"Acting on my own as a concerned citizen, in cooperation

with the Jericho Police Department, I have discovered evidence that conclusively proves that Ronald Lyle could not have murdered James Irvin. Because I intend to demonstrate my desire to be a model citizen, I have brought this information forward—"

Stevens punched the "off" button so hard it looked like his finger was going to go through the table.

"What the hell is this?"

"It. Is. The. Truth. What any good citizen—any really, really good citizen—would tell you. I am doing my community service, as you asked."

"You are trying to fuck up the system. And you are going to fuck up yourself. Do you have any idea what happens if anybody hears this?"

"Too bad. It's right there." Cassie pointed at the recorder. "On the tape. Or chip. Or whatever."

Stevens threw the recorder on the floor and stomped on it. "Not anymore."

"I bet it is," said Cassie. "I bet any good technician could take the memory card out and recover that. What are you going to do, Stevens, eat the evidence?"

"If I have to." He picked up the little pile of plastic, fished out the memory card, and popped the card into his mouth. Stood over Cassie, chewing and crunching and glaring at her.

He spat the pieces of card in her face. "Let them recover that."

"C'mon." He snatched Cassie up by one arm and she didn't fight it. He dragged her out of the room.

"I can't go to jail," she said.

"Should have thought of that earlier."

He dragged her out the door, past the booking area and into the parking lot and threw her into the passenger seat of his black Impala. Got in and peeled out of the lot.

"Jesus, Stevens, where the hell are we going?"

"Going to drive round and round till you get some sense in you."

"I've got sense. Listen, Ron couldn't—"

"Shush."

"Shush? Like you're talking to a little child. I'm going to tell the whole damned world." She rolled her window down and yelled at it. "Ron Lyle is—"

Stevens yanked her back in with one hand and clamped his hand over her mouth. Cassie bit it, hard, and he pretended not to notice.

"You get blood on my car, you're going to clean it up."

They blew threw a red light and Cassie pointed up at a small, four-blade helicopter hovering over the intersection, looking like a child's toy but holding rock-steady.

"QBot monitoring the red light. They got you, Stevens."

"Shit." He tried to find the QBot in the outside mirror. Couldn't. "Keep an eye on that thing."

"Why?" She laughed at him. "Think you can't fix a ticket?"

"Ain't the ticket I'm worried about. Watch him, see if he's following us."

Cassie turned and looked, bored. "Ain't budging. You're paranoid, you know it?"

"Yeah."

They rode up the mountain. At the top, Stevens pulled into the parking lot of an antebellum home that had been turned into a museum. He parked on the far side of the lot from a school bus that was disgorging kids. Stevens took his hand off of Cassie's mouth and got out and walked away. Cassie followed, slamming the door behind her.

"I am suing the hell out of you and JPD!" she screamed.

Over his shoulder, Stevens said, "Good for you. Told you not to talk like that around there. Not even in the car. God knows who heard what you said."

"How can the biggest and the baddest be scared?"

"Sometimes there's bigger and badder than even the biggest and the baddest. Who do you think you were helping with that crap back there? Yourself? You want to go to jail? Lyle? Look, let me tell you: Word gets out that Lyle has a fighting chance, any reason for people to pay attention to him, and he will wind up dead the next day. They will find his body hung in his cell, everybody will point and say he did it because he was guilty. You play this thing the way I told you. And you play it quiet."

"Or what? You're going to send that little squirrel-of-a-cop around to beat me up again?"

"I didn't tell him to do that. I told him to let you know we were there, that's all."

"Sure."

Stevens sat down on a bench overlooking the city and patted the seat beside him for Cassie.

Cassie stood in front of him with her back to the city and waved her finger at him. "You didn't even ask me about the evidence I found."

"What's the objection they use in the courtroom? Irrelevant. Nobody cares."

"You're going to hear it anyway. Ron Lyle couldn't have done it."

"Just decided to take a nap on top of a dead guy?"

Cassie made a face at Stevens. "Don't know about that. But I know that the killer was big and vicious. Ron's a little bitty weasel. Look at the crime-scene photos and convince yourself."

"Can't. You stole my photos."

"You can get more. Another thing: the hatchet was brand new."

"So?"

Cassie leaned back and crossed her arms over her chest. "So

you really think Lyle went to Home Depot and said, 'I better pick up a hatchet in case I need to hack somebody to death today?' C'mon. If the hatchet were lying around in the garden or a tool room at Irvin's, I might buy that this was just a drug robbery gone bad. I don't buy this, and you don't buy it, either."

Stevens looked past her and studied the city sprawled out below them through the pine trees. Cassie left him to his thoughts until she lost her patience.

"Are you listening to me?" she shouted.

"Not so loud," said Stevens.

"Oh, so now you're scared of fourth graders?"

She turned to the kids in the distance and yelled, "This man is a dirty cop. A dirty, sloppy cop."

Stevens leaned back and said, "Feel better now?"

Cassie glared at him, the city behind her and her finger shaking in Stevens's face.

"No. No, I do not feel better. I feel outraged. And one last thing, the thing your Keystone Kops couldn't be bothered to find. In the yard of the house next door was the plastic wrap from the hatchet. Says it right there on it, with a big label from Home Depot. So, after Ron stopped at Home Depot for the murder weapon, before he went into a house he'd never been in, going in to hack a man to death he'd never met, he took off the wrapping and threw it on the ground. Maybe you can add littering to his charges."

Cassie paused, waiting for Stevens to say something nasty, but he was just nodding his head with a funny little smile.

"But," she said. "But—and this is the part even you have to pay attention to—his DNA was not on that wrapping."

Stevens laughed at her. "DNA? You've got your own DNA lab? Can get a match done in a day when the state of Alabama takes a year? You're turning into a fucking Nancy Drew."

"Tell me I'm wrong."

He pointed down to the city. "See that?"

"What? The old Saturn rocket standing at the Rocket Park? Everybody's seen that. Biggest thing in the Jericho."

"Biggest and best. Everybody's seen it, and nobody notices it anymore. When I was a young pup on the force, full of piss and vinegar and sure that truth and justice would prevail—like you are now—the city was young then, too. Young and proud to be building the rocket that would take men to the moon. A proud moment for a proud city. Jericho's still high-tech now, but changed its dream from 'moon' to 'money.' And the Lyles of Jericho are getting squashed when they get in the way."

He patted the bench again, and Cassie sat down next to him.

"Of course you're right," he said, "and it doesn't matter. Not one damned bit. Why the hell you think I told you to keep quiet back there? The powers that be have decided this is the way it's going to be, and anyone who doesn't like it can go down with Lyle. They've got their patsy—damned if I know how or why they set Lyle up, but we both know they did. And they're going to get away with it, like they're getting away with everything else."

"You can't let this happen."

"Sure I can. I'm a paid employee of the Jericho PD: I do what I'm told. Been doing it for years, and I'll do it until I collect my pension and get out. And there are people watching to see that I do. I can't investigate this thing any more than I already have."

"Well, I sure as hell can," said Cassie.

Stevens shrugged. "Hey, if that's really what you want to do. Knock yourself out. I can stall your arrest until maybe Friday. Get something rock-solid, something we—by we, I mean, you— can take to somebody outside of the Jericho, and maybe I'll never get around to filing charges on you. Otherwise, you're sitting in that prison cell with Lyle this time next week."

Stevens got up and walked, ponderous and slow, back to the car.

Cassie called, "So I'm not going to jail?"

"Not today. Maybe Friday. If you can't deliver."

Cassie followed. "You think I can't do it? You may think I'm just some trashy little drug-dealing loser, but I used to be smart. Teachers said so, everybody said so."

Stevens smiled a little as he got in the car and cranked the engine. He pulled away before Cassie was all the way in.

"Hey!" she said. "What the hell's wrong with you? Let me in."

Stevens stopped the car and pointed at her. "You want to get in, get in fast, or get lost."

Cassie got in and Stevens slammed the gas, popping Cassie back in her seat.

Cassie said, "Show some consideration."

Stevens turned and glared at her and gave her a nasty little laugh as he peeled out of the lot, the car drifting out of his lane while he stared at her instead of the road. An oncoming car had to swerve to keep from hitting them. Horns squawked and Stevens ignored them.

"Get it straight," he said. "I ain't your friend; I'm your boss. I ain't your friend any more than you're Ron Lyle's friend. If you have to, you'll put him in jail. If I have to put your ass in jail to cover my own, that's just what I'll do."

He turned his eyes forward and pulled the car back in his lane. They didn't say anything until they got back to the JPD parking lot. Stevens stopped the car on the edge.

"Get out," he said. "You want to play Nancy Drew, then get the fucking job done. And I better hear progress from you every day. Twice a day, maybe. This is job one for you."

Cassie got out and held the door open, glaring at Stevens. She noticed a little self-satisfied smile playing on his face.

"You son of a bitch," she said slowly. "You planned this all along. You knew I wouldn't let Ron go to jail. You just want someone to do your dirty work for you. Why did you pick on me?"

He smiled. "I own you."

"You're willing to put Ron and me—two innocent people—in jail if you have to, and not even give it a second thought."

"Innocent?" said Stevens.

Cassie glared at him. "You know what I mean. Is there no limit to what you will do?"

Stevens smiled.

"This is Jericho, sweetheart. The sky is not the limit."

CHAPTER 16

When Cassie left Stevens, she wanted to feel clean and normal and smart and middle-class before she went to her job interview but she was still boiling with things she wanted to say to Stevens and the whole dirty world. She went to the coffee shop in the Barnes and Noble bookstore to sit and think.

She stood back from the counter and looked at the prices for the fancy coffee drinks and smoothies. More money than she had today. She shook her head, realizing that this was the first time she'd looked at the prices. When she was on top, she came here all the time with friends. Order a smoothie with every trendy ingredient on the menu, hand the clerk a ten, and not even notice how much change she got back.

This year had been different. On any given day, what she had in her pocket—after she paid Jill and paid Charles—was all that she had. If she had two lonely dollar bills keeping each other company, she could have a beer—maybe—or a really cheap dinner. Not both.

She hadn't been in Barnes and Noble, even to browse, since her first arrest. She realized now that the reason wasn't really money but shame. And not even shame over her arrests, or even the big red scar, but just the unreasoning shame of poverty. Standing outside the door and knowing that everything inside the store, and the other stores, was for other people with money.

Cassie stepped away from the line and sat down and people-watched. It felt good sitting here now, wearing her best outfit

84

from LA, the lucky blouse from a designer whose name impressed everybody, hoping it would bring her luck with the job interview. She smiled at the people in line. People in suits. Hipsters wearing torn jeans that they probably spent a hundred dollars on to get a look that said they didn't care about money. People glancing at watches and cell phones, in a hurry to get somewhere important.

Maybe it's the world she's coming back to. Real job, real money again. A world where strangers would look at her without wondering what she was guilty of.

She rejoined the line and stood there remembering her last order, getting what she wanted and not even thinking about the price. That seemed shameful in its own way to her now, just using money to show that she didn't have to worry about money. She wondered what it all meant to her today. Wondered what it would mean tomorrow, after she had a job and membership in the rich-folks club again. Assuming, of course, that she could get Stevens off her back. And Belva and those other things on her list.

She stepped up to the front of the line. The young girl behind the counter was cute as a puppy, with a silver bone in her nose and a genuinely friendly smile.

"Hi," said Cassie, smiling back. "I just wanted to tell you, thanks for what you do here in providing a warm, friendly place for people to get away and relax."

"Oh, that is so sweet of you to say that," said the girl.

Cassie said, "I know you mostly just hear a lot of complaints, people upset that their double decaf mocha was only a single decaf mocha and such. I just wanted you to hear about the good that you're doing."

"Thank you, ma'am. Is there something I can get you?"

"You know," said Cassie, "what I want is something really

simple and good with no pretense. Could I just have a glass of water?"

"Certainly."

Cassie turned to a woman in a red business suit behind her and beamed. "They just do such a good job here, don't you think?"

The woman smiled sweetly. "I'd like it if you would get out of my fucking way so I can get my first fucking cup of coffee before I fucking well kill somebody."

"Oh." Cassie turned back to the clerk, and then turned back around to the woman in red.

"You don't have to go around making everything in the world dirty."

CHAPTER 17

Cassie sat alone on the sidewalk at 11:45 and wondered if she was in the right place. The address matched the one Gene had given her, but the building itself was a rusting, corrugated-metal shed from the eighties with a falling sign that said "Gateway Storage." Someone had spray painted "to Hell" over "Storage." The building was out in the woods near the airport, overgrown with pines and kudzu and set so far back from the road that it looked more like a farmer's barn until you got close. An abandoned barn.

But it was the address that Cassie had been told held promise for her, so she sat down with her back and her good blouse against the rusty wall next to the small, glass front door and looked out over a small, black-tar parking lot with heat waves boiling up and weeds growing out of the cracks. The lot was empty but for a few faded yellow lines and her beat-up, old truck. Cassie reached into her ragged JU backpack, and pulled out James Gleick's classic text, *Chaos: Making a New Science*.

The spine was held together with duct tape and the book naturally fell open to a few favorite pages worn almost to the point of tissue. She loved the pulse of the book, the feel of smart but ordinary people discovering that the world doesn't have to be the way they were told. Discovering that most of the universe is hiding in the cracks between order and disorder in the world, and then building the mathematical tools to deal with it. Chaos. Cassie fell in love with the concept the day she heard about it, back in college when everybody still treated her like she was smart and fed her the best ideas and the toughest technical problems.

The glass lobby door clicked open and Gene stood there looking down at her and rubbing his eyes.

"Told you noon." He was wearing an old tee shirt and sleeping pants printed to look like they were jeans with a "Clark" belt buckle and the jeans pulled down to reveal "Superman" underpants. His hair was flat and bed-messed on one side and he was unshaven.

"They make watches, you know," he said.

Cassie scrambled to get to her feet.

"Yes, sir," she said. She felt silly calling a guy a year younger than herself "sir," but he was going to be her boss. Maybe.

He waved his coffee cup at her book and coffee sloshed onto it.

"Shallow," he said.

Cassie wiped coffee off her book with her hand and struggled not to lose her temper.

"Of course it's shallow." She started to put the book up but felt like that would be conceding the point. Keep it in her hand, maybe wave it in this jerk's face. "You can't get to the deep stuff without dipping your toes into the shallow end. You ever get out of the lab, go to the ocean, and see how the real world works?"

"Big deal," he said. "So you read something like this so you can use big words like 'Mandelbrot sets' and make people think you're smart?"

"No, if you're trying to make people think you're smart, you interview them in hideous pajamas; try to show them you're so smart you can do whatever you want."

She stood up and looked down on him now.

She said, "But if you care more about what you think than what somebody else thinks, then you follow this book up with nonlinear dynamics. You bug your math teachers until they've got nothing else to show you. You work with your comp sci teachers until you realize you can't solve a multi-dimensional, nonhomogeneous problem on a single-threaded linear computer. And you go back to your genetics teacher and tell him he needs to look at this."

She sighed. "But of course he won't listen. Assholes never listen to basketball-playing girls. So you ignore the assholes and teach yourself. And even when you're on the road playing basketball, you keep working at it because you love it and you know you're your own best teacher."

Gene said, "Huh."

Cassie pursed her lips. "You know, some people say that's pretty rude. Sounds like you think you're smarter than they are, don't even need a full word to show it."

Gene stared at her for a minute and smiled.

"People who think that can go fuck themselves," he said. "Besides, you ever think the sound might be directed at myself, might express surprise and momentary self-contempt because I didn't think of what you said myself?"

He held the door open and motioned her inside.

"Coffee?"

"No, thank you," said Cassie. "Caffeine's a drug to stay awake. I don't need it."

"Also boosts your brain, so you can keep up with me."

"Still don't need it. You keep the coffee for yourself."

Cassie bit her lip. *Watch your mouth, girl.*

Gene turned away, probably, she thought, so she couldn't see him smiling.

The door opened into a small lobby that was gray and empty except for a banged-up government surplus desk. Behind the desk was a blow-up doll wearing a blue uniform.

"Meet Officer Otto, security," said Gene.

"Looks like that blow up doll from *Airplane*," said Cassie. "That was his name, right? Otto? Yeah, 'Otto the Autopilot.' "

"That's him. Best security I can afford. Have to hope that anybody who looks in the only window here sees a uniform and goes away."

Gene walked into the interior and Cassie followed him into a quarter-acre of open space empty except for small clusters of old equipment sagging in random spots. They passed under a cardboard archway with the word "GENES" painted by hand.

"Ostentatious?" said Gene.

"Little." Cassie wanted to say something about small men and big egos and compensation, but she bit her tongue and congratulated herself on her restraint.

"Not my name," said Gene. "Well, of course, it is. But the company's not named for me but for what we're going to do here. Custom genes, genes to do anything you want."

"Another Jericho miracle," said Cassie.

"Yeah. But here's why I have a sign: nobody's going to take you seriously if you don't take yourself seriously. Someday, that sign's going to be neon, hanging in front of a big building. But it's never going to happen unless I treat myself like a billionaire genius today. Don't come here unless you're willing to treat both us and everything here that way."

"A big deal," said Cassie.

"BFD." Gene nodded.

"Maybe we'll change the name of the company to that," said Cassie.

"No." Gene walked away.

He walked past an area with a homemade raised floor for cables, empty except for two weathered picnic tables with old computers and an empty set of racks for servers. He waved at it without slowing down. He was walking two steps in front of

Cassie so he could talk over his shoulder and she'd have to keep up.

"We can build the genes after we get a grip on all the information we already know about genetics. I'm trying to beg or borrow the computers I need in here, get someone to do the math work." He turned back to her and didn't pause. "Of course, I might have to contract all that out, if I can talk a company into doing the work for an equity stake in a company with no sales and no product yet. There is more data in genetics work than most people realize."

Cassie stepped in front of him and kept walking, forcing him to follow her. "You mean like 25,000 separate genes, 23 chromosomes, 7,000,000,000 individual humans, each with 3,000,000,000 bits of information coded in their DNA? And that's just limiting ourselves to the living members of one species."

He froze in mid-stride and Cassie strode past him without pausing. " 'Course, I might do the work in house, if I find the right person."

They walked in silence until they came to a section walled in with Plexiglas held together with duct tape.

"This is actual genetics hardware, borrowed from Randy's company," he said. "Have to keep that in a clean room."

"Randy's generous."

"Ha. Gets thirty percent equity in my company for old junk they'd probably throw out. Much more generosity like that, and I'll just be an employee working at somebody else's company. You've got to be very selective about who you give ownership in your baby."

They passed an old pickup truck, and a tiny, black sports car in a corner by a garage door. He waved at them. "The truck's mine. My dad keeps his pride and joy here and lets me use it." He pointed to another area with an army cot and a table with a hot plate and a microwave. "My stuff," he said.

"You live here?"

"No, just crash sometimes when I'm working. I've got an apartment, but I might give it up and just stay here and save the rent money." Gene stopped at a cardboard box by the bed and pulled out a pair of jeans and a tee shirt and a pair of boxers.

"Anyway, I've got a lot of this worked out already. The Informatics part—the computer stuff—is what's missing. Everybody tells me how hard that is, but I don't get it."

"Probably because you don't listen," said Cassie.

"I mean, it's just calculations. No offense, but what you computer people do is just two times two, on a big scale." He was walking over to a rusty industrial shower in a clear, Plexiglas stall. He stopped for a minute and said, "I do listen."

"Well, listen to this," she said. "Two times two is easy, but you've got so many numbers in genetics, if you just do two times two over and over the universe will run out of time before you get the answers you want."

"So." He stopped in front of the shower and dropped the clean clothes on the floor. "What you need is a lot of computing horsepower. Still easy, if you can beg enough computers." He pulled his shirt over his head and reached for his pants.

"You need me to step outside for a minute?" Cassie said.

"No. At GENES, we take ourselves seriously. Treat a minute of my time as being worth five hundred thousand dollars. I— we—well, maybe we—cost more than an astronaut on orbit in the space station. At least in our own minds. Keep talking and don't waste time."

He pulled his pants off and stepped into the shower.

"Well, I ain't going to scrub your back," said Cassie, although the idea crossed her mind. *Too bad he's so short.*

"This time." Gene smiled at her over his shoulder. It was a good smile, kind of like a little boy getting away with something.

"Won't work," she said.

"Scrubbing my back?"

"No. I mean, yes, that certainly won't work. No. I mean your idea of just adding more horsepower."

"I'm good at begging. In a month, I'll have more computing power here than NASA."

"Still not enough."

"Are you one of those girls for whom nothing is ever enough?"

She looked at his body through the glass and thought, no sir. He was short, but with a compact, powerful body—a gymnast maybe. Thinking about Gene and exercise equipment led her to thinking about his body as exercise equipment and what she could do with it. She shook the image away and focused.

"OK," Gene said, turning off the water and toweling dry. "If everything's not enough, what do you do?"

"Two things. First, you flip the problem. Look at patterns, not data. Think fractals. Think patterns of fractals."

He stepped out and pulled his pants on and she felt like she could concentrate better.

"Second," she said, "you go somewhere that has more brainpower than you can buy."

"You mean like go to a Star Trek convention, tap into the Borg?"

"No. You want better than that. You want me."

"College girl slash drug queen?"

Cassie's mouth tightened. "You want answers, or you want snide comments? Believe me, I can do either."

He held up his hands. "Answers. For now, though, this is all talk. Won't need you till I figure out how to get computers without giving away my company."

"I can have your computing center up today, if you've got money. Just a little money."

He pulled the tee shirt over his head and looked at her a long time and seemed to make a decision.

"A little money is exactly what I've got."

Cassie turned and marched toward the computers on the raised flooring. Gene followed.

She sat down in a chair in front of a computer and found the chair was set high for Gene.

"Jesus," she said, lowering the height. "How do you sit in this?"

"I'm not oversized like you."

Cassie shot him a look. Even sitting down, her eyes were level with his. "Not even . . ." She bit off the rest of the comment. "How do I log in?"

Gene gave her a password.

Cassie pointed at the screen. "Look, the big users of computing power these days are the Amazons and the Googles of the world. They have to buy enough equipment to handle peaks—like Christmas season, for instance. Rest of the time, their equipment mostly sits idle, so they rent it out as cloud computing. Pretty cheap, actually, if you don't mind running your stuff at three A.M. when their computers sit idle. You set up your software, tell them how to distribute it among their unused computers, when to run it and, voila! You've got yourself more computing power, instantly, than you could build here in six years. Here, look." She logged onto an Amazon site and started filling out fields. She stopped, pushed back, and stood up from the chair.

"Your turn," she said. "Need you to put in your credit card."

Gene sat down. "Hope I'm not over my limit. Again."

His eyes were looking at desk level. Cassie giggled at him and he grinned back and raised the seat for himself.

"Moose," he said to her.

"Gnome," she said.

They both turned their heads so the other couldn't see they were smiling.

Chapter 18

The sun was just a red glow in the Sunday sky when Cassie left GENES and drove into town looking for someone to celebrate with. Her cell phone rang as she pulled up in front of the Greenacres house. She looked at the ID. Gene.

"I told you," she said, then giggled. "I've got uh . . . things I've got to do tonight. I'll be back tomorrow. First thing. It's seven o'clock at night—on a Sunday, I might add. You can't expect a girl to work till midnight on her first day."

Gene said, "There are going to be a lot of midnights here before we're done. Going to take a lot of dedication to accomplish something great here."

"Sounds wonderful."

"OK. But for now, I'm sitting at the computer by myself."

She shut off the engine and watched the lights in the house. "You mean my computer? Your computer's the one in the half-clean room."

"OK, your computer. But it's finished the run you started. How do I start the next one?"

"You don't. You don't mess things up on my computer. I'll do it."

"When?"

Cassie sighed loud enough for Gene to hear. "Tonight. I'll take care of my other things, then I'll come by and kick it off. Then I'm going to get some sleep."

"Wake me up when you get here."

"You sleep? Slacker."

"Now that's talking like a GENES girl." He paused. "Not that I meant . . . You know, there may be some disadvantages to this company name."

"It's a good name. See you later."

She let herself into the house and found Belva at her computer. "Where's your mother?"

"Out." Belva waved a hand. "Said she'd be back, sometime. Or not."

Belva looked at Cassie. "Business suit, makeup . . . doesn't quite go with the black eye. New look?"

"Oh, yeah. All goes with the scar."

Belva said, "I always thought the scar looked good on you. Kind of gets you a fierce warrior princess look."

"Just what I was going for," said Cassie. "When I picked the scar out at Macy's. C'mon, let's go get some dinner. We'll be back sometime, too."

Belva yelped and shut down her computer. She rolled out the door and up the ramp Cassie had pulled down at the back of the truck. Cassie clamped Belva's chair into place in the empty space next to the driver's seat. They went to a little Mexican restaurant on the corner and sat alone at a table, the place empty on a Sunday night except for a couple of Hispanic kids sitting at a table in front of the soccer game on the TV theoretically doing their homework while their parents ran the place. Belva attacked an enchilada; Cassie had beans and rice and water.

Cassie said, "Your mom out with the guy from last night?"

Belva snorted. "You think that loser would take Mom out, maybe even spend money on her? No way. That guy was only interested in what was lying around the house for free. Don't know what happened to him. No, she's out with Loser Number

2. Or two hundred thirty-three. I've lost count."

"Belva, I know that's tough on you."

"Things ain't tough on me; I'm tough on them. Nothing tougher than me."

"Look out, world," said Cassie.

"Damned right."

Cassie studied Belva. Belva looked uncomfortable.

"Cassie, Mom ain't so bad," said Belva. "Don't pay too much attention to my bitching."

Cassie didn't say anything.

"I mean, it's kind of the same thing for Mom as it is for me. World's tough, so Mom acts tough, like she don't care about nothing, particularly me. But you got to know, deep down, she loves me and would do anything for me if she could."

Cassie thought of what to say to Belva, settled on, "Good attitude."

Belva said, "Mom's just trying to find her way to get along with the world."

Cassie leaned forward. "Her way doesn't have to be your way. You can choose your own way, do things the way you think is right, not just the way the world or your mother says it has to be."

Belva laughed at Cassie. "Oh, hell, yeah. You think just because I cut Mom some slack I want to be like her? Hell, no." She leaned over. "Hell, hell, no. It's complicated, Cassie. I know Mom could be better, know things could be better for me, too. Someday, when I find a way to make things better for myself, I'm going to move out and not look back. Till then, I got to believe in what I've got. No matter what I see Mom do, I've got to try to believe she loves me." She leaned back and made a sound like a laugh with no joy. "Until I find a way out."

"Belva, you've got computer skills. You're good in school,

when you aren't getting into trouble. You can go somewhere someday."

"Think I don't know it? I got it all planned out. I'm fourteen now. I'm going to be walking again by the time I'm sixteen. Those doctors don't know as much as they think they do."

"I believe it."

Belva took a big breath. "You ain't going to believe this part, but it's going to happen just like I say. I'm going to play high-school basketball. Then I'm going to play at JU. Have my trophies right next to yours. Going to be somebody."

Cassie felt her eyes watering.

"You are somebody," she said.

When they got back home, Cassie parked her truck in the street. Angled the truck so the lights shone on the driveway.

Cassie got Belva out of the truck and Belva rolled herself onto the basketball court. Cassie picked up the ball, dribbled to the free-throw line, caught the ball, and squared up. She coiled into the shot and released. Felt her arms come up over her head, the sweet, smooth motion of her legs feeding energy to her shoulder, then shoulder to arm and arm to hand until she felt the ball spin backwards off her fingertips, her hand pointing straight and true to the goal. Every part of her felt good.

She chased the ball down and put it in Belva's hands.

"Here," Cassie said. "Let me show you how to do it right."

CHAPTER 19

Cassie left Belva's jazzed from her upbeat day and jazzed about where she was going right now. There was a song on the radio by a ballsy, new, redneck blues singer named Lizzie Borden from Florida, and Cassie was singing the chorus at the top of her lungs, rocking and shaking the old truck.

"I'm done playing nice with your bad."

She screamed and banged the steering wheel hard to the beat.

"Done playing nice with your bad."

She drove down to Pratt Street and took a side street to Moonie's. Cassie threw open the door and stood in the entry and howled like a wolf. Throwing her arms out like a singer at the climax of a song, she screamed, "Iiiiiiiii quit." She pointed at Charles, planted in his customary spot in front of the TV. "And I'm done playing nice."

Everything in the bar seemed to shake except Charles, sitting rock-still at the bar on her right, holding a beer, and watching whales on the TV. The white thug at the table stopped talking and tried to look bored without taking his eyes off Cassie as she walked over to Charles.

"Nobody quits unless I fire them," said Charles without looking at Cassie. "Thought you bought enough for a week. Must have had a good night moving product, back here to buy more coke. Good girl."

"Not here to buy. Here to quit."

Charles laughed. "Darlin', you're what I call unquitable. Most folks come in here, pay up front, buy a little, maybe buy a lot. They come back, don't come back. I don't give a fuck."

He leaned back, exaggerating how relaxed he was. Cassie started to say something and he held up his hand.

"But you're my All-Star. You move a lot of product. Folks in the upscale clubs downtown won't buy from anybody but you. So you're not just a small-time buyer to me. I own you. Probably have to get you medical insurance and a company badge, darlin'."

"Well, darlin'," she wrapped one arm around Charles's neck. "I'm done playing nice with your bad. Done with your bad, period. Sick of knowing the only way I can make someone I care about better is to sell other people shit that will make them worse. Going back to a good world where I can be proud of what I do, every day. And not have to deal with scum like you."

She slammed the baggie down on the counter.

"Preach all you want." Charles turned to her bored and expressionless. "But bring me my money. My boss wants money from me; I want my fucking money from you."

"That's another thing I'm done with," said Cassie, "saying 'fuck' every other word to show people like you how tough I am. Like I'm in some old movie, surrounded by wolves, and 'fuck' is like a pointed stick, only thing I've got to keep the wolves away, have to keep poking it at them."

She poked the air with an unseen stick, turning and poking in every direction.

"Fuck! Fuck! Fuck!" she yelled as she jabbed the air.

Charles laughed and motioned.

White Thug stood up and tugged up his jeans. "Maybe that's what this bitch needs, boss. Give this bitch a good fuck and she'll do like she's told."

"Maybe so," said Charles.

101

White Thug came toward Cassie, smiling and swaying a little. Cassie realized how badly she had overplayed her hand and looked around for a way out. Nothing here but the front door.

She backed up to the bar and forced a big inviting smile at him while she tried to think of what to do.

"Come on, big boy," she said.

He stopped, not sure what her smile meant.

Cassie reached over to Charles's beer bottle and slid her hand up and down it seductively while staying locked onto White Thug.

"You want some of this?" she said.

White Thug smiled back and stepped forward. "Hell, yeah."

In her mind, Cassie spun her arm around and smashed the bottle on the side of his head and it shattered and blood poured over his face as he fell.

In the real world, she feinted with the bottle and jumped around him. Black Thug was slow getting up. As she burst out the door into the night air, she heard Charles say, "Let her go, boys; she ain't going nowhere."

CHAPTER 20

Cassie bounced into Jake's bar, jumped up on a stool and waved her finger at him.

"Jake, I'm on top of things now. Well . . . almost, anyway."

Jake gave her a barman's skeptical look. "Yesterday, you were going to hell."

"I was. I took care of everything. Everything. Almost everything."

Jake sighed and picked up the glass he polished like rosary beads whenever he felt a tough conversation coming on.

"Stevens?" he said.

Cassie put her finger down.

"Maybe. He's going to let me slide."

Jake turned the glass over slow, looked around the almost-empty Sunday night bar, and looked back at Cassie for a long time. "I've never seen Stevens let anyone slide. What exactly did he say to you?"

"He didn't *exactly* say I was off the hook, but I showed him he was after the wrong man. That's got to count for something, doesn't it? The rest has got to be his job."

She looked at Jake for confirmation, saw he was looking down, couldn't look at her.

"Right," she said.

Jake gave Cassie a very tired look. "Lot of people in Jericho wind up in car accidents these days, or killed by muggers who never get caught by the police. Watch yourself, girl."

"I will. Anyway, I'm on top of everything now. Everything else."

Jake put his elbows on the bar and leaned into Cassie's face. "What, you made a big coke score? Not sure I want to hear about this."

"No. Here, look in my bag." Cassie shoved her bag across the bar.

"Not sure I want to look in a woman's purse, either. Particularly when her purse is bigger than my car."

She pulled it open and held it up to his face.

"What do you see? More important, what do you not see?"

"Starship Enterprise? World Peace?" he said. "Looks like everything else is in that mess somewhere."

She snapped the bag shut and pulled it back across the bar.

"Coke," she said. "You don't see little bags of coke. You don't see a roll of cash, either. I quit."

"Quit? You quit Jericho's drug bosses? In your dreams, darling girl."

She nodded furiously, a big grin on her face.

"What's that supposed to mean, 'you quit'?" said Jake. "You gave them two weeks' notice, turned in your ID badge, they shook your hand and wished you well? Think that's how it works?"

Cassie paused, then glared.

"Why are you being so dense? I quit. They can't *make* me work for them, no matter what they say. I've got a real job now. Can take care of Belva. Maybe a real boyfriend. Remember the tall guy from last night? I got a feeling that might be real. You think it's too soon for me to call him?"

Jake opened his mouth, started to say something, thought about it, and said, "I'd put that on the bottom of my list, Cassie. Sounds like you've simultaneously pissed off the Jericho cops and the Jericho drug dealers in a single day. Let me give you some un-asked-for advice."

Before Jake could continue, Cassie felt someone slide onto the stool next to her and heard him say to Jake, "Scotch and soda, easy on the soda."

She didn't look up. Whether the guy was looking for coke or company from her, he'd move on when she showed no interest.

This one did neither, just downed his drink and sat there. She could feel him staring at the side of her face, at the scar. Felt him smiling at her.

"Not that bad," he said.

She turned, tight-lipped, and said, "Not for you. Move on, jerk."

He laughed, kind of a Hollywood laugh, full and a little made-up. She glared at him.

"Answers my question," he said.

"If the question is, 'When should I leave?' The answer is, 'Now.' Before I get mad. Jake's got something I want to hear." She turned back to Jake.

"No," said the man. "Question I had was, 'Are you Cassie Luna?' Sure as hell got my answer, with that attitude. Besides, I've got something you want to hear, too."

Looking in the mirror at the two of them, she said, "Look. I don't know you. Whatever you want, I ain't got it for you. Tired of politely telling you to go away. If I have to tell you again, I won't be polite anymore."

She turned her back to him but the man kept on. "Maybe you don't know me, but I know a guy named Stevens. He wants to do some business with you outside."

Cassie turned back and glared at him for a long second.

"Tell him I'm busy. Had enough of being tough for one night."

"Tell those two." He nodded at the door, at two uniformed cops. One of them was Squirrel.

Cassie looked at the door. "Oh, yeah."

"He remembers you. What did he do to you, anyway?"

Cassie swirled her club soda and looked back in the mirror for a long time.

"Called me pretty."

He laughed. "He said there was more. In any case, I can see his point, even with the black eye and scar. He's still got a hard-on for you. I can see his point on that, too."

Cassie laughed in the man's face. "That's your approach? Come in here throwing your cop-weight around and tell me you've got a hard-on? Bet you get all the girls." She stood up. "C'mon. Let's go see my old pal Stevens. Get this over with."

Jake quoted the man a price for the scotch.

"Cops don't pay," he said. "Covers hers, too, tonight."

"Club soda." Cassie snorted at him. "I don't drink when I'm working. You might try it."

Cassie walked past Squirrel with her head down. As she passed, he muttered, "Bitch."

Cassie hurried past them and out the door. It was raining now, a cold rain that steamed as it hit the hot pavement and washed the street into a shiny scene of blacks and whites, little streetlight halos floating above it all. The rain washed over Cassie and transformed her carefully arranged hair and makeup into a street girl's face of tangles and haunted eyes and soaked the lucky blouse into a tattered rag clinging to her.

Stevens was sitting alone in his black Impala at the curb. He rolled his window down half way and shielded his face from the rain.

"Get in."

Cassie leaned her arms on the roof and put her face to the window and let the rain run off her ruined face onto Stevens.

"I'm good here."

"Yeah," said Stevens. "You look good. Get in."

"Not getting in. Leave me alone. Told you, I'll get you something."

"When?"

"Whenever. Get off my back."

"Whenever is now." He held up a plastic bag holding a small clear envelope of white powder. "You just got sloppy and tried to sell coke to an undercover cop at the bar. With two witnesses."

She looked at the bag and looked at him.

"Stevens," she said. "Let me go. Please. I got a chance now."

"No. This is your chance, and your only chance. You've got something you've got to do, right now. The wife of our murdered guy is a real piece of work. Stays drunk and screwed up. Goes to AA and Narcotics Anonymous meetings to pick up guys. I can't believe she's not involved."

"So arrest her. Plant that little white baggie on her if you have to."

"Ain't the way it works, if your family's got money and gives stacks of it to our beloved Mayor Strong. I want to know what's going on, but I don't want to lose my pension investigating it and wind up like you." Stevens shifted in his seat to see if Cassie was paying attention.

"Maybe this is a break for both of us," he said. "Mrs. Irvin's at an NA meeting now at the Baptist church on Whitesburg. Go there, maybe try to sell her something. Maybe get her high, see if she can tell you something. Bring me something we can use."

Cassie had a line that she was going to spit into Stevens's face but he interrupted her.

"Do something worthwhile with your life for a change."

She stood in the rain for a minute, thinking about that, forgetting the smart-ass comment she was about to give him.

"This is it for you and me," she said. "I'll solve your case, and that will be the end of my old life, and the start of my new.

I'll take care of this, then I'm done."

Stevens showed his teeth in the dark car. "Think it's that easy to wash your slate clean?"

Cassie said, "Maybe I deserve this. Maybe I deserve everything I've got. But Ron doesn't deserve it. He's a worthless little shit, true, but he doesn't deserve to be on this hook, this time. I'm going to get his innocence back. After that, I'm never going to have anything to do with you or JPD again."

Stevens gave a harsh laugh. "Innocence? Anything he might have had like that is long gone. Once you go to jail, you never get that back."

"I'm getting his innocence back. Mine, too."

CHAPTER 21

Cassie pulled into the parking lot of the Baptist Church. The yellow brick compound sprawled downhill for acres, looking more like a shopping mall than the broken-down St. Joe's church she had grown up in. Cassie crossed herself and wondered if Baptists did that.

She looked around at the size and money of the place. *God must be good to fundamentalist rocket scientists.* She found a small knot of cars parked beside a door to the church preschool and went in.

The room itself was empty except for a couple of tired-looking men stacking up chairs, working around one chair sitting alone in the middle of the room. The chair held a sad-eyed woman with styled, graying hair and clothes out of a high-class catalog, looking lost and confused. As Cassie walked up, she saw that the woman's lipstick was smeared and her eyes were glassy. She looked up at Cassie like a child trying hard to smile after the bus has already left.

"Isn't someone going to take me home?" she said in a small, brittle voice.

Cassie paused. "Are you Nancy?"

Nancy nodded and gave a weak, little, hopeful smile.

Cassie pulled one of the chairs off the stack and sat down next to Nancy.

One of the men stacking chairs yanked the chair out from under Cassie and she fell on the floor hard.

"Hey," she said.

The man put her chair back on the stack.

"You think you got a right to be here?" he said. "You think you got a right to be anywhere?"

Cassie recognized him as a former customer. Last she heard of him, he was going to jail after robbing a check-cashing store. At the time, most of his money went to her.

She tried smiling but he didn't smile back.

Cassie turned to Nancy. "Yes, I'm here to take you home."

Nancy started to stand up and Cassie had to help her. "I usually find a gentleman friend here. But not tonight." She looked at Cassie and tried to interpret Cassie's smile. Nancy's eyes fluttered open. "Oh, no, I don't do that sort of thing. Not with women. I'm sure you're a very nice young lady, but . . ."

"I don't either," said Cassie.

Nancy looked at Cassie. "Then Ann must have sent you."

Cassie thought quickly. "That's right. Ann sent me."

"Ann is my guardian angel."

Cassie thought about saying, yeah, Ann fluttered down to me on wings of gold while I was in church praying, asked me if I could do her a favor and check on you.

Instead, she took Nancy's elbow in one hand and reached down to pick up Nancy's purse in the other. She guided Nancy toward the door, while Cassie's former customer glared at their backs.

Nancy paused when they got to the parking lot.

"I can't go home," Nancy said. Cassie thought she was going to ask about going to Cassie's home and panicked at the thought of a visitor—particularly this visitor—in her mess.

Nancy said, "I'm staying in a hotel, over there, until the police let me back in the house." She waved vaguely in the direction of the parkway. "Which car should we take?"

Cassie tried to imagine Nancy standing up in her truck, holding on for dear life. "Yours," she said. God, what a crappy life. Don't have a home or even a car a decent person could ride in.

Nancy held up the keys to a 5-series BMW and Cassie took them.

Driving along Martin Road, Cassie tried to think of the polite way to ask a grieving widow if she had killed her husband.

"I'm sorry for the loss of your murdered husband."

Nancy didn't react. After a long pause, she just said, "Yes."

They drove on and stopped at Kroger so Nancy could get a bottle of wine. Nancy sat on the hotel bed while Cassie poured wine into plastic cups.

"Do you have any of Ann's pills?" said Nancy.

"No," said Cassie. Then she added, "Ann said not to give you any more pills unless you were feeling too guilty."

Nancy started crying. "He was the only one."

"Uh, Ann said you might be feeling bad. About Jim and all."

"Of course I do."

Cassie paused and thought about what to say next. "You know, the police don't think the guy who killed him acted alone."

"Well, of course not. Who could believe that a man comes into my house, kills my husband, and then passes out?"

Cassie took a breath. "The police think they may be getting close to finding out who helped the killer."

She looked hard at Nancy for a reaction.

"Good. Good." Nancy lay down on the bed and started to fade. Cassie sat on the edge of the bed and bounced up and down to keep her awake.

Cassie said, "So, you'll be glad when the police find out what you did?"

"Everyone knows what I did. All the things I do. And Jim was the only one who understood."

Cassie was losing her patience. "So you hired the man to kill your husband?"

Nancy's eyes fluttered open. "Do I look Chinese?"

She sat up. "Everyone knows all the things I do—the men, the alcohol, the pills. Everyone knows, and they all think I'm terrible. Except Jim. Even when I hurt him, he always kept loving me. He loved me, and he loved the company he built. Jim went to work every day and talked about battling the Chinese, how they were always trying to undercut his prices and run QBot out of business. He loved QBot, and he loved me.

"He was the only one who loved me. And now the Chinese have killed him."

Nancy lay back down and started snoring. After a minute, Cassie slipped off Nancy's shoes, and pulled the covers over her. On impulse, she bent down and kissed Nancy's forehead.

Standing alone and lonely in the parking lot, she called David and got his voicemail.

"Hey, lover," she said. "Really need you tonight; want to do last night all over again. Thought about waiting a couple of days to call you, but no point in being coy when we're both everything on each other's what-I-want list. Call me. Soon."

Walking back along Martin Road in the dark, waiting for the call back and dodging cars on the narrow shoulder, Cassie thought about what she had to tell Stevens.

"A billion Chinese did it. Arrest them all," she said to the darkness. She tried to imagine what Stevens would say to that.

CHAPTER 22

Cassie got back to GENES a little after three A.M. Monday morning. She pulled around back and used the key Gene had given her to open the garage door and parked next to the little black sports car.

The lights were on but the place was silent. Cassie got out and decided not to slam the truck's door, tiptoeing and feeling silly for trying to be quiet after making so much noise coming in. She heard a noise and froze, then saw it was Gene asleep on his cot. She crept over and stood looking down on him.

Snoring, sprawled on his stomach in a pair of boxers, he looked like a cute little boy and she smiled. Mentally traced the taut muscles in his back and the smile grew and changed. Looked at the curve in the boxers and decided she didn't need to keep looking. Cassie pulled up the blanket and tucked him in.

She walked to her computer and went to work setting up the next run. She reduced the data as much as she could on her own computer, trading her time to save precious, expensive seconds after she sent the run to the cloud. After a couple of hours of work, she submitted the run and watched to be sure it got started all right.

The tiredness of the day flowed up from her toes like a time line: clearing Ron Lyle (at least in her mind), getting a job, trading in drug dealing for saving an innocent man. Ending back here, the end of a proud, hard day's work. With a job. With a mission. Good tired, but so much still left to do. She put her head down, just for a minute.

The next thing she knew, someone was shaking her.

She opened her eyes and looked at Gene. Sat up and wiped the drool away from her mouth.

Gene smiled and waved an oversized coffee mug at her. "Thought you might need this when you woke up. Sure of it now."

She took it and then said, "Oh, no. I don't drink coffee." Handing the mug back, she said, "How long have I been asleep?"

"I don't know. How long were you working? It's about seven now."

"Not used to getting by on a couple of hours sleep. Can't wake up."

Gene waved the mug again.

Cassie said, "Maybe just this once." Took a big sip and grimaced.

"I really appreciate your jumping on this work so hard."

Cassie ignored him and focused on the screen. "Yeah, sure. Looks like it's going OK."

She pointed at one number.

"See, that's how I'm trying to do this. If we run it at a higher priority, it gets done faster but it costs more. I'm running it at the very lowest priority, which means it only runs when the cloud has absolutely nothing else to do and they charge us next to nothing. What is our budget on this, anyway?"

Gene tightened his lips and straightened up. "That's something I wanted to talk to you about."

"Yeah, sure—wait, what time did you say it was?"

"Seven. Little after."

Cassie jumped up.

"Why the hell didn't you wake me? I've got to get home and get some—things done."

"What about the things we've got to get done here?"

Cassie waved at the screen. "That's going to run for another couple of hours. Be back before it finishes."

Gene said, "What am I supposed to do if I need your help here? What's so important you can't do it here?"

She pulled up the collar of her ruined lucky blouse. "Among other things, I've got to get a shower."

Gene waved at the clear, Plexiglas shower.

"You can take one here."

Cassie looked at him a second longer than she needed to.

"You wish," she said.

He didn't argue.

Chapter 23

Cassie was driving back into Jericho from GENES, into the edge of Research Park, passing chrome and steel cathedrals to the gods of better living through business and engineering. Closed to her until now.

"Bam!" she pointed at each door as she passed it. "Cassie's coming. Got a job. Stopped selling drugs. Proved Ron's innocence."

She turned onto Greenacres Drive and parked in front of her parents' old house. She sat there for a minute calming herself. She took a deep breath and said, "And now, the best part. Morning intention. Today, I will make a difference in the life of a child. And I will be grateful for my new life." Her smile grew and she added, "Bam."

She walked into the house without knocking. The living room was dark and quiet. Belva was in her room on her computer.

"Bam!" Cassie said to Belva's back. Belva kept typing. Cassie looked around Belva's room. Nothing but a cot and a desk covered with scrounged computer parts. A couple of cardboard boxes for clothes. But everything neat: Bed made taut, nothing lying on the floor.

"Girl," said Cassie. "You ever get off that computer?"

"Only when one of you make me. Here, look at this." Belva clicked on an icon of a fist. The leftmost of the three old monitors filled up with a standard Hollywood-style dark and spooky forest.

"Where'd you get that?" said Cassie.

"I made it myself, from the background in the Wizard of Oz. You know, the scene where they're in the woods going to the witch's castle?"

"Got it."

Music came up, the opening zoom bass riff from the Stones' "Satisfaction," and a girl in a wheelchair faded into the scene. The girl looked like a cartoon with her face all sharp angles like knives and angry spiky red hair.

"Took her from a Japanese anime," said Belva.

"You're getting good at stealing."

Belva twisted her lip like Elvis. "Thank you. Thank you very much."

"Christ. Four convictions for theft from cultural icons before school. You've got a career ahead of you. You'll either be a criminal or a civic leader."

Belva said, "Did this part on my own."

She pressed a button on the game controller and the ordinary wheelchair grew rocket launchers and jets. A dragon swooped into the screen. Belva twisted the joystick and blasted it to bloody fragments.

"I've got a rocket launcher between my legs."

Cassie said, "Freud would probably have something to say about that. You remember Freud?"

Belva shut down the game and gave her a look.

" 'Course I remember Freud. I read all those books you give me. I wheel myself up to the used bookstore on the corner and read everything in there, too. So I know Freud. I like what Betty Friedan had to say about him, though."

Cassie ruffled her hair. "Smart ass."

Belva pointed at the screen. "Bad smart ass."

"Yeah. Except that we're not going to say 'ass' anymore."

Belva said, "You bet your . . ." and Cassie put her hand on her mouth.

"Really. We're back to the good world now. Your mom around?"

Belva laughed. "Asleep. Or drunk. Or high. Take your pick."

"Huh," said Cassie. "Well, I came by to see if you wanted a ride to school. Guess she won't mind."

Belva yelped and they loaded up the truck. The engine started with a groan and they lurched down the street. Cassie pulled onto Homes Avenue and headed to the high school.

"Going to miss this old truck." She looked sideways at Belva to see if she picked up on this.

"Bessie? You can't get rid of Bessie. Mom told me how you took Bessie off a user that wouldn't pay up after you were dumb enough to float a deal without getting cash up front."

"Your mom shouldn't tell you those things."

"She told me about the gun under the seat, too. I looked. It's there."

"Well, don't touch it. I won't touch it, won't have anything to do with guns. It was there when I got the truck, and I'm going to get rid of it. And your mom shouldn't have told you about that, either."

"She tells me everything. Everything that she thinks will make you look bad. So how you going to replace old Bessie? Free is the only price you can pay for a new car; they don't give you much for that."

"Got a job."

"You got a job? You got a job!" Belva reached over to high-five Cassie and the truck almost ran off Homes Avenue when Cassie tried to return the gesture.

"I got a job." Cassie was grinning. "A real job. With real money and real benefits and everything. I'm going to get a real apartment—maybe a little house somewhere. I'm going to get my scar fixed."

"Oh, man," said Belva. "You're going to become a citizen again."

"Told you, we're back in the good world again. And I wanted to pick you up this morning to talk to you about something, before I talk to your mother about it. Jill's got her hands pretty full these days."

Belva snorted.

"Stop it. That's your mother. And she deserves a chance to get straight, maybe have some time on her own." Cassie paused and looked out the window, trying to seem casual.

"I was wondering how you would feel about coming to live with me for a while?"

Belva jerked her head sideways and stared hard at Cassie.

"You ain't shitt—I don't know what the word is. Funning me?"

"Funning? What are we now, Ozzie and Harriet? But, no, I'm not."

Belva stared. Then her face crumpled and she was crying and laughing.

"Oh, yes. Oh, yes. You and me, Cassie, we can do anything. I can help out. I can clean. I can cook. We can go on trips, go to those historical places you teach me about. We can . . ."

"We can." Cassie looked at Belva and then Cassie was crying, too. She pulled into the parking lot of the Indian restaurant.

"Belva, I know your mother tries hard—in her own way, she really does—but I know things haven't been easy for you. I want things to be easier."

"No, Cassie, you don't know how bad things have been. Long as it's all I had, I made the most of it. But if you and I can carve out a life, I'll do anything. But I'll tell you this: I don't want things easy. I want to be tough like you. I don't mind hard; I want it hard. Kick life in the face; show it who's boss. I wish we were alive back in the bad old days in Alabama. You and me go to the Klan meetings, run my wheelchair over their toes, tell them to let people go."

Cassie laughed and felt giddy. "Bam."

"Yeah. You and me."

"C'mon, let's go home," said Belva. "Pack up my stuff and tell Jill."

"That's a hell of a start—heck of a start. Play hooky from school your first day with me. Not going to be like that, missy."

"No, this is Monday. One of those Monday holidays. President Somebody-or-other did something-or-other. I just let you give me a ride to get out of the house."

Cassie gave her a hard look. "You sure about this? I never heard about this holiday."

"It's a holiday for me, now. I'm celebrating this day every day from now on instead of my birthday."

Cassie sighed but couldn't help but grin. "All right. It'll give you a chance to pack up your stuff. I'll go in to work, get some stuff up and running, and then come back and get you." She paused. "Not much room in my apartment. Hadn't thought about that."

"Oh, c'mon, Cassie. How much room do I take up? I can sleep on the floor, least until we get some money from your job."

Cassie made up her mind. "OK, let's do it."

"Hip hip hooray!"

Cassie laughed. "Don't go All-American girl on me now."

Cassie put the truck in gear and drove back to Greenacres. Rolling Belva down the ramp, she told Belva, "Stay out here and shoot some hoops. I'll go in and talk to Jill."

Talking to Jill required waking up Jill, and waking up Jill took some effort.

"Get your damned self off to school," Jill finally said without opening her eyes. "Don't need me to do everything for you."

"No, Jill, it's Cassie, not Belva."

"What the hell you want?"

"We need to talk."

Jill sat up. She'd gone to sleep naked without washing her face and her eye makeup had smudged and run in black streaks, looking like a reject from a zombie porn movie. Cassie tried to pull the sheet up but Jill slapped her away.

"Coffee. Make me some coffee, then I'll talk," said Jill.

Cassie made coffee and brought it back. Jill had pulled on a dirty Auburn football jersey.

"Now, Jill, listen to me," Cassie said "We need to talk about Belva."

"Huh," said Jill. Cassie vowed to stop making that sound. "Whatever trouble that cripple bitch has got herself into, you can get her out. I'm tired of having my life ruined by her."

"Well, that's what I want to tell you. I'd like to take Belva, let her live with me for a while, let you get out and spread your wings on your own some."

Jill took a long slow sip of coffee and studied Cassie.

"No."

Cassie sat there, not sure of what to say. Jill ended the silence.

"You just want to stop giving me my money."

"Jill, c'mon, I can still give you some money to help you get started."

"Don't believe you. You'd just desert me." Jill started to cry, spilled the coffee in the bed and ignored it. "Everybody deserts me. Everybody feels sorry for that smart-ass bitch, nobody cares about me."

Cassie said, "Jill, don't do this."

Jill pulled the covers over her head. They both heard the basketball clank off the rim outside.

From under the covers Jill said, "What the hell's that bitch doing here? Supposed to be in school."

"She told me it's a holiday. We figured we'd get her stuff packed up, use the day to move her into my place."

Jill pulled the covers back and laughed.

"You can't raise no kid, Cassie. This ain't no holiday. That bitch will lie to you just to stay in practice. And you're too dumb to see it." She looked at her sister and laughed again. "You can't do nothing right, can you?"

Jill dove back under the covers. "Belva's going nowhere, not now, not ever. You take that lying, fucking cripple bitch to school and get out."

Cassie stood up. Belva was sitting in the doorway, listening.

CHAPTER 24

Back at Gene's, Cassie parked next to the black Tesla sports car again. She stood there and looked at the difference between the shiny miracle of high tech and her worn-out, falling-apart-before-her-eyes, piece-of-crap ride and felt like she was looking at the story of her life: disappointing Belva, disappointing Stevens. Hell, even disappointing Charles who was too low himself to have a right to be disappointed. When she tried to slide the door closed, it stuck and she gave up and left it hanging open.

She looked up and Gene was marching toward her, fists pumping, muttering to himself. Whatever he was saying didn't sound good.

"You!" He waved a finger at her. "Where the hell have you been? What was all that bullshit you tried to feed me about dedication and wanting something great here as much as I did? You can't take a goddamned two-hour coffee break, not when you're on the verge—"

Cassie burst into tears and threw herself at him. He put his arms around her. She let herself curl into him, sobbing on his shoulder.

"I just . . ." he said.

Cassie said something but it just came out as blubbering noises and random screeches.

"I just . . ." Gene paused. "I was afraid you were going to kick my ass when I chewed you out about this. Big fight, walk out, everything scorched behind you. I even put up some of the fragile stuff so it wouldn't get broken."

"I know," said Cassie, although it came out as "a-ow". "I destroy everything. I'm terrible at everything."

"I wouldn't say that. Not here, anyway."

She could feel that her tears were soaking her boss's shirt. She wanted to stop but she couldn't and she felt like this was just one more thing she was messing up.

"I'm a monster." She cried like she hadn't cried in years.

"No," he said, gently lifting her chin off his shoulder and meeting her eyes. He wiped her cheek dry with his thumb. "Is that what this is about? My making fun of you Sunday because you're so tall and all? No, I mean, really, Cassie, you're beautiful. I mean—I'm not trying to come on to you or anything—but you're the most beautiful woman I've ever met. And you're sweet. I know you come on tough and everything, challenge the whole damned world to some kind of apocalyptic cage match, but you're really the kindest and sweetest person I've ever met. You don't know how much I need you here."

"You don't need me. I'm terrible at everything," she said, more tears flowing. "My big sister said I will never do anything right. And she's right. I won't. I just try and try and I just keep screwing things up and it's always my fault. Everything I touch just turns to—"

"Gold," Gene cut her off. He pulled her head back and stroked her hair. "Like your hair. I'm sure everybody tells you your hair is blonde, like, bleached-blonde, beach-girl, spoiled party-girl, princess blonde. But it's not. It's gold. Like real value, the real thing. Like you."

He pulled away and held her arms with his hands and looked into her eyes.

"And you sure as hell aren't terrible at everything. That's what I wanted to tell you, even if I was doing a lousy job at it.

You're on to something good here. I was looking at your runs while you were gone. You're doing something good." He paused. "Maybe even something we can sell back to Randy."

"Really?" Cassie wiped her face with the back of her hand, felt makeup and tears and wiped it on her jeans. "I don't know. It was just a stupid idea I had back in school. Nobody else thought much of it. I had fun showing it to you yesterday but I was going to tell you today that we may need to stop wasting our time on it."

Gene looked deeper in her eyes. "Hell, no. Look, you've got a different way of looking at this stuff, that's where breakthroughs come from. I think we can build a product on this, if we work really, really hard at it."

She didn't know what else to say, so she said, "Really?" again.

"Yeah. I mean, maybe. We've still got a lot to do and you never know how these things will turn out. But, after only one day at work, this may be something we can make some money from. Pretty fucking good for a fresh-out-of-college intern that nobody'll hire. Definitely not terrible. Terrible is the last thing you are."

"Wow."

Gene took a deep breath. "You know, we never talked about money, but we both know that I hired you as an unpaid intern. We've got no money in the company—not yet anyway. And you've got all your basketball money and don't need money as much as you need an opportunity."

Cassie started to argue, paused, and realized it should have been obvious that Gene didn't have money to hire anything but an unpaid intern. And realized that Charles and drugs were still the only way she had to make money. *Shit.*

"Of course," she said. "I knew that."

"But I don't want to do things that way," said Gene.

Cassie pulled back a little.

"Look, I want us both to be really dedicated to doing something special and really, really good. I know you're just an intern, and I've only known you for a couple of days, but I want to make this company yours, too. I'm going to give you a five percent stake in the company. Randy's company will have thirty percent, you'll have five, and I'll have sixty-five. That OK with you?"

Cassie stared at him with her tears drying and her mouth open.

"If we make something of this," she said, "that could be real money someday."

"Someday."

"More than just the money. I know how much this means to you now. I heard you complain about giving Randy a piece of it for all his help. Right now, today, this company is the most important thing in the world for you."

"Us," he said. "I want it to be the most important thing in the world for us. Don't take it unless you want it to be the most important thing in the world to you, too. Nothing else ahead of it."

She started to say something but Gene put a finger on her lips.

"Think a second," he said. "Be sure you want this to be yours."

He took his finger away and she looked around at Gene and the broken-down shed in the woods and smiled.

"This," she said, "is what I want."

"No money," Gene said, "until we get our butts in gear and build something we can sell?"

She pushed him away. "Then let's go to work."

CHAPTER 25

Tears dried, Cassie said, "I gotta go for a walk."

Gene was still excited, bouncing around the lab like a puppy. "Hey, don't be long. You're an owner now. We've got great stuff to do here."

Cassie smiled back at him. "Doing it as we speak. I've got runs churning away. I need to go clear my head and make a couple of phone calls. Be back before I'm needed here."

Before she left, she looked around the lab at sheets of Plexiglas duct-taped together to make a semi-clean room, a computer center with less power than the laptop she'd had in LA, and an unmade cot with Gene's dirty laundry piled on it. Not the stainless-steel counters and white lab coats she had imagined when Gene offered to interview her in his lab. But now, she owned five percent of this. She decided this wasn't the time to explain to him how much she needed real money. And real results for Stevens.

Cassie threw open the garage door with a clang and stepped into the darkened, pine thicket.

She pulled her phone out and looked up the number for Nancy Irvin's sister Ann. Walking along the country road, she dialed the number.

A girl's voice like molasses answered. "Gurley Sells."

"Yes, ma'am. My name is Cassie Luna. I'd like to speak to Ann Gurley, please."

"Miss Gurley is out. Can I take a message?"

"Sure. I met her sister last night. Tell her I need to talk to her about her sister. Let me give you—"

"Just a minute."

A minute later a louder voice came on. "This is Ann Gurley. Were you the girl harassing my sister last night?"

Cassie said, "Yes. Well, no, I wasn't harassing her. I just wanted to talk to her, like I want to talk to you. Hey! I helped Nancy. Gave her a ride to her hotel, tucked her in, made sure she was safe. I did not harass her."

"Tried to sell her drugs, that's what you were trying to do. I've heard about you, Cassie Luna. Heard about all of you over in that corrupt Jericho. Dirtiest city in the world; why I stay over here in River City. You keep your hands off Nancy."

Cassie said, "Nancy said you supplied her drugs."

Ann said, "Well, I never—I only give her what she needs. Now you just stay away."

"Gladly. Look, I just wanted to ask you a couple of questions about your brother-in-law."

"You don't ask me anything."

Cassie looked at the phone and snapped, "Fine." Started to hang up. Instead, she said, "Ma'am, I don't mean to be rude, but you need to talk to me. And I don't take no. If you don't talk to me, I'll be in your face every second until you do. I'll be on your doorstep, in your conference room. I'll be—"

Ann laughed. "You remind me of me, young lady." She paused. "Fine," she said, imitating Cassie's tone of voice. "We can talk, but on my terms. When I call you, you better be ready."

"Always ready."

Cassie heard Ann say "Fine" again and slam down the phone.

She stared at the phone until it beeped dead and she felt like staring at a dead phone was just what her life felt like now. She needed a friendly voice. She dialed David. He answered just before it went to voicemail.

"Hey," she said, purring.

"Yeah?"

"Haven't heard from you. Wanted to know if you wanted to get together tonight for a little pick-me-up? The other night felt like a nine. Want to go for a ten this time?"

"What I need is for you to stop calling me," he said.

She paused, listening to what he had said a couple of times in her head before she really heard it.

"Well," she said. "I mean, I've only called like—"

"Five times. I've got five messages on my phone. Getting tired of apologizing to people when I interrupt them to send you to voicemail."

"I'm sorry," she said. "I mean, I thought we were like everything on each other's list."

"Well, yeah," he said. "Sleeping with a big blonde was on my list. One-time thing. Now that's done."

Cassie's phone went dead. Again.

CHAPTER 26

Cassie hung up the phone and yelled, "Fine" at the piece of metal and plastic in her hand as David's number disappeared from the screen. Thought about who she blamed for her miserable life and dialed Stevens.

"Hey," she said. "Get your fat, donut-destroying ass out of your chair and do your goddamned job so I can get you off my back and get on with my real life."

There was a long pause, then Stevens said, "You got the wrong number, child. Ain't nobody here that works for you."

Cassie found a stump and sat down.

"Good. If there's nobody there working for me, then I ain't working for nobody there. Glad to retire from that job."

"Trust me, you don't want the retirement package. Enough of this tough-girl act. What you want?"

Cassie stood up and paced down the road. "You Jericho fake-police keep all your files on a case in some kind of folder or something?"

"It's called a murder book. You need to learn the language."

"Don't care what it's called. Care that I don't have it."

There was a long pause.

"You're a civilian. You can't see that."

"That what you think, I'm a civilian now?"

After another pause, Stevens said, "I get your point. I'll bring it to you, let you look at it sometime."

"No. You'll bring me a copy, right now, or you can find

130

another six-foot-two girl to solve all your problems."

"All right. I'll meet you for lunch somewhere, bring you a copy. But you got to be careful with this."

"I got to be careful? I'm the one whose butt's on the line here. No. Get me a copy, now. If you get it to me tomorrow— even lunch today—then my schedule slips a day and I'll have you an answer Saturday, not Friday."

"We got to have this cleared by Friday. Not Friday. By Friday."

"Then you have to get me that book, now. And you have to bring it to me, now. I'm out in . . . No, you don't need to know where I am now. Not going to meet you in that corrupt Jericho. Meet me out in the sticks, in fifteen minutes. There's an old convenience store, just a shack with a bunch of old bicycles and junk out front, down on Tri-Forks Highway, mile south of the Interstate. Be there in twenty minutes, with my copy."

Stevens was screaming as she hung up and looked at the time on her phone. The phone rang immediately. She looked at Stevens's name on the ID and turned her phone off.

She stood in the middle of the road, trying to get her bearings to the junk store. No way to walk there in time on the road. She was going to have to cut through the woods, trust she'd get it right.

She was studying the sun, trying to remember how to get her bearings from it, wondering what direction she was even headed, when she heard a noise like a wailing child. She turned and looked down the road. The noise came closer, and a speck appeared and grew as it came toward her and turned into a beat-up pickup truck. She planted herself in the middle of the road and put her hand up.

The old man at the wheel tried to go around her and Cassie slapped his window so hard he flinched. He stopped and rolled down the window.

Cassie had to yell over the squalling noise from the engine. "I need you to take me to the store, sir."

The old man studied her through red-rimmed eyes tired from years of long days spent barely holding things together.

"I can't, missy. I got to get this old truck up to NAPA 'fore that fan belt tears itself plumb up. Get back home and jack-leg my neighbor's washing machine so she can get her laundry done."

"Please, sir. I know you got a lot to do. Probably don't have enough of nothing to do it with, either. And I can't pay you or anything. But it sure would help me if you could give me a lift."

He studied her. "Reckon this old truck can go a mile out of its way before it breaks down."

She climbed in the passenger door. "Thank you, sir. I apologize for stopping you."

"No problem, miss. Been a long time since I've had a beautiful blonde beside me."

Cassie leaned over and kissed the old man on the side of his head. "Thank you."

They got to the store a minute before Stevens, just enough time for Cassie to plunk herself down on a rusty lawn chair out front and turn on her phone to check the time.

Stevens pulled up in front of her, almost running over her toes. His window was rolling down as he stopped. He shook a finger at her, and opened his mouth to say something.

"Nineteen minutes," she said, talking over whatever it was he was trying to say. "One more minute and I'd have been gone."

"Gone?" Stevens said. "Where the hell you think you're going? Think hiding out in the woods'll keep me from finding you and arresting your ass?" He looked around the lot. "Where's that piece of shit you drive anyway? How'd you get here?"

"That's for me to know," she said. "You to worry about. Got my stuff?"

"Christ, you sound like one of your own customers, desperate for a fix."

"Desperate to get rid of you, get on to a real life. Where's the book?"

Stevens reached over to the passenger seat and scooped up a loose pile of Xeroxed pages. Cassie held out her arms and he dumped them on her.

"Jesus," she said. "You call this a book?"

"I call this a violation of department regulations. Don't lose these, and don't show them to anybody else. And get this done by Friday."

"What the hell is this stupid Friday deadline?"

"For me to know." Stevens mashed the accelerator as he pulled away. "You to worry about."

CHAPTER 27

Gene was peering over Cassie's shoulder, perched on a blue exercise ball two feet across, sitting on it like a chair.

"Your algorithm does not converge," he said. His feet were pulled up close to his butt on top of the ball with his arms out for balance, swaying back and forth.

"Stop that." Cassie shoved her chair back into Gene and sent the ball rolling away, Gene hand-walking furiously to stay on top of the rolling ball. Hand-walked the ball back beside her.

She said, "You're making me nervous and I'm trying to work."

She was trying to solve a problem. Had been locked in a death-struggle with it since she had walked back in and shoved Stevens's murder book into a cardboard box under her picnic-table desk where Gene wouldn't see it. But she couldn't solve this problem. She felt so close to a solution, but it just wouldn't work.

"Does too converge." Cassie spun her chair away from her computer and faced Gene. "Would you put your feet down before you crash into me and ruin everything? Or better yet, get a chair like a normal person."

Gene said, "Ommmmm," and pulled his hands together in a prayer pose. The ball stayed rock-steady.

"Or better yet, just go away and let me get my work done. Work I'm doing for you, let me remind you, and for free. Sooner as I figure this out and send the results to your appropriately caged-in part of the lab, the sooner you can get back over there and get your own work done. And the sooner we can get a product working that we can sell."

"Should be easy," he said.

"Is this more of your computing-is-just-two-plus-two speech? Look, we made a breakthrough yesterday. Correct that: I made a breakthrough. But, before we can sell this, I've got to get this down to an algorithm that works every time. And I've spent all morning hitting my head against the wall and getting nowhere. And you're not helping."

"Ommmmm."

"How do you do that without falling?"

Gene opened his eyes and smiled. "Years of gymnastics and dance."

Cassie snorted "Dance," and turned back to her computer. The display showed the number of Amazon servers consumed by Cassie's operation. The number—and the cost—doubled as they watched.

"Shit," she said.

"Told you," said Gene, closing his eyes again. "Your error bounds are widening. Every cycle your routine makes things worse instead of better, gobbles up more processors. Soon your algorithm will take over all of Amazon, then it will spread to the White House and the power plants and then the world will go dark and the monsters will come out and it will be World War III and everyone is blaming you."

"Oh, shut up." Cassie punched a button and the display cleared and the number of servers she was using dropped to zero.

"Hey, loosen up. It was a joke, an awkward attempt to get you to laugh."

Her eyes were filling up and threatening to overflow.

"It doesn't converge," she said.

"For now. Give yourself—and the problem—some time."

She was working hard to hold back that last tear that would start the flood. "It doesn't work," she said. "Nothing I've done for the last year works. I can't even . . ." She thought of all the things that she couldn't make work right now. Belva. Stevens. Charles and the thugs. She realized that she couldn't even tell Gene about them. That last tear was pushing harder.

She said, "I told my professors as loud as I could that if they'd just give me the computing resources, I could prove this could work. They told me I was wasting my time, and the university wouldn't pay for it."

"Bet that pissed you off."

"Hell, yeah. I got lucky with the basic idea. I was reading the Chaos book at the same time that my Informatics professor was explaining how hard genetics computations were. The two ideas collided in my brain and I spent years working out the details of using chaos theory on genetics problems and trying to convince the university, but they wouldn't give me the resources I needed. Now I've got the resources, and I still can't do it. Big mouth Cassie screws up again."

Gene pounced off the ball like a cat.

"Enough of this pity party. You need a meeting."

Cassie's tears turned to anger in a heartbeat. "Really? Really? Like I don't have enough to do? To fix this, you're going to rent out the Von Braun Center, have me sit in the audience by myself while the Fearless Leader of our company stands at the podium with a Power Point presentation sure to amaze and inspire? Think that's going to change the screw-up that I've become?"

But Gene was walking away and she followed while she ranted. Gene stopped and pointed at the Tesla. She looked down at the tiny, almost invisibly black sports car.

"That," he said, "is our conference room."

Cassie looked at Gene and scrunched up her eyes.

"All right," said Cassie. "Five minutes of inspirational

wisdom, then my enthusiastic corporate ass better be back here working. I may be a stupid screw-up, but I don't quit."

She opened the passenger door and wedged herself in and bumped her head on the ceiling.

"Jesus Christ," she said. "Do they make these things in real-people size?"

She looked at Gene, buckling himself in and grinning at what he was about to say.

"Don't," she said. "What you're about to say would not be considered inspirational."

His grin didn't fade. "Buckle your seat belt tight. That'll pull you down into the seat."

Tightening the belt pulled her head away from the ceiling and she was comfortable. She waited for the engine to crank. Instead, the car burst toward the open middle of the lab without a sound.

"Electric," said Gene.

"I knew that."

Gene flicked the wheel to the left and the Tesla made a precise ninety-degree turn and accelerated almost instantly toward the open door, the only sound the wheels chirping in the turn.

"Fast," said Gene.

"I knew that."

The Tesla cleared the garage into the darkness of the grove. Gene nudged the wheel again and they exploded out of the pines into dazzling sunshine.

Gene hit the four-lane with the speedometer passing 100. They flashed around a big, green minivan and dropped onto a side road so fast the minivan driver probably wondered if the silent, dark streak was real.

"So that's the agenda for this meeting? Show the new girl the real world? Or just try to slide in a snarky comment? Maybe we can go back and try something simpler?"

"No, stop that. This is a thinking ride. Clear your head, focus the front of your brain on something fun and let the back part of your brain go to work on your problems."

"Don't think the back part of my brain is big enough for my problems."

They hit an S curve and Gene held the Tesla on the edge of the pavement.

"Jesus," said Cassie.

"Eighty-five," said Gene. "Fastest I've ever made that curve." Without taking his eyes off the road, he added, "And your mind is now focused on the road."

"My mind is on survival."

"That's the idea. Focus the doing part of your brain on something that takes your full concentration, like driving. Talk about something other than your problem so you're brain is completely off it."

"OK," said Cassie. "So—in our last moments alive—what do we talk about?"

"You pick. Any question you want to ask me, I'll answer. Keep the driver's mind occupied on two things at once."

She thought a minute and giggled. "Dance lessons."

"Christ," he said. "OK, we're going to pretend you're writing my biography and I'm dictating to you."

"Lucky me."

"When I was a kid, I didn't speak when the other kids did. My mom took me to about a hundred different specialists, who had a hundred different diagnoses, mainly autism. Most of them shrugged their shoulders at Mom, said you're stuck with him, not much you can do. Mom didn't buy that. She put me in every wild-ass therapy she could find. Nothing worked. I was the stupid lump in the corner. You can't believe the crap people do to you when they think you can't fight back.

"I got to be ten years old, still the lump in the corner, and they tried dance therapy. Another hopeless waste, they thought, but they were always glad to take my mom's money. They were dragging me around the floor, doped up on meds and half asleep, when it suddenly clicked: dancing was just a pattern. Then I saw it was a pattern within a pattern. I was good at it. They thought I was just some kind of one-skill dance prodigy, but it wasn't that at all. Numbers had a pattern, too. I knew that all along, but nobody asked the dummy about smart stuff like math."

They came back onto the four-lane and blew by a truck.

"Anyway, after that everything opened up for me. Language is just patterns. And biology—particularly genetics—is just the biggest pattern of all. And I'm—with your help—going to be the one to figure it out."

"Thank you for acknowledging the little people. Will I get a footnote in your Nobel Prize speech?"

"Probably. So I spent the first part of my life with everybody thinking I was worthless; now they think I'm a hero."

"Sounds to me like your mom was the hero, battling all the experts and so-called friends who told her the expensive treatments were a waste of money."

"Yeah. Yeah, she was. Worked her ass off for me. Nobody ever gave her a chance because she was just the dumb kid's mom. She took every shit job she could find to pay for it. Nothing she wouldn't do."

The Tesla bounced up a short, steep hill and dropped down to a parking lot by the river and stopped with a chirp of the tires. Looking through the branches of a fresh-flowering persimmon tree, Cassie watched the Tennessee River flowing without hurry through the green hills.

"Beautiful," she said.

"Yeah." Gene unsnapped his belt and bounced out. "Your turn to drive and talk."

"The way I'm screwing up these days, not sure I should be behind the wheel of anything faster than an old postal truck. Besides, you said this was your dad's car."

"He'd approve. I only met my dad a couple of years ago, but he's cool."

"Wait—how do you not know your dad?"

"He's a musician. Left not knowing Mom was pregnant, Mom was too proud to tell him. I tracked him down my junior year. He's got money. He's taking care of Mom, which is a load off for me. Would give me money, too, but I want to make it on my own. Kind of dumb about that, aren't I?"

"I don't think so. So he gave you the car?"

"Wanted to. I said no. He asked if I could hold onto it while he's on the road. He took me to a performance driving school in California to teach me real driving, and we spent a week driving the Tesla back to Alabama. So it's kind of our link. You're the only other person I've let drive it."

She walked around, got in and strapped in and sat there. Sat there, afraid to touch anything.

"C'mon," said Gene, slumped in his seat. "You're stalling."

"I can't do this. I'm afraid of hurting something that means this much to you."

"I believe you won't."

She faced him and punched the "D" button and stomped the throttle like she was used to in her truck. The Tesla spun towards the river and she panicked.

"Gene!"

As the river was rushing up, he said calmly, "Brake."

She touched the brake and the car stopped instantly.

"Gene," she said. "I can't—"

"Yes, you can." He reached over and yanked her seat belt so hard she felt like she couldn't breathe. "That driving school I went to spends the first day drumming two things into your

140

head: It's how you sit and where you look. If breathing doesn't hurt, the seat belt's not tight enough. No control if you're sliding around in the seat.

"Second thing: Cars go where you look."

"Sounds like magic," she said.

"Magic is just science without explanation. Here's the explanation: Hands follow eyes. Car follows hands. Car goes where you look. Never, ever take your eyes off where you want to go."

"Very Zen."

"Race-car drivers are a pretty un-Zen bunch who only care about things that will keep them alive. Try it. Relax your hands on the wheel, stop thinking about how to drive. Just ease down on the throttle and try driving with your eyes."

She touched the throttle and the car shot forward. She looked to the left and the car turned with no conscious effort on her part. Tried a few more turns and gained confidence.

"Hey! This works," she said, just as she hit the throttle too hard and went into a spin in the middle of the empty lot. She braked the car to a stop.

"Of course," said Gene. "It does take some practice. Stay in the lot until you've got the feel of things."

After a few minutes, she pulled out of the lot and shot past the river houses.

"OK," said Gene. "Now, can you drive and talk at the same time? Need a question to get you started? Like how old were you when people discovered you were smart?"

"I was lucky," she said. "I didn't have to wait till I was older for people to think I was smart."

"Must have been a public school."

She stuck her tongue out at him sideways, not taking her eyes off the road flying by faster as she was gaining confidence.

"No, it was my parents. They thought I was something special from the start, made sure everybody else knew it, too."

She pulled onto the four-lane and around a truck.

"So, I was special. Never wanted to disappoint a teacher or a coach or ever, ever disappoint my mother or father. Especially not my father."

"They still around?"

"No."

There was an awkward silence.

"So," said Gene, "you were like an All-Star?"

"Was an All-Star. Being merely 'like an All-Star' would have been like getting a 'B' on a test."

She laughed.

"I remember my freshman year in high school; the *Jericho Times* put me on their second-team All-City team." She paused. "Sounds good for a freshman, right?"

"Right."

"Dad gathered up every old newspaper on our street, took them down to the *Times* and dumped them on the sports editor's desk. Told him to read his own crap."

"Explains a lot," said Gene. " 'Course being born tall, smart, rich, and gorgeous couldn't have hurt."

"Wasn't tall until I was a senior in high school. And my parents were medium-poor."

She ignored the "gorgeous" part and wondered what to do with it. "Anyway, got a college scholarship at the local college, Jericho University, played one year in the WNBA. Did some commercials. Then it all changed."

"Was that your—ah," Gene searched for the right phrase. "Youthful indiscretion?"

Cassie paused. "That's what you think I am, some airhead girl at a party, busted by the cops?"

"Uh . . ." said Gene. "Let's change the subject. Your driving's getting better. Good even."

"Feels good," said Cassie. "When you relax and trust your body and the car, it's partly just an eye-hand coordination thing. Like basketball. Feels good, like a lot of it's coming back to me."

She hit the S curve Gene had gone through earlier. The car felt like it was on rails.

Gene leaned over. "Sixty-five. Pretty good for a sort-of beginner."

They pulled back into the garage and Cassie parked the car.

Gene sat back and said, "Driving's one part focus—which you found today—one part eye-hand coordination—which you developed by years of practice and hard work—and one part mental. You've always had a good brain. You're good at stuff, Cassie."

She beamed and leaned over and kissed him on the cheek.

Gene beamed, too. "Look, I didn't mean to pry back there. Your story, your business. I don't have to know about that old stuff."

"The youthful indiscretion?"

"Yeah. As long as it's in the past."

Cassie exhaled. "Look, I think I'm losing sight of something important here. Every day, I set an intention of what I'm going to be that day. I'm going to add to my intention today. I will make today a day to open up to you. And I will be grateful to have a friend who understands all I have to do. Let's talk now."

Gene looked at her and waited. Cassie paused, her mind focused on how to tell the story. Then her eyes got big.

"It does converge. My algorithm was right. I just didn't set it up right. You were wrong."

"Was not."

They got out of the car and marched over to her computer, arguing as they went.

CHAPTER 28

Cassie had her elbows planted on her picnic-table desk, her new processes running on her computer and feeding data to Gene in the clean room. She had Stevens's murder book spread out on the desk. Her eyes couldn't stay still; darting to her computer screen, and feeling excited when the new approach seemed to be working, then flicking to the clean room, feeling guilty and hoping Gene wouldn't come out and catch her stealing time away from their work. Finally, turning back to the murder book and feeling lost in the avalanche of bureaucratic minutiae.

She looked at her watch. Three o'clock in the afternoon. And she still needed to get this process finished. Find a killer. Save a girl. And then there was that really nasty thing she knew she had to do tonight.

Cassie's cell phone buzzed and she jumped. She picked up the phone without taking her eyes off the screen.

"Hello," she said. Before there was a reply, she yelled, "Hold on" and slammed down the phone.

Shit. The whole screen was flashing red. Something had gone wrong in the process she had running for Gene, and needed to be fixed right now. The clean-room door cracked open with a hiss of escaping air and Gene came stomping toward her.

She swept the murder book into her bag away from Gene. The phone was making angry little yelps and she picked it up. Wedged the phone between her shoulder and ear so she could talk and type at the same time.

"Go," she said to the phone. Gene jumped up on the raised floor and stood over her, shaking his finger at the red light on her screen. Cassie nodded furiously and typed as fast as she could.

There was a tinkling soprano laugh on the phone. "Well, land's sakes, I think I must have the right number, if you're as rude as people say. 'Go'? What is that? Urdu for 'Good morning to you. How can I help you today?' "

Cassie ignored the voice and kept typing and the red light turned to green. Gene threw up his hands and marched back to the clean room. Cassie closed her eyes tight and concentrated on the phone.

"Sorry," she said. "Who are you?" Felt rude, but at least she hadn't said "hell."

The laugh tinkled again.

"We have got to work on your manners, child. Why do I have to be somebody important for you to talk to me? Why can't I just be a new friend who wants to get together for a cup of coffee? You do like meeting new friends, don't you?"

"Got plenty already." Cassie thought about it and couldn't name two friends who weren't either children or people currently mad at her for one thing or the other. Still.

"Well, look here, missy," the voice was high, musical, and Southern, but it was starting to acquire an edge. "I am the woman you called yesterday, begging for me to talk to you. Ann Gurley. I'm sure you remember me. I would like you to come over for coffee so we can discuss my sister."

Cassie sat up straighter. "I just had coffee. We can talk on the phone."

"For crying out loud, young lady. Are you always this difficult? Is it asking so much just to come to my house for some information you need to know?"

"All right." Cassie pulled a pad of paper over and picked up a pen. "I'll come see you in a couple of hours when I get a break. Where are you?"

"Now. I'm by the golf course in River City."

"River City? That's twenty miles from Jericho. Pick a place in town."

"I don't come to that dirty, corrupt Jericho."

"Then I'll miss out on your valuable information. You're probably just trying to sell me life insurance or a time-share in Destin anyway."

Cassie put her bag on her table and started to pull out the murder book.

"I guess this answers the question of how difficult you are. Very well, then." Ann sighed. "How about Bunbakers, in Madison, halfway between?"

Cassie left the murder book in the bag.

"Sure, I can do that."

"See now, that wasn't so difficult. You must be one of those people who always have to have the last word."

"Am not."

"Then I will see you there in twenty minutes."

"Thirty." Cassie hung up the phone.

She postponed telling Gene she had to leave as long as she could. Finally sent him a quick computer message.

"I've got . . . an errand. Got to go."

She walked to her truck as fast as she could go, but not fast enough. Gene was flying out of the clean room as she touched the truck's door.

"Errand? Cassie, come on. We're on the verge of something big here."

Cassie looked at him and wondered how to explain that her real-estate gig was really a half-assed murder investigation to keep her out of jail. "I have got to get other things cleaned up until you can pay me some real money. Make it up later."

"There is no later. It's always here and now. What you've got to do is make up your mind."

"Don't get all Zen on me. Back as soon as I can."

CHAPTER 29

Cassie got to Bunbakers thirty-five minutes after she hung up the phone, picked up a large cup of coffee in a paper cup, and sat down in a Formica booth and looked at her watch and wondered if she had time for a nap.

It was forty minutes after the phone call when Ann swept into the coffee shop. Big smiles, cheerful hellos for everyone behind the counter, like the kindergarten teacher Cassie once knew who made a point, first thing every morning, to let every child know that she loved them, and that she was in charge.

Chattering gaily to anyone who would listen and several who would not, Ann took her coffee over to Cassie's booth and set it down and stood there smiling.

"I take it you're Ann?" said Cassie, intentionally not looking up.

"Well, of course I'm Ann. Everybody knows Ann. And you don't need to introduce yourself, because Ann knows everybody." She looked at Cassie's cup and made a clucking sound. "This just will not do." She spun and skipped over to the counter, complimenting a waitress on her Mark Twain High School tee shirt, picked up a plastic top and popped it on top of Cassie's coffee.

"You are not going to spill coffee on my nice new Cadillac." She stood there waiting.

"We can talk here," said Cassie.

Ann's smile faded from the I'm-so-glad-to-see-you variety to the cold, I'm-the-teacher-with-a-ruler-behind-my-back variety.

"I need to talk to you about my sister. And I am not going to do it here." The smile dropped away entirely. "You need to listen," she hissed.

Cassie stood up and tried to shove Ann aside but the little woman was rooted to the ground like a rock. Ann spun and led the way to a pink Escalade parked illegally at the curb. The car chirped and Cassie got in.

Ann got in the driver's side. The smile was back.

"Now I won't keep you more than just a few minutes, Cassie dear. It just seems to me that we both know a little bit about what it means to be a sister. The more I've heard about you, the more I'm sure you're someone I want to get to know."

Ann pulled away from the curb without looking and almost hit a pickup truck. The truck's horn squalled. Ann wiggled her fingers in a wave and smiled back like the truck was just saying hi.

"I'm not a person most people want to get to know," said Cassie.

Ann turned to Cassie and smiled as she pulled out onto Madison Boulevard heading west. It seemed to Cassie that Ann did most of her driving watching the passenger rather than the road.

"And that's why you may be exactly the person I want to know." Ann turned her head to the front briefly and saw that she was taking up both lanes. Stayed there and jacked the Escalade up to seventy.

"Where are my manners?" She smiled back at Cassie. "This is supposed to be about you. I understand you have some questions about my sister Nancy, so you just go right ahead and ask me. I'll tell you anything you want to know."

"Did she kill her husband?"

Ann stomped the brakes and they screeched to a stop in the

middle of Madison Boulevard, tires squealing around them. She turned to Cassie and snarled.

"I will not have my sister's name dragged through the mud. And I will not have people like you trying to sell drugs to her."

A car behind them honked his horn but the Escalade didn't budge. Ann muttered something toward the car's driver, yanked her door open and stomped out toward the driver. The car went around her and she yelled at him as he went by. Ann got back in the car, put the smile back on, and hammered the gas.

"I wasn't trying to sell Nancy drugs. Looked like she'd had enough," said Cassie.

Ann's smile stayed frozen while she thought about something.

"I take care of Ann. I don't approve of drugs, but I see that she has enough of what she needs to get by, and no more. She doesn't need anyone else adding anything else."

"Like I said, I won't sell her anything," said Cassie. "And I don't want to drag her name through the mud. But a lot of people don't believe Jim Irvin's murder was as simple as it seems. Nancy's going to get plenty of mud on her unless someone comes up with a better story."

Ann stared hard at Cassie and said nothing for a long time while the car weaved at random from one side of the road to the other.

"You don't know what I've gone through for Nancy. I know you've got your own story with your sister—I do my homework. But you just don't know. The first time I had to put Nancy in rehab, I had to come up with a lot more money than I was making then as a nurse. That's when I started selling houses, just to raise money for my sister. Money changes everything. Even after she married Jim I still took care of her. Still do. Got her out of more jams than you can imagine. But we're sisters. Nobody takes care of my family but me."

Cassie said, "I can imagine."

Ann smiled a sad smile. "No, you can't."

Cassie smiled back. "Yes, I can. You have no idea what I've been through."

"Sure."

Cassie glared at her. "I am sick and tired of all you people thinking you know what I've been through and looking down on me because of where I am now. When I was back in LA, I had the whole American dream—and I deserved it because I worked for it. Movie-star boyfriend. On TV endorsing natural foods and stuff, helping people—helping them because they looked up to me. Had more money than I thought I would ever need.

"Turned out I was wrong. My sister wrapped the family car around a tree back here in Alabama. Killed my mother and father. Paralyzed my niece. My sister, Jill? She was drunk, and she was the only one not hurt—not even prosecuted because she was sleeping with a cop and a district attorney and God knows who else. She hadn't bothered with insurance for Belva. Jill's money went for her own drugs and booze and anything else that felt good.

"I gave Jill every dime I had to help Belva, and that wasn't enough. More money than I could have made selling a couple of houses like you, too. In LA, there was a guy always hanging around, told me I could get money if I'd take a load of drugs from LA to Jericho, just one time. I was a big star; who was going to search my bags?"

Cassie smiled a wry smile at Ann.

"Look," said Cassie. "If you're going to keep looking at me instead of the road, you mind pulling into that gas station, keep me alive long enough to finish my story?"

Ann pulled into an off-brand station and stopped and didn't say anything.

"JPD was waiting for me when I got off the plane. Hell of it was, I actually got away from them and ditched the bag. Didn't matter. Another bag magically appeared and I was busted."

She touched her scar.

"Got this in a fight with the cops. Got bounced out of the WNBA, out of LA, back in Jericho. No job, no life. And, oh yeah, you remember that crack of yours about not being able to imagine being tied to your sister? Soon as I got out of jail there were more bills for my niece, and no help from my sister. I had an honors degree with two technical majors from JU, but no company would touch me with a drug bust. Had to start selling drugs just to pay their bills and try to hold enough back to keep myself alive."

Ann nodded. "What happened to your niece after she didn't get the surgery she needed?"

Cassie laughed. "That's the worst—or best—part. When it all came out, the team owner in LA paid for it out of his pocket. Would have done it all along, if I'd only asked him."

Cassie looked out the window at something far away.

"If I'd only asked." She looked back at Ann. "But that's not my way. Stupid me. Still, someday I'm going to get back to that fairy-tale life, and I'm taking my family with me, and I'm doing it on my own. Nobody takes care of my family but me."

Ann reached over and patted Cassie's cheek. "You're a good sister."

Cassie snorted. "Good sister. Bad detective. Bad dope dealer. Trying to learn how to be a good mother and a good employee in my spare time and fucking up at both of those. Probably going to be a bad jailbird or a bad corpse after Friday."

Cassie paused. "I don't know why I'm telling you all this, but it feels good. I've never really told anybody all this."

Ann patted her hand. "Maybe you need a good sister, too."

Ann pulled the car back on the road. They crossed the bridge over the Tennessee River into River City. Ann pointed up to a billboard with nothing but Ann's smiling face and the words "Ann Sells" in hot pink.

"You'll see those all over River City. I stay out of that corrupt Jericho. But, by God, I run things over here in River City."

Ann turned the car around and they headed back. They rode in silence back to Bunbakers.

As they pulled into the parking lot, Ann patted Cassie's hand. "You are so lucky today. I am the world's best at recognizing and developing talent, and you have talent, I can tell. We need to work together to put my brother-in-law's killer in jail. Stevens and those other Jericho crooks have ruined enough lives."

Cassie laughed. "Yeah, Stevens and his band of Keystone Kops mess up a lot of things."

Ann said, "Keystone Kops? Think Stevens is something to laugh about?"

Cassie looked at Ann. "You don't think Stevens had anything to do with your brother-in-law's death?"

"Who else? It's common knowledge that there's some unknown powerful somebody who is sitting on top of all the drugs and corruption in Jericho. Nobody knows who. Might as well be Stevens. Why do you think he was so quick to arrest that guy they found at the scene, announce the case was closed?"

"No. I mean, Stevens didn't want to do that. They made him. Told him it would take a year to get DNA tests done; told him to close the case."

Ann said, "They've got DNA evidence?"

"Yeah, I found the wrapper from the handle. Killer left his DNA on it. The tech guys already said they couldn't run any DNA tests because they were told not to."

"So, you're the one who found the evidence. And who was the one told them not to run with it?"

"Stevens."

"And how did you find this wrapper?"

Cassie looked out the window. "I was helping Stevens. He told me I had to."

Ann pulled up to the curb at Bunbakers.

"Missy, you are being set up. We've got to get you out of that rotten Jericho . . . get your life back where it belongs."

She reached over and took Cassie's hand. "You and me. We've got to stick together. We're both good sisters. And we both fight hard in a tough world."

Cassie smiled. "Except you smile a lot and I say 'Fuck you' a lot."

Cassie got out of the car at the curb and looked back at Ann.

Ann gave her a megawatt sales smile.

"Child, see this smile? That's just the nice way to say 'Fuck you.' "

CHAPTER 30

"Hope you got your errands done," said Gene as Cassie walked back to her computer. "We're not going to make any money here unless you get to work and stay at work."

Gene was sitting in her chair, facing her computer.

"Move." Cassie hip-checked Gene and he and the chair skittered across the plywood platform, stopping just before he went over the edge to the concrete.

Cassie stood in front of the computer with her bag and her keys still in her hand.

"Looks like you didn't mess anything up," she said.

Gene crab-walked the chair back.

"Nothing to mess up. You left me hanging with no idea of what to do."

"You had data. Told you I'd be back."

Cassie studied the screen, made some adjustments, and kicked things off again.

"There. That ought to keep you busy. I'm going to rewrite the main process. I think I can get the cost down on it by thirty percent."

"Maybe if you'd been here working on it, it would already be down by forty percent. Maybe we'd be ready to take this thing to Randy, see if we can sell something to him and get some eating money. For both of us."

"Well, I can't do everything for everybody, all the time."

"What the hell's that supposed to mean?"

"I've been here one day and my work's the only thing that we might have to sell anytime soon. And you're bitching at me. Can't anybody do their own work?"

"Jesus Christ. Are you really going to play that card? It's going to take years to figure out how to build genes to order. We— I'm trying to do something here that none of the big companies have ever done. Trying to stretch a couple of thousand in college savings to keep me alive until I do. Don't have a lot of Hollywood money in the bank to live the high life like you do. Maybe if you think you're such a hot shot, I ought to take my five percent back. Let you go off on your own and run errands."

Cassie didn't look at him. "Fine. Take the five percent back. Just leave me my computer."

"Fine." Gene stood up, shoved the chair at her, and stalked away.

Cassie yelled, "Fine" at his back.

She sat down at her computer.

"Men," she said, loud enough for him to hear. "They're all alike. I'm just going to deal with women I can trust."

She focused on the screen. She opened up an editing window and went to furiously typing in code.

She didn't know how much time had passed until she realized that Gene was standing beside her again.

"Hey," he said. He set down a cup of coffee and a paper towel with a slice of microwave pizza. "Thought you might need this." He hesitated before he said, "You're still here."

"Of course I'm still here." Cassie reached for the pizza and took a bite.

"God, that's good," she said.

Gene raised an eyebrow. "Nobody says microwave pizza is good. When's the last time you ate?"

Cassie thought. "Coffee count?"

"I'll get you another slice." Gene smiled and walked away.

"Make it two."

He came back with two slices stacked together.

"Look," he said. "Back there, earlier—"

"No need to apologize," said Cassie. "We need each other on this. I'm not going anywhere."

"I wasn't going to apologize," he said.

"Neither was I."

Gene said, "It's after ten o'clock at night. Why don't you go home and get some sleep? Get back in here early."

"Shit." Cassie looked at the clock. "I gotta go. Got some . . . I sell real estate. I've got some real-estate business to do."

"Real estate at ten o'clock? Who are you showing houses to, Dracula?"

She looked at him.

"Jealous?"

CHAPTER 31

Cassie tried to ease open the door to Moonie's and peek in to see who was there. Didn't work. Someone ripped the door open from inside, laughed, and said, "Your girlfriend's back."

She stood there with her hand hanging in the air and the eyes inside focused like rifles on her head.

White Thug was sitting just behind the door at the usual table. Black Thug sat next to him with the door in his hand, laughing.

"Shut the fuck up," said White Thug.

Cassie tried to smile but it came up weak and fake.

"Hey, Charles," she said, stepping in. "How you been?"

Black Thug slammed the door behind Cassie. She jumped. Both thugs started laughing.

Charles was sitting at the bar with the TV off and a speaker box in front of him. He turned to Cassie with a genuine smile before he turned back to the speaker and said, "Forgive me. I need to attend to something here for just a moment."

A distorted voice that sounded like a robot said, "Make it fast. And leave the speaker on."

Charles turned back to Cassie.

"Pissed," he said.

Cassie tried to stand up straight but the energy wasn't there.

"Fuck. Get over it," she said. "We got business to do."

Charles smiled even wider while the thugs laughed harsh, dirty laughs behind her. She heard them push back their chairs and stand up.

Charles said, "You quit, remember? Quit saying 'fuck,' too, but here you are."

"Changed my fucking mind."

"Oh, I like that. C'mon, say 'fuck' some more for me."

"Fuck." She paused. Charles waited for more. "Fuck. Fuck," she said. Then, "Fuck, fuck, fuck, fuck . . ." She could feel tears starting to well up in her eyes, wanted to stop her eyes and her mouth, but she couldn't control either so she stood there chanting "fuck" while they laughed at her.

Charles pulled out a gun from his jacket, set it on the bar, and she stopped.

"Tell you what," he said. "Kiss and make up with my boy, here in front of us all, we'll do some business."

White Thug turned her around and threw his arms wide and stood there leering and hard-eyed. She wanted to bring her knee into him, but she just stood there and waited as he put his arms around her and squeezed hard enough to hurt and she could smell his sweat and beer.

He breathed into her. "Say 'fuck' to me."

The speaker box said, "Enough," the voice distorted enough so that all emotion and tone were squeezed out. The room got instantly, eerily quiet.

"Charles, is that the girl you were talking about? The one you were whining about, one that does half your sales, losing her was going to make you buy less from me until you could replace her? The reason why you were crying that I had to cut my price until you could get back on your feet?"

Charles paused. "Wasn't whining and crying. That was just business."

"I've told you before I don't like the way you do business. Let me show you what you do in a business when someone under performs."

There was a long pause.

"Young lady, you want a job?" the voice said.

Cassie hesitated. "Me?"

"Yes, missy. You."

Cassie said, "Fuck, yes."

"You don't have to talk that way to work for me. This is business. As of now, you've got the clubs downtown. The whole downtown. Half of Charles's territory is now yours."

Charles said, "You can't—"

"Yes, I can. Hand her that case that was dropped off earlier."

Charles reached across the bar and pulled out a brushed-aluminum briefcase like the head of an aerospace company might carry. Slid it to Cassie and locked her into the stare again.

The voice said, "Open it."

She popped the latches and saw a bunch of plastic bags with cocaine.

"Your new good friend Charles has just fronted you the money for this, so you can go to work for me. You'll have to pay Charles back. For now, I don't care if you sell it all yourself, or set up your own network. But soon you're going to have to set something up, because, by yourself, you won't be able to move as much as you have to buy from me now.

"Charles will give you a number. Get yourself a burn phone. Call that number tomorrow. Give the guy your name and number."

Charles said, "She pays me back five thousand for that suitcase by tomorrow night, or I come for her."

"Friday night," said the voice. "Four days from now."

Cassie took the briefcase.

Charles looked at Cassie, holding the case for a second before he released it.

"Be careful," he said. "Watch out for accidents."

"Don't touch her, Charles," said the voice. "Unless I say so."

Charles hissed a slow, "Yes, sir."

Put his hand over the speaker and whispered to Cassie, "Like hell."

CHAPTER 32

Cassie sat in her truck studying the door of the Red Rock Inn, the place where Ron Lyle had said he was the night of the murder. Just two days ago when she heard his story, but it felt like a lifetime.

The Red Rock was a red-brick house built in the sixties, part of the building boom Jericho experienced when money flowed freely to put men on the moon, converted now to a blue-collar bar. The crumbling neighborhood around it was a mix of neat houses well-maintained by older couples who had lived through all the boom and bust years of the city, and other houses need-ing help. A few, like this one, converted to bars, tattoo parlors, and a video store. The grass on one side of the Red Rock had a trampled path leading back into the neighborhood itself.

Cassie looked at the path and tried to imagine Ron walking it. Saw a ghostly figure shambling along, maybe planning to have one beer with friends before bedtime. Maybe just bored and looking for a way to get out of the house. Not planning on waking up the next morning covered in blood, a cop shaking him awake, stiff and sore from sleeping on something uncom-fortable, looking down horrified when he saw the body he had slept on, then looking up at the angry cop and feeling like he had spun down the rabbit hole into a life he'd never imagined possible.

Maybe somebody in the Red Rock knew how that could hap-pen.

Cassie took the briefcase from Charles and put it on her lap and opened it. There was more coke in the briefcase than she had ever seen, more than she had ever moved in a month. And she was supposed to move this by Friday, or at least enough to pay Charles back.

She took a handful of packets out and put them in her beach bag. Closed the briefcase and put it under the seat and took the beach bag with her.

She walked into the bar and nobody but the bartender looked up. The interior of the house had been opened up into one room. Booths around the perimeter, a quiet couple sitting at one of them. She looked over to make sure there was a dark corner booth free if she needed it, and walked over to the bar and took a stool as far from the one guy at the bar as she could.

The bartender slid over and jerked his chin at her.

"Club soda," she said.

"One dollar."

Cassie said, "For club soda? Nobody charges for club soda."

The bartender shifted toward her, moving out of the shadows into a pool of light in front of her.

"If it costs me, I charge you. Nothing free. Kind of like you, Cassie."

"You know me?"

"Everybody knows you. Don't know why you're expanding your business down here. We don't have the money here they have downtown."

"Maybe I just came in for a club soda."

"Maybe. Maybe not. No skin off my ass either way. Still one dollar."

"Jesus." She fished in her jeans and laid a crumpled-up one on the bar.

"Tip?"

She looked at the bartender for the first time. He had a

beat-up looking face, not fresh beat-up, but like he'd been beat his whole life and was tired of fighting and losing. She wondered if he was joking, decided he wasn't, started to give him a smart-ass answer and remembered why she was here. Fished out another dollar and put it on top of the first one.

The bartender scooped it up and something like a smile broke his face.

"For that, you get free refills. Even a lime."

"Goody."

The couple from the booth came over to her.

"Hey. Uh." The man wavered in front of Cassie, not sure of what to say, but wanting to impress the girl hanging on his arm. They were both fresh-scrubbed, college-student young, smiling and trying to be cool.

"I mean," he said, "like, how much."

"Not here," said Cassie. She picked up the glass that had appeared in front of her. Waved it at the booth in the corner. "Over there."

The girl giggled, the boy tried to look tough, and the three of them walked over and slid into the booth.

"How much," Cassie said, "for what?"

"You know. Cocaine." He tried to look cooler. "Coke."

Cassie looked at him. "Let's say for the record: I do not sell drugs nor have I ever sold drugs. Do both of you swear that you are not now, nor have you ever been, affiliated in any way with any police force?" She studied their faces. "Or police auxiliary?"

The boy nodded eagerly. "We do so swear."

"OK. So if either of you are police, this is now entrapment." *Or at least that was true on a TV show once. And Friday's coming.*

Cassie sighed. "How much do you want?"

"I . . ." He looked at the girl and got no answer. "I don't know. We heard it made sex really great, so we thought we'd try it, you know? So just enough for that, I guess."

Cassie reached into her beach bag and pulled out one of the small envelopes and poured half of it into another envelope. She handed them the half-hit and charged them full price.

As they stood up, the girl leaned on the boy and giggled.

"Does it—you know—work? Make things better?"

Cassie looked the girl in the face for a long second and thought hard about snatching the drug away and getting them a glass of milk.

Instead, she said, "Sure. Makes everything better."

She went back to the bar and sat down.

The man on the end said, "Coke virgins?"

Cassie snapped, "How the hell would I know? Not my business."

"But you got them started," he said.

She turned to the bartender.

"I'm looking for a friend of mine, says he comes in here some. You seen Ron lately?"

The bartender's face hardened.

"Don't know a Ron."

The man on the end said, "Sure you do. You know little Ron. Came in here the other night. Pretty wasted when he left."

The bartender gave the man a hard look but the man was too drunk to notice.

Cassie turned to him. "You didn't happen to see who Ron left with, did you?"

"Yeah," he smiled at the bartender. "He was with that big, bald guy that comes in here—"

"That's it," snapped the bartender. He pulled out a baseball bat and put it on the bar in front of Cassie.

"We don't serve drug dealers in here. Get out. Now."

CHAPTER 33

Cassie sat in her truck and dialed Stevens. *Monday night. Please, God, let me get Stevens off my back so I can get on the forty-seven other things I've got to get done.*

"Yo," said Stevens.

"Yo? Is that any way to answer the phone? Whatever happened to manners?"

"Manners? I'm getting etiquette lessons now from a fucking drug queen? Probably dealing as we speak?"

"Am not." *Well, not right now.*

"So, you called to tell me what I need to know?"

"Yeah. Ron left the Red Rock Inn with a big, bald man. The bald guy did it. Go find him. I'm off the hook."

"Like hell. What am I supposed to do with that? Arrest every bald man in Jericho? Shit, this is worse than your idea that the Chinese did it. You've got to blow the roof off this, you've got to do it yourself, and you've got to do it by Friday. And you need to watch your ass."

"From who, you? Hey—wait, I just realized. You're a big guy, with really sloppy hair. You sure you aren't wearing a wig? Maybe you're the big, bald guy."

"I do not wear a wig. Jesus Christ, your detective skills suck. Don't know why I picked you for this anyway."

"Then let me go. I won't tell anyone that there are people saying you did it."

"Sounds like a Cassie maneuver: attack whoever's putting

166

pressure on you. Look, I'm not the one you've got to worry about. There's been rumors about that guy before. Big, bald guy with a porn-star mustache. Shows up when people get threatened, shows up when they disappear. Lately, he—or whoever's behind this—has gotten meaner. Couple of people set on fire, no clues on how it happened. Watch yourself, girl."

"So, I'm supposed to catch a murderer you police can't even go after without hurting anyone's feelings?"

"You used to be Cassie Luna, Wonder Girl. Remember?"

CHAPTER 34

Cassie hung up the phone and decided to stake out the Red Rock door. Her head kept nodding and she kept sneaking glances at the convenience store up the street. She could leave the Red Rock parking lot for five minutes, run up to the store, and then sit here with a 32-ounce coffee to keep her awake.

But that might be the five minutes when she would lose her opportunity. So, she waited. Five minutes before closing, the door opened and the customer she had seen at the bar came out. Cassie got out of the truck and left the door open to stay quiet. He looked in her direction and jumped.

"Jesus!" he gasped.

"Can I talk to you, sir?" she said.

He leaned against a car and put his hand on his chest.

"Damn, girl, you almost gave me a heart attack there, just coming up out of the darkness like that, gigantic figure in the night." He looked up at her and said, "No offense."

"None taken. Can I have just a minute of your time? Please?"

He was silent for a while and Cassie tried to study his face in the light of a lamppost a hundred feet up the street.

"Got to get home soon," he finally said, turning to the path. "Wife's expecting me."

"You walking?" she said. "I could give you a ride."

The man turned. Cassie could see a flash of white teeth in the darkness.

"Maybe," he said. "If you was to give me a ride. A ride, and a free taste of what you was selling back there."

Cassie said, "The ride's free. Anything else depends on what you can give me."

"Ain't got much to trade. Don't know much more than what you heard back there. Long Tom—bartender in there, owns the bar—he's the one you ought to be talking to. But I think he's too scared to talk."

"Then I'll talk to you." She motioned at her truck.

He climbed in the door, stepped across the seat, and stood where the passenger seat would have been, and said, "Where am I supposed to sit?"

"Floor, if you want. Just hold on to the dashboard if you're too finicky to sit on the floor."

She cranked the truck and he folded himself onto the floor.

"Gave up on being finicky about stuff years ago." He looked around the truck. "I ain't never seen nothing like this. A couple of long boards pulled up in the back, a couple of clamps bolted to the floor here where a chair's supposed to be. What you do, give rides to Frankenstein's monster?"

"Maybe. It's kind of a long story. Where we going?"

"Turn right up here at the light."

Cassie put on her blinker. "OK, what happened to Ron?"

"Got happy."

"Don't look happy now, sitting in jail."

"Well, he come into the bar that night, sat there nursing a beer. Bald guy and a friend of his come in. They talked to Long Tom a minute. Long Tom and the bald guy didn't look too happy with one another. Thought the bald guy was going to walk out, then he got a big grin. He and his buddy sat down on either side of Ron and bought him a beer. Ron got drunk off it—that's what I mean by saying he got happy—and the bald guy and his friend had to help him out."

"You ever see the bald guy before?"

"Sure. He comes in about once a week. Never drinks anything. Talks to Long Tom a couple minutes. He laughs, Long Tom frowns and gives him something, the guy leaves. That night, he decided to stay and have a beer with Ron."

"How'd Long Tom take it?"

"Didn't like it. Scowled at them, but didn't do nothing but bring them beers when the bald guy snapped his fingers."

"Bald guy. Did he have a mustache?"

"Yeah, yeah he did. One of them droopy ones." He pointed. "That one's my house, right there."

They pulled up and he waited for Cassie. Cassie fished in her bag and brought out a packet and held it up.

"I don't know," she said. "You haven't given me very much."

"All I got."

"You remember anything, anything at all that the bald man said to Long Tom?"

His face lit up. "Yeah. Yeah, I do. When they was leaving, holding Ron up by the arms, the bald guy pointed his finger at Long Tom like it was a gun, and said, 'Sim.' "

"What's that mean, 'sim'?"

"Danged if I know."

Cassie handed him the packet and he got out.

Cassie pulled away. Still time to hit the after-hours clubs and make some money. And get some coffee.

CHAPTER 35

Cassie thought, *it's coming together now.* Not her life, God knows. Or her amateur, half-assed detective work. But, sitting here in the lab, her process was humming. Her approach could sort through the mountain of raw numbers implicit in every human being, and find the critical information buried there. Find it faster, cheaper, and more reliably than anyone ever could before.

She looked around the lab and wondered where Gene was. She had come to work in darkness; now it was mid-morning and she still had their lab to herself. She thought about that: their lab. Hers. She looked around the lab. Nothing shiny. Nothing here that would appear on a publicity shot in a glossy magazine.

But she was smiling and proud. Wished that Gene was with her, the two of them sitting on the rump-sprung couch that Gene had picked up on the side of the road. Sitting there like an old married couple, talking about their work victories and dreams together. She pictured the two of them in the old American Gothic painting, maybe holding test tubes instead of a pitchfork.

She snorted at herself. *Too bad he's so damned short.*

She turned back to her computer and clicked on a music app, Susan Tedeschi's tough blues filling the lab around Cassie. She sang along at the top of her lungs, feeling powerful. An idea came to her unbidden to make her process work even better.

She didn't hear the door open, didn't hear Gene come up

behind her until she felt the raised floor vibrate. She turned around with a big smile, ready to tell Gene her good news.

Her smile crashed when she saw his broken and bloody face. She jumped up. "Gene! Oh, my God!"

His face was bruised purple, a neat row of stitches with dried blood on his forehead and the right side of his face swollen twice as big as the left. One sleeve of his shirt was cut away, his arm bandaged and in a sling.

He stood there with a lopsided grin on a lopsided face and said, "I've got great news."

CHAPTER 36

Cassie looked at Gene's lumpy face and said, "This is good news?"

Gene's smile widened and blood trickled out of one corner of his mouth.

"Yeah." He spat a little blood.

Cassie stood up and cradled his head gently in her hands and examined him. "Well, not this," he said.

"We've got to get you cleaned up."

"I'm clean. They did that down at the emergency room."

"They didn't finish the job. I spent too many years with basketball trainers to think this is good enough." Cassie led him over to the sink and pushed him down into a folding chair. "Sit. Sit still."

She went over and pulled the first-aid kit from the wall.

"Christ," she said. "Who did this?"

"Told you, the ER nurses. Don't blame them. I left before they were finished, wanted to get back here and tell you the news."

"No, I mean who messed up your face in the first place."

He tried to talk and she waved away a spray of blood.

"Never mind. Shut up until I get you back together. Don't want to catch AIDS from you."

He put his hand over his mouth and said, "You wish."

Cassie laughed. "So that's how you get girls? 'Hey, baby, want to get AIDS from me?' "

He smiled a red-toothed smile. "Probably just 'Hey, baby.' "

"And that works?"

"I struggle to keep my life free from distractions."

"Effective."

She reached into the small refrigerator and cracked a couple of slivers of ice free.

"Here. Rinse your mouth out in the sink, then suck on these, see if the cold will stop the bleeding."

With a mouth full of ice, he said, "Grue juize."

She shook her head. "Glad to hear it, whatever that was. Now keep quiet and let that ice do its job while I do mine."

She dabbed at the stitches with an alcohol swab.

"Not bad," she said. "Let me put a little antibiotic and some gauze over it."

Gene was looking around. He jumped up.

He swept up a pad from Cassie's table and came back, put it in his lap, and scrawled, "NEWS" in big letters.

Cassie took a gauze pad out of the kit and cut it to size. She glanced at the pad.

"Oh, yeah. You've been out getting into fights with the other little boys and now you want to know what progress I've made while I was here working like you should have been. I've got great news. I've got the cost of a run down almost fifty percent; now I'm building a kick-ass GUI front end. Wait till you see it."

Gene started to write something, looked at her, and scratched it out and wrote "50%?"

Cassie nodded furiously. "At least." She taped the pad in place. "Now hold still." She started picking through his hair.

Gene gave her a thumbs-up with his good hand. He flipped the tablet sheet over and drew a big dollar sign. In front of it, he wrote, "We have."

Cassie was still digging in his head and didn't look at the pad. "Huh. They missed one here. Need a couple of butterflies."

Gene shook the pad at her.

"Hold still." She glanced at the pad.

"Oh."

He shook it at her again.

"Good." She went back to his head. "Really good news. Second most important thing in the world, right now. We'll talk about it when you're not bleeding."

She worked on his head but kept glancing at the pad in his lap.

She couldn't stand it any longer. "Really? Real money?"

He nodded and she took his head in her hands to hold it still. She studied her work and said, "OK, now talk slowly and quietly. Don't open your mouth too much."

He whispered, "We've got money."

"I got that. I'm ready to do cartwheels. How much? Who?"

"Randy. I went to him early, only time to catch a guy like him. Actually talked to him in the parking lot. Showed him the results we're getting. You're getting. We're going to run some of his data. If he likes what he sees, he's going to give us up-front cash and then pay us to run their data for them. He wants to buy our process, but I told him we're not going to give him that."

"Wow." She grabbed his head and kissed him on the forehead hard, tasting the blood and sweat and antiseptic. She stepped back and did a long cartwheel, graceful, flowing, and seeming to fill the whole lab.

Gene mumbled, "Wow."

Cassie said, "How much?"

"Don't know. It'll depend on how well the test goes."

Cassie paused. "So not right away?"

"No. But someday. Someday soon. Maybe next week."

"You know," said Cassie. "Much as I'd like to have the money for myself—and have it right now—I think that, when we get it, some of it needs to go into the lab."

"Plenty of things we need around here."

Cassie balanced on one foot, folded her hands in a prayer, and brought herself into a yoga tree pose.

"Today," she said. "I will be patient."

"What's that?"

Cassie closed her eyes and said one long "Om."

Opened her eyes, unfolded herself, and smiled at Gene.

"Told you, I do morning intentions. Every morning, I say an intention for the day."

Gene tried to grin, his teeth mostly white now. "Cool. Like, I will get my work done."

She stuck her tongue out at him. "How much money have you brought in today?"

"True."

She looked at him and said, "Hey! We're forgetting the important part. What happened to your face? Did Randy literally demand a pound of flesh?"

"Not Randy. But yeah, someone wanted a pound of flesh. I was standing in the parking lot talking to Randy when this bald guy came up, smiling this big salesman smile. Randy tried to put the guy off, told him he'd meet him in his office. The guy wouldn't leave, glad-handed us both, wanted to know who I was. Randy downplayed it; tried to tell the guy I was nobody. I told him about our company and the stuff we were doing."

"Oh, Gene. No."

"What? I thought it was just advertising, tell everybody I see. Like handing out business cards."

"How'd that work for you?"

"Not too good. Guy told Randy to go inside, he wanted to talk to me privately, would talk to Randy later. Randy started to object, then shut his mouth and went inside. Bald guy turned this big megawatt chamber of commerce smile on me. Congratu-

lated me on the business, pumped some sunshine up my skirt
on how big we were going to be. Told me I needed to join the
Good Government Committee like other businesses did, give
them ten grand to get started.

"I actually was polite, told him maybe when we were bigger.
He said, 'Ten grand, by Friday.' I laughed and his smile went
away. He beat the crap out of me, left me lying on the pavement. He pointed a finger at me, laughed, and said, 'Sim.' "

"Gene, don't brag to people like that."

Gene laughed. "C'mon, Cassie. He's just a punk in a business suit. I can handle things like this. Even the cops didn't
want to be bothered. Cop in the emergency room took a report;
when I tried to describe the bald man, he just put it down as
'unknown mugger,' told me that nothing ever happens with
these things."

"Hell, no," said Cassie. She pointed a finger at Gene.
"Something's going to happen this time."

Gene stood up and smoothed Cassie's arms down by her
sides.

"C'mon, Cass. Shake it off. We've got work to do here."

His mouth was bleeding again. Cassie looked at his battered
face, still trying to smile at her, face full of blood and bruises
and bandages and all he was thinking about was her and their
dream here. The next attack on Gene would be worse unless
she stopped it. Now.

She shook him away and headed for her truck.

"Gotta move," she said. "Be back when I'm back."

"Hey," he said. "What about patience?"

"Patience, hell."

CHAPTER 37

The confused young receptionist frowned at Cassie from behind the plastic window looking out over the QBot lobby.

"You're not authorized," she said, looking at a list.

Cassie had left GENES on a mission to kick somebody's ass. After driving around a while, she realized that she didn't know whose ass to kick or how to do it and that, lately, every time she tried to kick somebody's ass she got kicked back harder. But she did know that the murder victim had been the president of the QBot Company and there might be answers there. So she went home and put makeup on her black eye and put on her interview suit from LA to try to bluff her way in. So—while she still felt like coming across the window and grabbing the woman's throat and demanding answers—she smiled her biggest smile at the woman.

"Oh, I know what I'm doing," she said. "I'm here to interview with Mrs. Walker in Personnel. I'm almost late."

"Nevertheless," the young woman said, "I need you to sign in, let me make a copy of your driver's license. I'll call back, and Mrs. Walker will come out from Personnel and get you. No one goes back there without a badge."

"Oh, I know where Maggie Walker sits." Cassie headed for the doorway. "I can't be late for my interview. She'll be mad at you and me both. You know how she is."

Cassie stepped through the doorway into the hall and the woman burst out of a side doorway.

"Stop!" She yelled and Cassie kept walking past her, fast, raising her hand and wiggling her fingers like she was just a ditzy airhead.

She heard the woman yell, "Security" and then, at her back, "And don't you go anywhere but Ms. Walker's office."

Cassie took the first left and took off running while the yelling behind her grew louder. She made a guess about where the president's office was and kept going until she was outside of a suite with just a modest "Jim Irvin" on a brass nameplate by the door. She scanned the hall, saw it was empty, and prayed the door was unlocked as she reached for the doorknob.

The knob turned in her hand and she whispered a quiet thank you. She quick-stepped inside and leaned her back against the closed door and looked at her watch. *Maybe two minutes. Maybe not. Not even enough time to stop sweating.* There was an empty assistant's desk with another door behind it. Cassie tried it, stepped inside, and shut that door behind her.

Her heart was pounding as she tried to catch her breath. She looked around.

The room was dressed to impress with thick, dark claret-colored carpets and dove-gray walls. Behind a walnut desk there was a wall of glass looking out over the parking lot, with a private door to the outside off to the left. The walls had a few pictures of Irvin with important people: the governor, generals. One picture showed Irvin with Jericho's mayor. In the background, at the edge, was a bald man with a drooping mustache. The mayor's head was turned that way, like he was trying to keep an eye on the man while he smiled for the camera.

Nothing on the desk but a closed laptop computer. No file cabinets to rifle through. Certainly no grinning Chinese assassins crouching by the desk.

She walked over to the desk and flipped open the laptop. Drums pounded out a heavy war beat and Cassie hit the mute button on the laptop. On the screen, a soldier stood alone and at risk on a stark, brown hilltop at dawn wearing a large backpack. As the sun came up at the soldier's back and bad guys popped up at the base of the hill in an armored truck, the soldier tapped a keypad strapped to his left forearm.

The backpack sprouted four propellers, one at each corner, and flew off of the soldier's back. The three-foot-long helicopter rotated ninety degrees, hovered over the soldier's head, and a small rocket pod and machine gun extended from its underside. A rocket fired and the bad guy's truck exploded into flames. The soldier saluted as the logo came up: QBot.

A log-on box appeared. Cassie tried a couple of simple log-ons and gave up. Easier on TV than it was here.

She sat down in the chair and looked out over the room. Right now she felt lost, without a clue what to do next. She considered putting the laptop in her bag and taking it back to go through it later. A missing laptop would probably be noticed. Besides, anything important would probably be kept out on a server somewhere and not here. Maybe.

She pulled open the file drawer on the right of the desk. It was clean, with only a few manila folders with dates on them. She opened one. It looked like Irvin's assistant prepared his agenda for him each day and gave him what he needed in a folder for the day. There was a folder for the day after he was killed and one for the day before. She flipped through them both, found nothing of interest, but put them in her bag anyway.

She pulled open the middle drawer of Irvin's desk. There were a few random pages, handwritten notes, some gum and paper clips. When she scooped them up, a white thumb drive with "Fueltown" written on it in Sharpie fell out. She dumped them all in her bag and noticed a rectangular piece of plastic sitting by itself in the front of the drawer. She turned it over. Irvin's badge.

She studied his face. He was a young man in the picture, and she looked at it and wondered what life had been for him then. *Had he already met Nancy? Were they young lovers, still full of hope and innocence? Or had they already started the slide down into compromise and acceptance of things unimagined in those young dreams?* She looked at his face, young and bright and smiling, and wondered who had wanted him dead.

She glanced at her watch. Two minutes gone already. No smoking gun so far. There was a private door to the outside.

She thought of something she had seen on TV. Maybe it would work. With all the stupid things she was doing lately, why not try one more?

She took the gum out and jammed as much as she could in her mouth and chewed furiously, watching the door and praying for the gum to soften. When it was one step better than rock-hard, she cracked the outside door open as little as she could, trying to keep from setting off the alarm. She fished the gum out and shoved it into the lock and eased the door shut.

She eased back out into the hall and made it to the first turn. As she rounded the corner, the badge woman and an armed man in a uniform and an older woman marched toward her. She put on her biggest smile and hoped the sweat didn't show.

"Mrs. Walker," she said, "I have been looking all over for you."

CHAPTER 38

The QBot security guys kept Cassie locked in a little room for half an hour, threatening to call the cops or Homeland Security while she smiled and ignored them and breathlessly gushed about how much she wanted to work at QBot and how she had read that Mrs. Walker valued aggressiveness and confidence and that was why she decided to just barge in and get a job. They had finally given up and thrown her out after telling her the terrible things that would happen if she ever did that again.

She sat in the parking lot, panting and splashing water on her face from a water bottle, and tried to think what to do next. Too many things to do, all of them needing to be done at once and not enough time for any of them. Leaving QBot, Cassie ran through the list: Nothing she could think of to do right now to solve the Irvin case. Belva was in school. No one to sell drugs to at 11 A.M. So she went back to GENES, where she had plenty of work that needed to be done and that she wanted to do.

She stood in front of her computer at GENES, tapping her toe and refusing to sit down. She checked her inbox and saw that the first of Randy's test data was in her inbox. She banged at the keys, not sitting down, hammering so hard the table shook. Set up the runs and then turned and glared at the garage door, blaming the door for not telling her what to do next. Her phone rang and she snatched it up and snapped, "What." Listened for a minute and said, "OK," and stabbed the phone off.

A few minutes later, she shook Gene awake. He rolled over, opened one swollen eye and saw who it was.

"Hey," he said, opening his arms.

"Give me a break," she said. "I've got to go sell a house. Be back when I can."

Gene dropped his arms. "Do we need to have that same fight again? You're supposed to be here getting your work done."

"Yeah, while you're sleeping. Fire me. You can hire me back later at twice the pay, and I'll accept your apology."

"Fun." He grinned a sleepy smile and Cassie wished she could take his offer and stay. "But I won't apologize."

Cassie said, "Should. Never know what it might get you." She walked over to the truck and drove away.

Ann was parked in the fire lane at Bunbaker's when Cassie pulled up. Cassie parked her truck and climbed in Ann's Escalade. Ann was on her cell, held up one finger to tell Cassie to be quiet.

"Well, I have got to go." She listened for a half-second and said, "Yes, I know this is important. You will just have to figure it out and get back to me. And do the job right." She smiled over at Cassie and said to the phone, "I told you I have got to go. Someone very important just walked in."

She snapped the phone shut and roared away from the curb, looking at Cassie.

"I have been waiting for you for five minutes. Do you know the last time I waited that long on anybody?"

Cassie had a comment but Ann kept talking.

"Never. Never. I have walked away from million-dollar deals because buyers were not there waiting for me. You are the first."

Ann was smiling, almost giggling.

Her smile fell and she put her face in Cassie's.

"Don't. Ever. Do. That. Again."

The smile came back. "You are going to be so happy, young

lady. Fairy-tale land's waiting for you today."

She paused to catch her breath.

"Oh, goodie," said Cassie. "Takes all the pressure off, know my fairy godmother's going to fix everything. Look, on the phone, you promised me something important."

Ann laughed. "I just love this feisty attitude of yours."

"Ain't an attitude, just me. Look, I don't have time for another ride-around. What you got?" Ann pulled out of the lot and put the Escalade half on the road, half on the shoulder. Cassie pointed.

"What?" said Ann. "Something I need to see out there?"

"The road. See that light? That red light? That's a hint."

Ann's laughter tinkled like cute little bells, but she stopped.

"Only for conformists. I was thinking about this over breakfast and this is just so, so perfect."

"Have you found out something about your brother-in-law's murder?"

Ann laughed again. "No, of course not. This is way more important than that."

"Pretty important to me right now."

"Not anymore. Not anymore. I'm thinking we should just let that drop, leave well enough alone, you know. Besides, you are going to be far too busy."

Cassie tried to say something and got cut off.

"This is just such a perfect idea. I am so proud of myself. We are going to have so much fun."

"OK, look, if this isn't about the murder, I've got to get back."

Ann laughed again, but there was less of a smile. "Must you always be so difficult?"

"Yeah. Tell me what's up, or I'm getting out."

"No." Ann pushed a button and locked the doors. "You'll ruin the surprise."

She went back to chattering and didn't slow down until they crossed the River City Bridge. She pointed up at the "Ann Sells" sign.

"Remember that," she said. "That's a hint."

They parked in front of an A-frame house sitting on a point of land jutting out into the Tennessee River.

Ann giggled. "Isn't it just too, too charming?"

"Nice house," said Cassie.

There was a big sailboat passing behind the house and a smiling, middle-aged couple waiting patiently by the front door. They smiled nervously at Ann but she brushed by them, unlocked the door, and walked in.

"This has just come on the market," she said to Cassie, with the couple trailing behind them. "Look at all this. Beam ceilings. Boathouse. I won't tell you the name of the former owner, because you'd recognize it."

The entourage walked up and down and over and around the house with Ann chattering with breathless amazement at every feature until they wound up in the kitchen. Ann leaned over the black granite island toward Cassie and said, "So what do you think?"

"Nice house."

Ann laughed. "You and I are going to get along so well. Your sense of humor is so . . . understated." She paused, smiled again, and said, "Better than where you're living now?"

Cassie thought of a burned-down family house, an apartment full of roaches, and a warehouse full of broken toys.

"Little bit."

Ann laughed again. "Welcome home." She stared at Cassie's expression and clapped her hands.

"I knew you'd just love it," she said.

"I can't afford this," said Cassie. The couple looked relieved.

"Yes, you can. Drop this stupid pretend-detective business

and come to work for me. The house is yours. Today. Before long, we will have signs up with 'Cassie Sells' all over."

Ann paused. Her smile was big enough to split her face.

"That's the idea that came to me. You and I are perfect together. Sisters, although I'm the big sister, of course. I need someone to be my right hand, tough enough to get things done for all my businesses. You can do it."

Cassie looked out at the boats on the river. "Selling houses? Ann, this is nice of you, but I can't sell houses. At least not enough to afford anything like this."

Ann's mouth got tight.

"Very well; you don't like the house, there are other houses."

"No," said Cassie. "Really, I've got my own job and my own . . . place. This is so nice of you, but I can't—" Cassie stopped. "Why are you doing this?"

Ann spun toward the couple and put her back to Cassie. The man reached into his coat and pulled out an envelope. Ann opened it and flipped through the bills.

"All right," she said to the man. "Go to the office. Tell Thelma I said you've got the house."

The couple left fairly bouncing with excitement and Ann, without a smile, turned back to Cassie.

"They said you'd be like this. I told them we'd try nice; if it didn't work, they could handle things their way. Brought this on yourself, missy."

Cassie said, "So that's how you do things here in clean River City? Have to bribe and threaten people?"

"Put on your big-girl pants. Underneath all the smiling TV faces there's a big dirty machine that runs things. Join it, be ready to get your hands a little dirty yourself, and you get your fairy-tale world back."

"I've got a shot at something clean now," she said. "Hard work don't scare me."

Ann's face turned to stone. "Nobody tells me 'no.' " She stamped her foot for a minute. "Look around you. This is everything you said you wanted: everything custom made, just for you. Perfect. Just perfect."

Cassie didn't budge.

"You made your own bed," Ann said. "Now lie in it and don't blame anyone else." She marched to the door and said over her shoulder, "Find your own way back."

CHAPTER 39

It took Cassie an hour to hitchhike back to Bunbaker's from River City. It would have taken longer except for the trucker who picked her up and grinned at her with a mouth full of more spaces than teeth. When they stopped at the light at Tri-Forks Highway, he turned to her and flashed a smile in all its tobacco-stained, empty-gummed glory.

"I'm going to stop up here and get a motel room for us and everything." He winked. "I like 'em big."

Cassie hit the door and rolled onto the shoulder and walked the rest of the way to Bunbaker's. Picked up her truck and drove back to work.

Gene wasn't there and the place felt empty without him. She fired up her computer. The runs with Randy's data were coming in and they were spectacular. Churning through the mountains of genetic data Randy had supplied, her process was gleaning more useful information at a lower cost compared to Randy's company's process. And Randy's company was the state of the art.

She looked at the data for one woman, known only as A34783. Randy's process had identified her as not at risk for breast cancer. That was good, but Cassie's had identified her as not at risk for breast cancer, but at risk for Type 2 diabetes. It was a small thing, catching one more piece of information in a sea of data. But with that information, this woman might be able to control her weight and her diet, and avoid a life-threatening disease.

Cassie felt herself smiling and proud. She looked around and realized that she wanted to share this with someone who could understand and who cared about what she had done. Someone who cared about her and understood what she was. Gene.

But Gene wasn't there.

She got up and had another cup of coffee, took a sip, and realized that her hands were shaking from the coffee she had already had today. She poured the coffee out.

She couldn't stand still, but she also knew she was exhausted and wouldn't finish the day unless she could find a way to wake up. She had two hours before she had to pick up Belva and take her to rehab. Maybe one hour for a nap; one for work.

She went to Gene's shower, stripped down, and felt the hot soapy water flow over her. She got out and toweled dry.

Gene's bed was still unmade. She pulled up the sheet and was hit with the aroma of Gene. Cassie lay down on the bed, pulled the sheet over herself, reveled in the man-smells, and fell asleep.

When she awoke, Gene was standing over her smiling. She smiled back.

"How's the wounded warrior?" she said.

"Pretty good, right now."

"It's working," she said. "Really well."

Gene grinned. "I can see that."

Cassie noticed she had kicked off the sheet and was naked. She pulled it back over her.

"Not that, you pervert. The reduction process. It's working like a charm."

"Huh." Gene looked in her eyes and nodded. "That's huge. That's one of those small improvements that will put a company like ours on the map. Better than that: someday, somebody's going to come up to you and thank you for saving their lives."

She smiled an easy, sleepy-eyed smile and snuggled down into the sheets.

"So what do you want to do," said Gene, "to celebrate?"

Cassie held the smile.

"If we're going to save somebody someday, I want a knight in shining armor to come save me now. What was that great pickup line of yours earlier?" She pulled back the sheet. "Hey, baby?"

At first, it was just a single, awkward kiss. Gene bent over her, slowly, gratefully, and kissed her shoulder worshipfully, like she was his own private goddess.

Cassie was used to Hollywood sex with her Hollywood lover: athletic, powerful—a performance to be scored. She had made a few attempts at duplicating that since then.

But this was different. Gene moved on, spreading soft kisses all over her. Each place he kissed said to her: this is a holy and a wonderful place. The kisses spread until she felt holy and wonderful and hungry herself.

Gene's clothes fell off as she responded. They took to their own private sky together and she moved on top of him and they became a single prayer. Prayer and response, prayer and response, prayer and response over and over until the whole church collapsed and they lay together, gasping and grateful to be who they were, grateful to be with who they were with, and, simply, grateful.

When she woke again later, Gene was propped up on one elbow, smiling at her.

"What's that smile for?" she said.

"The smile's for you, for the us-ness of this moment." He stroked her cheek. "But I've got more good news, too. When Randy got nervous about talking to me about the bald guy, I went and talked to some other guys running small tech companies. The word is that someone is running all the drug operations in North Alabama, and expanding into extorting money from businesses. Nobody—not even the drug lords or the owners—knows who that person is, or what they're doing with the money. Some of us owners are getting together to stand up to them."

Cassie sat up.

"Gene, that's harder than you think. You can't just crash around with these guys."

"Can't just walk away."

"No." She paused. "Look, I don't want to get all tender here, but be careful. Be really careful."

"Aw."

She wanted to change the conversation. "So why you telling me this?"

He leaned in and kissed her. "Give us something else to celebrate."

She woke up again later and Gene was snoring next to her. She reached over lazily and turned his arm so she could see his watch.

"Shit." She jumped out of the bed. Gene woke up with a lazy grin.

"So what are we going to celebrate this time?" he asked.

Cassie was throwing on her clothes.

"Celebrate my getting my ass kicked for being late to pick up Belva. Again. Honestly, I don't know why you made me late."

"Me? You're mad about that?"

"Yes. No. I'm mad about falling asleep, fucking up again." She smiled, more to herself than Gene. "Well, not mad about . . ." She giggled. "Never mind." She leaned over and kissed him on the head. "Look, I kind of took advantage of you there."

"I didn't mind." Gene still had the grin.

"No. I mean, I just don't want you to think . . . I mean, I've got too much going on in my life right now for a real relation-ship or anything."

Gene held up his hand. "Just a friendly service of the com-pany."

"Yeah," said Cassie.

"We can think of it as a perk for our long hours here. You know, at Google they have pastry chefs and massage therapists. At GENES, we have . . ."

They locked their eyes for a long second, both trying to read the other's expression.

"Yeah," they both said in unison.

CHAPTER 40

Tuesday night was rounding into Wednesday morning. A slow night at Jake's, Cassie sitting across the bar while Jake worked a crossword puzzle. A few couples looking for a mid-week party, some kids in to listen to the band. No business for Cassie so far and no sign of any.

"Jake, can you make money doing crossword puzzles?"

"Oh, yeah," he said. "I just come in here for my health."

"I've got to have five hundred dollars by tomorrow. Got to."

"Cassie, that voice inside your head that keeps telling you that you've 'got to' do things is going to be the death of you, if you don't get a grip on it."

"The director at Belva's rehab says no more sessions until she gets at least five hundred paid on the bill."

"So sell. Or find some other way to make money. Just don't do something stupid."

Cassie sighed. "Selling this shit feels stupider and meaner every day. Sometimes, I wonder what Mom and Dad would say. I think I'm getting soft."

Jake had a finger pointed at her and a big smile on his face but Cassie wouldn't let him talk.

"And itching to do other things, too." She laughed. "Itchy and soft. That's kind of gross, isn't it?"

Jake's smile was warm and proud. "No, it isn't."

"Gross or not, I gotta get over it, at least for now. Rehab wants five hundred tomorrow; the guy who owns that briefcase wants a lot more than five hundred by Friday. I gotta hustle before he comes for me. I'm afraid he might be so mad at me he may say the hell with it and come for me without waiting for the money."

"Cassie, you scare me sometimes."

Cassie was going to say something but a young boy broke away from the group of kids and came up to her.

"Hey," he said. "One of the guys in the band said you were the person to see."

Jake and Cassie stared at the boy without saying anything.

"You know," said the boy. "To see about buying, you know, some stuff."

Cassie snorted. "You mean, like some baby food or something? I don't sell to kids. If I sold." She looked at Jake. "How old is this kid?"

Jake looked at the kid.

"I just let you in to see the band. Told you, no booze. And certainly nothing else."

The boy went back to his group. Cassie could see the group making fun of him, the boy turning red.

"Kids." Jake shook his head and moved down the bar to wash some glasses. Cassie turned back to the band. The boy was at her elbow again and she jumped. His eyes were moist and gleaming.

"Look," he said. "They're laughing at me. I told them we were going to party."

"I don't sell to kids."

"I'll pay you double. Ma'am, I can't go back there empty handed."

"Beat it. I haven't sunk that low yet."

"Please, ma'am. I can't go back there empty handed. I've got five hundred dollars. I'll pay it all, just for enough for us all to get high. Everybody knows coke isn't really bad for you anyway.

Please, just this once."

Cassie couldn't believe she heard herself say: "Where's the money?"

Jake cleared his voice loudly. The boy got a big smile and reached into his windbreaker pocket and pulled out a roll of bills. He was smiling to his friends and decided to make a big deal out of it. He looked around, trying to look cool but just looking obvious, and dropped the hand with the money under the counter at Cassie. Cassie took it, and passed him a couple of small plastic bags.

Jake leaned across the bar, his face red.

"You," he said, pointing a finger at the boy, then slashing it at the door, "out." He motioned to the boy's friends. "All of you. Out." The boy backed towards the kids.

Jake glared at Cassie.

"You, too," he said. "Out."

"I'm thinking."

"Think outside."

She stood up but stood rooted. She looked at the kids, standing up and shuffling around the table, staring at the baggies in the boy's hand. She told herself: I'm doing it for Belva. And I'm not hurting them. As she looked, the kids' chairs turned into wheelchairs. And she thought, no, I'm not doing it *for* Belva. I'm doing it *to* a lot of Belvas.

"Don't just stand there," said Jake. "Move."

She marched over to the table of kids. The boy had put the coke on the table, all of them admiring the rare jewel. She snatched it up.

"Hey," said the boy who had bought the coke. "That's mine."

"Call a cop." Cassie stomped away, then whirled around and shook a finger at the boy. "What would your mother say if she knew what you were doing?"

CHAPTER 41

Jake's coffee was wearing off as Cassie turned off of the interstate into the Greenacres neighborhood. Wearing off, or maybe kicking in: it was hard to tell. Her head kept falling toward the wheel but her hands were shaking. She threw her head back and howled like a wolf to wake herself up.

She parked in front of the house at a little after two A.M. Wednesday, stopping to check on Jill and Belva before hitting the after-hours clubs. The lights were on, which only meant that Jill was awake or she had gone to sleep and left them on or gone out and left them on. *It was as useful and clear as every clue she was finding playing detective these days,* thought Cassie. She drug herself up the walk.

As she put her foot on the first step, she groggily remembered that she had left the truck unlocked. Thought about leaving it, but decided that she couldn't afford to have Charles's briefcase run off in the hands of a neighborhood kid. She turned around, feeling like everything was slow motion.

The first two steps back toward the truck were a massive achievement. But then something big kicked her in the back and threw her high into the air and a giant bang shattered her eardrums and the night bloomed into fire around her.

She landed on the ground on her back watching the door of the house swallowed up in flames. To her tired brain, it felt like a movie and she wondered why she couldn't remember the first part of the film. Somebody grabbed her shoulders and dragged her to the street. A face came into view an inch away, yelling, but her hearing was gone and the yelling came through as a jumbled whisper: "We've called 911. Someone's going to roll your truck down the hill away from the fire. Are you all right, miss? Are you all right?"

Well, of course I'm all right, thought Cassie. And then it hit her that the house was on fire and her back was singed and that this was no movie.

"Belva!" she yelled. The adrenaline kicked in and she pushed the hands away and stood up, shaking and unsteady. The people were making noises but she couldn't make it out and didn't care. Someone put his hands on her shoulders and tried to lead her away but she shook him off and started toward the house.

"Belva!"

He grabbed her again.

She pulled free and ran around the flames to the corner of the house but the back door was a wall of flame now, too.

"Belva!"

She ran back to the front. The door was now a gaping hole ringed with fire.

Cassie made it to the porch and dove inside.

"Belva! Jill!"

A wall of flames filled the little hall that led to the back bedrooms. Cassie wrapped her arms over her face, and jumped through the flames for the back of the house.

She landed on her face on the tile floor of the tiny bathroom between the two bedrooms and found a little pocket of breathable air in the first foot above the floor. She gulped a deep breath and screamed, "Belva!"

Every time she raised her head it felt like her face was on fire. She pulled a towel from a rack and crawled to the toilet to soak it in water but the dry towel burst into flames in her hands. She pulled herself up on her knees and kept her face on the floor for air. Her butt seemed to catch fire as she tried to hurl herself through the flames to Belva's bedroom.

Then she was choking and something was pulling her back. She tried to kick it away but it was a losing battle and she choked on one last lungful of smoke and lost consciousness.

Cassie woke up lying in the yard across the street, watching clouds of smoke drift casually among the stars and wondering again where she was. She sat up and saw the burning house and remembered.

There was a plastic oxygen mask over her face. A young fireman sat on the ground next to her breathing through a mask, too. His left arm was in a splint.

The EMT watching them waved to a big fireman standing without his helmet in the street. The fireman came over and Cassie could see he was older, probably too old for this part of the job anymore, but his face was streaked with black soot and red marks anyway. He was trying to stay expressionless. He pointed at the broken arm of the man next to Cassie.

"That's the way you thanked him, ma'am. He shouldn't've had to risk his life for you. He came in the bathroom window and saved your ass, pardon the French."

"Thank you. Thank him." She looked at the house. "Are they there?"

"Who?"

"My sister and her daughter. They live there."

"We're trying to get in to search the inside now. Were they at home?"

"I don't know," said Cassie.

The tears started. Instead of cooling her cheeks they felt like little rivers of the fire itself and she sat there as the tears burned her face and the smoke rose from her hair and her clothes. She rocked back and forth and said it over and over again and again.

"I don't know."

CHAPTER 42

Cassie sat on the curb across the street from the burning house, as close as the firemen would let her, close enough for the flames to sear her face through her tears. A dark shadow drifted between her and the fire and she looked up at a black sedan.

"You!" she yelled. Her tears dried up.

"Of course it's me." Stevens filled his car like a giant slug, talking through the open window without bothering to get out.

"You did this." Cassie stood up. The EMT tried to pull her back down but she threw his arm off her. She pulled the oxygen mask off of her face, the bands snapping, and threw it on the ground.

"Why the hell would I do this?" Stevens pulled out a cigarette and lit it, drew a breath, and exhaled smoke at Cassie.

"Put pressure on me, maybe. Help your buddies, maybe. Maybe just because you're so fucking evil you make houses explode for the fun of it." Cassie wiped at her face with the back of her hand, but all it did was smear soot and water and tears everywhere.

Stevens froze, the smoke just curling out of his mouth. "What you mean, explode?"

"You know exactly what I mean. I'm walking up to the front door and boom! Whole world turns to fire."

Stevens stared at Cassie.

"Was hoping this was just a grease fire or something," he said. He turned and looked at the fire and turned back to Cassie. " 'Fire of unknown origin.' That's what they're going to call this." He went inside himself for a second. "We've had a couple of those lately."

Cassie snorted. "You mean you set a couple lately."

Stevens ignored her and stared at his cigarette. "Anybody inside?"

"Maybe sister. Maybe niece. What the fuck do you care? You're ready to burn Ron and me both already. What's two more?"

"Yeah, what do I care?" He looked at her. "Look, I want you to drop this thing. Drop it, get out of town, go somewhere and change your name."

Cassie shoved her head in his window. "I'm supposed to trust you now, walk away from this. Leave my family in whatever shape they're in. Let you and Charles's drug thugs and the bald man get away with whatever it is y'all are doing. You'll probably have me picked up at the state line and shot."

He threw the cigarette out the window past Cassie's head.

"Don't expect you to believe this," he said. "Never meant to get you in this deep. Meant for you to stay in the background. The bald man's bad news. The people who make houses and small businesses disappear into flames are bad news. If we—and by we, I mean me, not you, you are off this case as of now— don't stop this by Friday, then Jericho's going to have a lot more 'fires of unknown origins' and a lot more killings done by unknown muggers. But you are off the case. I catch you anywhere near this, your ass is in jail. At least I can keep an eye on you there."

Cassie reared back and yelled at Stevens. "Make up your fucking mind. First you're going to put me in jail if I don't do your job. Now you're going to put me in jail if I do." She leaned back down and put her face in his face, still yelling at the top of her lungs.

"I don't care. I'm coming for you. All of you."

"Keep your voice down. I was never here."

She stood up and threw her arms up and howled, "Stevennnns is in the house."

Stevens cursed and pulled away. Cassie kicked the side of his car as hard as she could as he left.

The EMT started to put a hand on Cassie's arm and hesitated, his hand hanging in the air an inch away from touching her.

"Miss," he said. "We need to get you in the ambulance and take you to the hospital."

Cassie turned to face him and tell him where and how he could take his ambulance. Over his shoulder, she saw something coming up the street.

She pushed him aside and ran past him.

CHAPTER 43

Cassie sprinted down the street, face full of tears, smoke trail boiling off her back. The EMT stayed with her for a few steps, then gave up and went back to the ambulance.

"Belvaaaa!" she screamed.

Cassie crashed into Belva's wheelchair and they went down in a pile in the street with Cassie's arms around her and Belva flailing away.

"You're alive," said Cassie. "Thank God, thank God." She had pulled her right hand free and crossed herself.

"Well, of course I'm alive." Belva was slapping at Cassie. She pointed up the street. "What the hell did you do to my house?"

"I didn't do—they did."

Cassie wiped her eyes and nose with the back of her right hand and pushed the wheelchair upright. She wrestled Belva into the chair, Belva's eyes glassy and locked on the flames.

Cassie said, "Jill?"

"Gone."

Cassie hesitated. "Where?"

"Just gone. Said she'd had enough. Dumped me on Courtney's mom and took off."

Cassie said, "At least she got out before Stevens or Charles set the place on fire."

Belva glanced at Cassie and went back to staring into the flames.

"That place has been on fire for years, Cassie. It just didn't show on the outside."

"What's that supposed to mean?"

"A lot of things happened there. Things you don't want to know about. Things that don't fit your fairy tales."

Belva stared into the flames for a long time while Cassie watched the tears pour down her face. She tried to hug Belva and Belva pushed her away.

Belva snapped, "That's not my house. Never was my home. Let it burn in hell. Jill's not my mom, neither."

"Belva, you don't mean that."

The tears were like a wall over her face. "The hell I don't. The hell I don't. Gonna move on now."

She looked at Cassie.

"Jill dropped me at Courtney's like I was a sack of trash, told me I was on my own. Supposed to break my heart, but it didn't. Jill got pissed when I didn't cry."

"You're crying now."

"Hell, no. Hell, no. Glad it's over. Glad Jill's gone. Glad hell came up and claimed that god-damned house. Glad . . ."

She was crying too hard for the words to make sense. Cassie wrapped her arms around her. Belva tried to push her away a couple of times but Cassie was stronger and they stayed there in the middle of the road until the shaking stopped.

"Let's stop all this Oprah nonsense," said Belva. "Go get my stuff from Courtney's, go to my real home. Time to move on."

She pushed Cassie away and Cassie let her.

Belva turned and started to wheel away from the flames. Stopped and spun back to Cassie.

"Oh, yeah," she said. She reached into the pocket of her sleeveless hoodie and pulled out a wadded-up note and handed it to Cassie.

"My mother said to give you this."

CHAPTER 44

Cassie unfolded the note.

Cassie,

I won't call you dear because you haven't treated me like a
dear in a long time and we both know that's a fact. All you
care about is that little bitch and now you're going to get
your wish. You said you wanted her and now you got her.
Jim and I got a chance to go to Florida and make a new
life without either one of you so now you can have Belva to
yourself and not have to pretend anymore that you care
anything about me and how about that, missy. I hope you
find out what a monster she is so you'll know I was right
all along. You just don't know all the things I've done to
try to help her crippled body and her evil mind but I have
and it's just too much and it's your turn now. I tried to
give her custody back to the state but you know Alabama
has never given a damn about its citizens anyway, except
for its athletes like you who the whole damn state treats as
gods just 'cause you grew up like a freak and could throw
a ball through a hole.

It's your fault things never got to be good between you
and me like they were when we were little girls and I used
to take care of you but after I birthed the Spawn From
Hell when I was fourteen and Mom and Dad stopped lov-

ing me and gave everything to you I just couldn't see my way to forgive you. Maybe I will someday because I am a Christian woman.

I am now going to fly away with Jim and chase after a happy life like you have and that you never let me have. Don't come after me because I deserve this chance.
The Monster is now yours.

Sincerely,
Jill

Cassie looked over the note at Belva.

"What do you know about this Jim?" she said.

"You met him Saturday night."

Cassie breathed, "Shit."

Belva said, "He left me alone, after he met you. That was enough for me."

Cassie stared at Belva but the girl's face was tight and blank now and held no answers for the questions Cassie had. No point in asking them now.

The older fireman had walked down the street to talk to Cassie. "We were able to get a camera into the two bedrooms. No sign of anybody there. You went through the front of the house and the bathroom and didn't find anyone. Too soon to say for sure, but maybe your family's OK."

"Thanks," said Cassie. "This is one of them here."

The fireman turned to Belva. "Are you OK, miss?"

Belva nodded.

Cassie said, "She was staying at a friend's. Her mother should have been the only one at home, and she left this." She handed him the note.

He took a long time reading it.

Cassie said, "You need to keep the note for the investigation, that's OK by me."

The fireman looked at her a long time. "See that man standing up there, writing on a clipboard? Clean suit, never even had the smell of smoke in it, let alone soot from fighting a fire, now he's the expert on fires? He's writing the report from the 'investigation' now. 'Fire of unknown origin.' "

Cassie said, "So it's like that?"

"Don't know who you pissed off, ma'am, but did you ever consider moving somewhere far away?"

"Every day."

He shrugged. "Well, if you need someone to watch your little one while you go to the hospital and get checked out, we can . . ."

"We're fine."

"We can keep an eye on her . . ."

"I'm taking her with me," she said. For the first time she scanned the street looking for strangers. "We're getting away from here now."

The fireman sighed. "Sign a release with the EMT. Leave a number where you can be reached." He walked back to one of the fire trucks.

Cassie signed the forms and loaded Belva into the truck. As she was cranking the engine, she got a glimpse of herself in the mirror: smoking hair, black-and-red-streaked face, bloodshot eyes. She reached under her seat for a box of tissues she kept there.

Her hand bumped up against the rusty pistol and she wondered how to use it.

She drove to Courtney's and leaned against the back of the truck and closed her eyes while Belva got her stuff. Belva came out with a big duffel bag of clothes and books, balancing her laptop on top.

They drove out of the neighborhood, Belva coming to life now and chattering about where she was going to sleep at Cassie's and how much fun they were going to have.

It sounded like the conversation they had Monday morning, not quite two days ago, when Cassie thought she would just work at GENES and ask Jill for Belva and live a normal happy life.

Even when you get what you want, she thought, it's ruined before you get it. You always wind up tired and dirty and angry, and all you can ever do is just fight back and hit as hard as you can.

CHAPTER 45

Belva said, "This isn't the way to your house, Cassie." She thought about it a minute and smiled. "Our house."

"We're not going there," said Cassie. "He'll be waiting for us there."

"Who? Boyfriend?"

"Hell, no. The man who did this."

"Jesus, Cassie. You think someone set fire to the house? You know who?"

"Houses don't explode on their own. Stevens and Charles and the bald guy are in on this. Any of them may be waiting for us."

"So we can't go home. Cassie, you don't have to take me to a fancy hotel or nothing. I can sleep in the truck."

"Hell, no," said Cassie. "They'll find us anywhere, unless they know not to f— not to mess with us."

"What does that mean?"

"I don't know. Let me think."

Cassie stared out at the road and drove in silence. She pulled into a Circle K convenience store and got out. She looked back at Belva and said, "Stay here."

Cassie was worried the clerk would remember her later, but he barely looked up from his girly magazine. This time of night, this neighborhood, maybe a six-foot-two blonde with smoke boiling off her hair wasn't that unusual. Cassie went to the ladies' room in the back and closed the door and looked in the mirror.

She was braced for a bad sight, but she didn't expect the sadness and tiredness she saw. She turned on the water and dunked her head in the dirty sink and held it there as long she could. Came up for air, and dunked again and again until the water coming off of her no longer tasted of smoke. Looked back in the mirror and saw a drowned rat with filthy arms and a filthy tee shirt. She stripped off the shirt and dropped it in the sink, let it soak while she worked on her body. She grabbed a handful of paper towels and wiped down the soot and sweat as well as she could.

She checked herself in the mirror and noticed her body for the first time in a long time. In LA, her body had been her life: weight room and conditioning and practice for basketball, and then hours spent standing still while prissy photographers and their assistants poked and prodded and measured and selected outfits for her modeling. It was still a good body: chunky-muscled but girl-curvy with glowing, golden skin. Should be doing something more than standing pitiful in a dirty convenience-store bathroom in the middle of the night.

She looked at her black eye and her scar and the soot-exaggerated wrinkles.

"You look fifty-fucking years old," she said to the mirror. The mouth in the mirror tightened. "Somebody needs to pay for this. All of this."

She wrung out the shirt and pulled it over her head. The coldness of the shirt felt right; just another tough thing to be ignored.

"Happy hour?" said Belva as Cassie got back in the truck.

Cassie looked at the beer bottle in her hand and back at Belva. "No," she said, giving Belva a dirty look. "You're too young for this stuff."

"Courtney's mom lets her drink Magnum Malt all the time. It's all right, but I don't like the taste."

"Good. Don't get used to it." Cassie twisted the top off the bottle, turned the bottle upside down, and emptied it in the parking lot.

Cassie held up the empty. "If I catch you with one of these, I'm going to send you to your room. Without your computer."

"No problem."

Cassie pulled the truck up to the road and Belva brightened.

"So we're in Ozzie and Harriet world from the fifties? You're going to come home from the office every day and make sure I've got my homework done, fix us meatloaf and mashed potatoes and a green vegetable every night? That might not be so bad. Hey, I can do the cooking."

Cassie laughed. "Can you just shut up and let me think?"

She pulled out into the middle of Government Drive and said, "Shit" and stopped the car in the middle of the road.

"Harriet wouldn't talk like that," said Belva.

Cassie pulled on out before traffic got to them.

"Forgot something. Can't get it here anyway."

They drove to the Wal-Mart on Universe Drive, the only place Cassie could think of that would have what she needed this time of night. She went in and came out with a garden hose.

Belva laughed. "Is that what you think you're going to beat me with, if I disobey your 1950s rules?"

"No. I'm going to need a chain for that," Cassie said. "A big chain. Don't think I won't get it if I need it."

They drove to a run-down neighborhood. Cassie stopped in front of a darkened house. Took the hose and cut a six-foot length with a knife from under the seat.

"What you going to do with that?" said Belva.

"I need to do one very un-Harriet thing. Don't pay any attention to anything I do until we get out of this neighborhood. And don't make a sound. Got it?"

Belva nodded.

Cassie went behind the truck and came back with the bottle full of gasoline and the hose she'd used to siphon the tank. Belva wrinkled her nose at the smell. Cassie took some tissues and stuffed them into the neck of the bottle.

She reached into Belva's bag and pulled out a schoolbook. She whispered in Belva's ear, "Keep your nose in this book and don't look up at anything. I don't want you seeing anything that goes on until we get out of this neighborhood. You got it?"

Belva nodded, grinning.

Cassie put the bottle between her legs, started the car, and crept along the street with her lights off. Made a couple of turns and then paused, looking down the street until she saw what she wanted. *First time I've been glad this old postal truck has the steering wheel on the right-hand side rather than the left,* she thought.

She started forward again, picking up a little speed. Steering with her knees, she pulled back her door. Picked up the bottle with her right hand, lit the tissues with her left and held the burning bottle out the door.

The truck was moving as fast as she could control it with her knees when she came up beside Charles's bright red Ferrari. She slammed the bottle down on the roof hard and it exploded into flames. The car alarm screamed, she grabbed the wheel and pushed the truck hard until they rounded the corner.

Cassie muttered, quiet and bitter, "Teach Charles not to burn my shit down."

"Cool," said Belva, with her nose still in the book.

CHAPTER 46

Belva babbled all the way to GENES. Cassie tried to turn off the voices shouting in her own head and focus on Belva but she couldn't. When she pulled the truck into the lab she felt as worn-out and old and dirty as the piles of equipment around her.

"Oh, my God," said Belva. "Man, look at all this cool stuff you've got here."

Cassie looked at Belva's eyes darting from one junk heap to another and smiled at the brightness in her face.

"Some people would just see junk."

"Some people don't know diamonds. Look, you've got a computer center there. Lab over there. Cute little apartment there."

"Yeah, cute."

Belva looked at Cassie. "You're trying to act like this is no big deal, but I see that big smile."

"Yeah. I guess I'm proud of it. When I'm not in zombie-mode. Look, we need to talk more about tonight. You've been through a lot."

"I'm fine." Belva snapped it out like it was one syllable. "Told you, when I got the chance to go, I was going to move on and not look back."

"Good. At least, good for now. We may have to talk about this some more later. Look, let me explain about this place. Belongs to—"

"I've got to get out and see all this." Belva unsnapped the clamps and rolled to the back of the truck and threw open the doors.

"You're saying this is all yours, right, Cassie? Telling me it isn't mine so I've got to be careful? See, I didn't even say 'ain't.' Nothing but the King's English from me from now on. New life, new rules. You're going to be proud of me."

"I am, right now," said Cassie. "But let me talk to you about this place and its owner."

Belva had the planks down, ignoring Cassie. Went skittering down them like a kid in a skateboard park.

"I knew Jill was lying about you, knew you had some secret place where you did cool things."

"Yeah, well, it's not exactly mine. It belongs to—"

Cassie heard Gene's voice. "Your aunt. She's being modest. That little pile of Plexiglas over there is mine. But, yeah, she pretty much rules this place." He walked up to Belva and put out a hand. "You must be the famous Belva, computer genius and budding basketball star?"

"Yes, sir," said Belva. "You must work for my aunt?"

"Belva," said Cassie.

"Sometimes," said Gene. "What brings you out here to your aunt's lab so late on a school night?"

"Moving in." Belva wheeled past him.

He watched her go and smiled back at Cassie.

Cassie said, "Look, it's just for tonight. She was staying with me and they were . . . painting my apartment."

"At three A.M.? You've got better luck with contractors than I ever had."

"We'll sleep in my truck."

Belva yelped when she got to the computers.

Gene pointed at Belva. "She doesn't look like she's going down anytime soon. No, give her the cot. You take the couch next to her. I'll sleep in my truck. Believe me, it won't be the first time."

"OK, but just for tonight. We'll be gone in the morning."

Gene was watching Belva scrambling, trying to find some way to climb up on the raised platform.

"No rush. Might be nice to have some kid energy around."

"Thanks for . . . you know. Covering for me and letting Belva think this is mine."

"Wasn't covering."

Gene turned away, called to Belva, "Let me show you something."

Cassie said, "Gene, wait a minute."

Gene turned back to Cassie.

"There's one more favor."

He smiled. "I figure I owe you one, after the afternoon."

"Let's call that one mutual. No, this is real. I need to go out for a while."

"Three A.M. real estate?"

She didn't answer.

"Hey, no problem. The kid and I'll have fun. Go."

"Thanks. I mean, really, you could give me a lot of shit about this."

"Hey," he said. "I've got your back." Grinned a little impish grin and added, "And your front and your—"

"Shush," Cassie grinned and pointed at Belva's back.

Cassie said, "I need you to be proper. Keep your back turned while I shower and get my clothes changed."

"We're going to be prim after this afternoon?"

Cassie pointed back at Belva.

"I get it." Gene walked away. "Hey, kid, Belva. Let me help you up there, show you your aunt's massive computer center, tell you what she's done with next to nothing."

Cassie went to the back of her truck, wishing she had gotten a nap or at least a cup of coffee. She grabbed the makeshift ramp and threw it in back into the truck. One corner of the truck was piled with dirty laundry waiting until Cassie had time for the Laundromat or until the smell became unbearable. She sorted through, throwing things from one side of the truck to the other. Found a pair of dark blue jeans, held them up and looked at them.

"Not dark enough." Threw them on the reject pile.

Held up another pair of jeans and looked at them.

"Yeah. Black." Dropped them on the floor at her feet.

Found her tightest sports bra and a long-sleeved running shirt.

"Black." Dropped it at her feet. Sorted through the pile for one other thing and found it: a balaclava, thin running cap that could be worn as a cap or pulled down like a ski mask.

"Black." Dropped it on the pile. Carried them all over to the shower.

The shower felt like a warm and soapy-clean heaven. For a moment, she had no problem that couldn't be scrubbed clean with Ivory soap. She didn't want to come out but she knew she had to hurry. As soon as the shower smelled more like soap than smoke, she jumped out and dressed and walked over to Belva and Gene.

Gene had dragged another picnic table next to Cassie's, set up Belva's computer, and leaned a piece of plywood on the edge of the raised floor so Belva could get up and down on her own. Cassie had to clear her throat to get them to take their eyes off Belva's computer and pay attention to her.

"Cassie," said Belva. "You look like a dude."

"Wouldn't say that," said Gene. "But I've never seen a real-estate agent dressed like a ninja with a black cap before. Selling a house to a midnight superhero? Or villain?"

"Something like that. Hey, thanks. I'll be back as soon as I can." She turned to Belva. "You mind Mr. Gene, young lady."

"Yes, ma'am."

Cassie looked back at her truck. Stevens, Charles, and God knows who else would be looking for it. She stared at it a long time.

"Hey," said Gene, following her stare. "If you're going with a dark avenger look, why not take the Tesla? Needs exercise anyway."

Cassie looked at the Tesla and smiled.

"Black."

CHAPTER 47

Cassie flicked off the Tesla's lights and felt invisible and silent. Wrapped in black clothes and driving the black Tesla through a moonless night, she was just a disembodied ghostly face flashing faintly as it passed by streetlights, blue eyes and pale, scarred skin and a slash-mouth tense with mission tonight.

Gliding into town through the empty city streets, she passed an old man hunched over his wheel. He never looked back at her.

"Cool," she said.

She came to the last major intersection, caught up in the thrill of her invisibility, and was almost sideswiped by an eighteen-wheeler that never saw her. She pulled over and waited for the heavy breathing to stop. Apparently, invisibility wasn't the same thing as invincibility.

She cruised slowly and carefully until she found a stand of pines in a vacant lot two doors down from Red Rock. She took her time backing into a spot completely hidden and sat watching.

The outside lights of the Red Rock were out but an inside light was on with a shadow moving around, blocking the light randomly so that it flashed like a code signal. Good. Hopefully the owner was still there. She got out of the Tesla and pulled the black mask down.

She found a dark corner by the door, faded back into it, and listened to the noises inside. Sounded like one person cleaning up with the TV still on. The noises seemed to move around, close to the door now, then off to the back.

While she was looking, the TV went off and the noises moved toward the door. Long Tom stepped out and pulled the door closed. Cassie grabbed him by the shoulders as he stepped out, turned him, and used her hip in an old basketball move to smash him face-first into the concrete wall and then shoved him down on his knees.

Cassie made her voice as low and hoarse as she could. "Don't scream."

Long Tom shook a cloth bank-deposit bag in his hand. "Money's in the bag. Take it and go. Don't need to get rough. I do what you guys want."

Cassie decided to play along with the confusion. "Yeah. This time we want a little more than money. Give me what I need, and you can keep your money, this time."

"When has anybody in this town not given y'all what you want? You point your fingers at us like a gun, say 'sim,' get whatever you want. I get it. No need to get rough. Folks like me gave up long ago. Gave up or died."

"Yeah," said Cassie. "Let's start with that, 'sim.' What's that supposed to mean?"

"You're asking me? What's this supposed to be, a test? See if I got it right?"

"Yeah. A test. Now shut the fuck up and see if you get the answers right. Like a quiz show. Get the answers right, you go home with the prize in that bag. Get them wrong, and you win the door marked hospital. Sim? What's that, like some kind of computer simulation?"

"Still don't get why I got to tell you what you already know—"

Cassie ground his face into the concrete. "Ain't going to tell you again."

"No, not computer sim. SYM. Shut Your Mouth. You boys

ain't that clever."

Cassie snorted. "No, we're not. Let's talk about Ron, the other night."

"You know I haven't talked to anyone about that. A girl came in asking about that, I told her to take a hike."

"Good." She bent down, her face an inch from his, the side of his face shoved into the concrete, his one free eye wasn't even trying hard to get a good look at her. Beaten before she got here. "But now tell me about Ron."

He jerked and his eye spun in the socket, trying now to read her face. She turned away.

"Why you ask me a thing like that? I'm not telling anybody anything."

"Wrong answer. You don't ask questions. One more and you win our lovely Emergency Room prize."

"All right. The guy who calls himself the Enforcer—your guy—came in for his pickup."

"This Enforcer—does he work alone?"

"No, they—you've got a whole organization, call yourselves Raiders after Bedford Forrest's Raiders from the Civil War. You take money from the Yankee businessmen down here and give it to the Good Government fund. Supposed to be a big organization, but the Enforcer is the only one folks are scared of. But you know that."

"Sure. So the Enforcer came in. Then what?"

"You sure you want to hear this? Really, I don't remember enough to tell anybody anything about it. I'm no threat."

"Then tell me what you say you don't remember."

"He came in for the weekly pickup, said he didn't want to wait until closing time. I bitched a little and he didn't like it. He smiled and sat down next to Ron, told Ron he was going to buy him a drink. Put something in his beer when Ron wasn't looking. Ron got a lot drunker a lot faster than he should have.

Enforcer stood Ron up, a big smile on the Enforcer's face. Told me that this was a warning to me and everybody else. Told me to read the papers tomorrow, know that this could happen to me and anybody else who gave him backtalk. Pointed a finger as he went out the door. Said, 'SYM.' "

The owner paused, his eye rolling around crazy again, searching her face for any hint of a reaction.

"Hey, I got the message," he said. "Got it before. Y'all didn't have to fuck up Ron like that, just out of meanness to somebody who happened to be at the wrong place at the wrong time."

The eye locked onto Cassie's eye.

"You ain't the Enforcer, but you look like him. His eyes, blue like yours, but cold and sharp like an ice pick. Yours are, like, warmer. Almost pretty."

"Don't call me pretty."

"Didn't mean nothing, Mister."

The eye rolled around crazy again, searching for anything.

"Wait. You ain't one of them. This don't make no sense. They don't never ask no questions. You can't be one of them. Cop? No—you can't be no cop neither."

The owner squirmed. "There's been talk. Some of the other owners—not me—getting together to hire somebody from the outside to come in and take down the Raiders. That you?"

"What if I am?"

"Shit, Mister, I blow with the wind. I can't tell if you're with the Enforcer or if you're something new. I just keep my head down, either way. SYM. But maybe, maybe you are somebody new. There's a lot of people looking to get behind anybody new. Just need somebody big enough to get the job done. Just saying."

Cassie said, "Maybe there is a new wind coming."

She paused and wondered why she had said that.

She turned his face away. "We're done here. You don't give

me any trouble, I'll make this easy on you. I'm going to dis-appear. You stay there for ten minutes. Don't look around. What you going to tell people about this?"

"Nothing."

"No. For real, if your best friend asks, what did you see?"

"Honestly, not much. I can't see enough of you to describe you to anybody. Blue eyes and black clothes."

"Good answer."

She brushed the bits of concrete out of the side of his face.

"Sorry."

"It's OK," he said.

She stepped back to the corner. Just as she stepped out of the light, he got brave and turned and looked straight at her, and got a big grin on his face.

"Damn," he said. "You're a big 'un, dude."

CHAPTER 48

Cassie rolled the garage door open at GENES and looked out at the early morning fog playing in the woods around outside. Cassie stood watching the shapes float by, imagining them turning into thugs and firebombs and worse. She decided that fog was just fog and that the morning wisps would be enough of a disguise for her to take Belva to Crimm High School without worrying about being seen.

"Thanks for the coffee," Cassie said to Belva when they were driving into town.

Belva gave a quick nod, no big deal. But she grinned.

"And, Belva, thanks for washing the dishes before I got up. And mopping the floor around the, uh, apartment at GENES."

"No problem," said Belva. "I'm going to earn my keep. You'll see. You and Gene won't have to do anything but get your work done around there. Speaking of which, what do you want for dinner tonight? If you'll stop at the store after school and let me buy ingredients, I'll fix y'all anything you want."

"Now who's trying to play Ozzie and Harriet?"

"Not playing. We're going to have a real life. I'm not going to waste this chance to live in a good world and be somebody."

"Good attitude."

Belva said, "Speaking of attitude, I get to do the intention today."

Cassie smiled to herself. "Go for it."

"Today, I will begin to build a life, and respect the lives of all living things."

Cassie beamed.

The last traffic light before Crimm High glowed red in the fog. Cassie stopped, took a sip of coffee and glanced over at the parking lot of the Indian Restaurant. A random breeze blew a hole in the fog and her eye caught a black SUV idling next to the street, a smile on the face of the man sitting in the passenger seat and looking at her. A bald man with a drooping black mustache, smiling at Cassie while he reached inside his jacket.

Cassie jerked the wheel to the left and slammed her truck onto the cross street, horns blaring and tires screeching around her.

"What the . . ." said Belva.

"Never mind. Just . . . relax. Taking a . . . shortcut to school today." Cassie glanced in the mirror and saw the SUV pulling behind her.

She had a lead, but the SUV was closing it fast.

"Shit," she yelled.

"Some shortcut," said Belva.

Cassie yanked the truck onto a side road. The SUV turned and came up beside them, the bald guy's head a foot from Belva. The SUV's window slid down and he pointed a black Glock across Belva at Cassie and waved her over.

Cassie stomped on the gas and the old truck gamely pulled two feet ahead. The SUV caught back up. Cassie looked over in terror as the bald man stretched out the window and put the gun almost to Belva's head. Cassie yanked Belva's head down and stomped on the brakes as hard as she could.

The cheap tires on the truck screamed. Cassie looked up in time to see a fireplug looming in front of the truck. She jerked the wheel and the truck screeched down a side street, its speed bled down to a walk. She looked in the mirror and saw the

SUV closing again.

She juiced the truck and jerked the wheel. The truck stood for a moment on two wheels then righted itself into the parking lot of a cheap apartment complex.

The cars were parked close here and the SUV could not get around Cassie. The SUV rode on Cassie's tail, pushing up and dropping back. Cassie caught them coming up fast and slammed on her brakes.

The SUV smashed into them and the heavy steel bumper of the truck chewed a big hole into the SUV's grille and steam poured out. The truck jumped forward and the SUV swerved into one of the old cars with a crash. Cassie stomped the gas and put distance between them.

Belva turned around and watched as they pulled out of the lot.

"They're coming again, Cassie."

Cassie looked in the mirror and saw the SUV coming for them in a cloud of smoke with one headlight dangling like an injured eye. She jerked the truck down a foggy street. The eye followed. Cassie reached up and flicked her lights off, pulled on the parking brake, and tucked the truck behind a Dumpster. The eye went by and disappeared.

"We did it," said Belva. "I told you, Cassie. You and I can do anything."

Cassie looked down the road and saw nothing. She put the truck in reverse and started to back out until she felt something on the side of her head. Turned and saw the bald man holding the Glock to her head.

"Out," he said.

Cassie got out. The bald man looked in at Belva strapped into her wheelchair and said, "You stay. Watch. Tell people what you see here."

A wisp of fog blew by and a young man, barely more than a

boy, appeared beside him and said, "Think you're the only one smart enough to turn off your lights?"

"Tell Charles I said to go to hell," Cassie said.

The bald man laughed. "I don't take my orders from Charles." The bald man lowered his Glock and jerked his head at the boy. "You take her. Let this one be your first."

The boy hesitated and looked at the bald man. Cassie stepped back to the car door, putting him between her and the boy. She snatched her gun out from under the seat and put it against the bald man's head.

"Maybe it will be my first," she said. *If I can do it.* She had never killed, had never even fired a gun. *Please God, let them just drop the guns and walk away,* she prayed.

He seemed to read her mind. He smiled.

"Think this is easy, missy? Pull the trigger. Turn the nice girl into a killer."

She froze. The bald man threw an elbow into her gut and laughed. Cassie stepped back and his next elbow missed and she pointed the gun at his head. She closed her eyes and felt her finger tighten on the trigger.

The gun went "Pop." Cassie opened her eyes and saw a small flag saying "Bang" waving from the barrel of her gun. The bald man had a cold smile and the boy was laughing at her.

"Toy gun," the boy said. "Tried to kill the Enforcer with a toy gun, after all the people he's killed. Wait till I tell people that."

The Enforcer said, "Do her now. Let's get out of here."

The boy pointed his gun at Cassie's head and Cassie stood there with her joke of a gun hanging limp in her hand. The boy's hand was shaking but his eyes were hard.

Cassie saw Belva on the ground, crawling toward the boy with something in her hand. The Enforcer and the boy saw her eyes and started to follow them.

"C'mon!" she screamed. "Do it." They looked back at her.

There was a crack and the boy collapsed, grabbing his knee and Cassie snatched the Enforcer's gun out of his hand when he looked away. Belva was lying on the ground at the boy's feet with a crowbar in her hand. She dropped the crowbar and grabbed his gun.

The boy slapped at his ankle and pulled out a small gun that looked like a toy but wasn't. He raised up and pointed the gun at Cassie and Cassie tried to get a grip on the Enforcer's gun but she was too slow and Belva pointed her gun first and fired, flinching with the blast. The boy stood motionless for a moment as bright red blood bloomed across his chest. He folded back onto the ground.

Cassie jumped over to Belva, took her gun and stuck it in the back of her jeans. She reached down with her free hand and snatched up Belva by the waist of her jeans and leaned her against the truck.

"How did you . . ." said Cassie, watching the Enforcer but talking to Belva.

"Crawled out. Nobody was watching the crippled girl. Crawled out with the crowbar and broke his knee. Crawled out and . . ."

Belva was looking at the body.

"Cassie, I didn't mean to . . . He was going to . . ."

"Baby, you saved my life."

Cassie motioned at the Enforcer with her Glock.

"Walk away from here while you can."

"What?" he said. "You're not going to kill me?"

"No," said Cassie. "We're not killers."

He backed away. When he got to edge of the Dumpster, he smiled at Cassie.

"One of you is," he said as he disappeared.

CHAPTER 49

"Going to jail," said Belva.

"No, you're not," said Cassie, shutting off the engine of the truck now that they were back in GENES. Crimm High School was just a far-away dream for now.

Belva unclamped her chair and rolled backward between the two wooden ramps. Reached back and pushed the rear door of the truck open and bent down and slid both planks into place.

"Know what they be doing to crippled bitches in prison," she said as she sailed down the ramp.

Cassie slammed her door and came around and caught Belva's wheelchair.

"You. Are. Not. Going. To. Prison. And stop lapsing back into that stupid street talk."

Belva tried to shake her off and couldn't.

She glared at Cassie. "I. Killed. A. Man."

Repeated it. "I killed a man. Bust a cap in his ass." She raised an arm. "Got his blood on my sleeve. Probably got guts all over me."

"That's not blood, it's magic marker. You weren't that close to him."

"Yeah, well, he be close to God now. Whispering, 'Get that little white bitch.' God saying, 'Damned right, my will be done.' "

"Jesus, Belva. It's bad enough that you get this gangster vibe when you're stressed, but now God's a rapper?"

"Might be. You don't know. Know I don't need your Ozzie and Harriet talk in jail."

Cassie started to say something and Belva interrupted.

"Don't you laugh at me."

Cassie saw that Belva was crying.

"Cassie, I killed a man. Killed a man. First morning of my new life, set an intention to do some good, and I killed a man. Look at it this way: More than anybody else, I know how shitty it is to have dead legs. I pretend it isn't, but it is. But now I killed someone else's legs. And I killed the arms he probably hugged his girlfriend with, I killed his—"

"You killed the hand he was using to point a gun at me with. Killed the brain that thought it would be fun—"

"Yeah. You heard what the bald guy said, this was going to be the first killing for the man I killed. Maybe he wouldn't have done it. Maybe he would have said, 'I'm not going to become a killer.' Only thing I know for sure is this: I chose to become a killer. I've got to live with that, whether I wind up in jail or in hell."

"You saved my life."

"Maybe. Put that on my tombstone: Maybe."

"Whatever. We'll talk more later. For now, take a shower and let me have your old clothes."

"Destroying the evidence?"

"Being careful. Now shower."

"Huh. Ain't going to shower out in the open like that. May be last shower I get without some bull dyke guard bitch waiting for me to drop the soap."

"Jesus," said Cassie. She grabbed a spare sheet and draped it from the shower to the bed, making a little tent.

"Happy?" she said.

"Oh, yeah, I be happy when—"

"Go!"

Cassie watched Belva roll herself to the shower and arm-hop her way into the seat they had put inside. Gene had come out of the clean room for the last of the exchange, stood there beside Cassie sipping his coffee.

"Sounds pretty tough," he said, "this school you're sending her to."

"I'm not sending her—oh! Look, never mind that. We need to talk. A lot."

Gene held up his cup. "I've got half a cup left. That long enough for this talk?"

Cassie reached over to take his cup. Paused with her hand over his and let it linger before she took the cup from him and drained it. He smiled as she emptied his cup.

"I'll get us two more," she said. "Meet you over there." Gestured to the picnic table by the computers.

He was watching her as she walked up to the table with the full coffee pot in one hand and two cups dangling from the other.

"What?" she said.

"Nothing. Just looking."

"Looking at a worn-out hag who's just come from hell and may be going back."

He focused on Cassie. "Hag? No. You do look tired. Maybe we should back off on our hours here, let you get a little more rest. But you are very un-haggy."

Cassie snorted. "Maybe yesterday, the pressure here was in my top three problems. Maybe even an hour ago. Not now. My problems just got bigger. And you need to know."

She searched Gene's eyes, wondered if this was a mistake, trusting someone she barely knew. *Is this just a cute guy and a one-night stand? Laying myself bare. Nothing good ever comes of that.*

Gene set his cup down, looked into her eyes.

Well, maybe some good, some times. Maybe now. Maybe this once.

"Just came from a killing," she said.

His smile was gone now. "You witnessed a killing?"

"Belva's in the shower washing off gunshot residue."

He tilted his head back, studying her for a long moment. She let him have the time to absorb what she'd said.

Finally, slowly, he said, "Belva's a good kid. We talked a long time—was that just last night? My bet is that—whatever happened—that girl had a damned good reason."

"They were trying to kill us."

"That would be a good reason." He sat and thought. "So what do we do now, come up with the money for a damned fine attorney, go with her and the attorney to the police?"

She looked at him and flickered just a tiny smile at him. "We?"

"Hell, yeah."

"The problem is, the police are in on it. The police, the city—hell, maybe the whole damned world, for all I know."

Gene sat up and took a long sip of coffee. "We do need to talk."

So they talked. Talked for a long time until Gene knew it all: her drug busts, Stevens, the Enforcer. Friday coming.

"Still don't get the Friday thing," Gene said. "Sounds like this has been going on a long time. Don't know what's special about Friday."

"Maybe Stevens is just blowing smoke, putting pressure on me."

"Maybe."

"Maybe Stevens is dirty, just using me somehow, maybe setting me up for something. Ann says so."

"Maybe. Maybe not. But there's more. I told you, I went to a meeting of small business guys, trying to get out from under this Good Government scam but mostly just grumbling, too scared to do anything. SYM means a hell of a lot more than just 'Shut Your Mouth.' "

Cassie leaned forward. "I'm all ears."

Gene grinned. "No. You're not." She smiled back and he said, "But let's stick with your ears for the moment. Ears and brains. You know James Morrison?"

"Dr. Morrison? From JU?"

"Yeah."

Cassie said, "He was my Simulation and Modelling professor. Till they had that fire."

"The small business he was starting burned down, and his daughter died."

"Yeah. He kind of went to pieces after that."

"No wonder," said Gene. "You don't know the half of it. The fire was no accident. He tried to stand up to them, refused to pay. They put his wife and one of his daughters in the building and torched it. Left him with one other child still alive so he'd be too afraid to say anything. Got him fired from JU. Made sure he couldn't get a job anywhere. Cleans bars at night for money now."

"Jesus."

"Yeah. They left the burned-out building as it was, still standing on Tech Drive where everybody coming into Research Park can see the big sign still out front. Remember the name of his company?"

"There were like three professors went in on that. Dr. Stevens, Dr. Morrison, Dr. . . . uh."

"Yankova. SYM, Inc. Three giant letters every Jericho engineer and business owner sees every morning and every night."

"Gene," Cassie said. "We've got to help Dr. Morrison. Maybe the other guys, too. Get them out here and put them to work."

Gene smiled. "You've got guys shooting at you, police

persecuting you, drug dealers fire-bombing your house, and your concern is helping your old teacher?"

"Yeah," said Cassie. "I'm going off half-cocked again, aren't I? No safer for him here."

Gene said, "They're probably safe enough where they are for now. And we're safe enough for now. We're so small I don't think anybody knows where we are out here in the woods. But they'll find us soon enough if we don't take the fight to them, find some way to break their backs."

They heard the shower stop.

"My turn for the shower." Cassie stood up.

She looked at Gene. He was chewing his lip, lost in thought somewhere.

"You know," she said. "The smart thing to do here might be to pack up and run, go to some far-away land and be happy."

Gene was staring into space. He turned to her and his face was hard.

"Hell, no. This is war."

Chapter 50

The greasy spoon next to the bait shop had been painted white long-ago, but now it was a featureless gray like the neighborhood around it. There were a couple of broken-down pickups in the lot, and a brand-new, red Shelby Mustang. Cassie looked at the plate-glass window and saw Charles staring out at her.

She smiled and reached into her bag and pulled out the Transformer magnet she'd taken off of Belva's backpack. She dropped it on the ground behind the Mustang and bent down. Reached under the bumper and fiddled until she was sure Charles had seen her hide something under the car, let him worry what it was.

She stood up and waved at him. She marched in and sat down on the stool next to Charles. He didn't look at her.

"What you do with my ride?" He stared ahead at the grill, pretending to ignore her while they talked.

"Your ride? Thought you had that red Ferrari?"

He turned and met her eyes. "Used to."

Cassie turned to the grill like he had. "My sister used to have a house."

Charles glared at the side of her head. "Who cares about your sister? You got my money?"

Cassie reached into her bag and pulled out a roll of bills and started to hand it to him.

"Not here," he hissed. "Not like that."

The waitress slapped a plate with a hamburger and fries down in front of Cassie.

"What the hell's that?" she said. "I don't touch that stuff. Do you know how those cows are killed? How much grease is in those fries?"

Charles jerked his chin at the grill. "Now pay the lady for your lunch. She'll count it in the back, and then give it me as my change."

Cassie laughed but handed the girl the bills. The girl disappeared into the back.

"This is your idea of a secure handover?" she said. "Look out that window. There could be seventy billion cops out there filming us. Hand a big wad of cash to a girl who walks away with it? What could possibly go wrong with that?" She turned and stared at his face. "Unless you and the cops are working together."

Charles watched the grill and said nothing. The girl came back, set the roll down in front of him and said, "Twenty-seven dollars."

Charles looked at her without expression.

"You owe five thousand. Six, now that I got to charge you for making this extra trip."

"You don't want my money? Here. Take this instead." She hefted the briefcase up on the counter.

Charles swept it off the counter and put it on the floor in front of his feet.

Cassie snatched the bills. "You take your 'product,' I'll take the cash. We're done. For good, this time."

Charles looked at the grill with a bored look plastered on his face. "Don't care. Six grand, or we take it out of your hide."

Cassie laughed at him. "You tried that. Remember?"

"I remember somebody firebombing my car."

"You remember somebody firebombing my sister's house?"

He turned and stared at her and didn't say anything.

"Remember?" she said. "The whole house exploded into

flames. But you missed me."

Charles stared at Cassie a long time.

"Cassie," he said. "You don't know what the fuck you're into. Stay away from me. Don't want your money, now. Don't want to be anywhere near you."

He stood and picked up the briefcase.

"You might," she said, "want to get somebody to check that car of yours before you get in it. Cars can explode out of nowhere, too."

Charles stopped and stared at Cassie. She stood up and pushed past him. At the door, she turned and looked back. "We're coming for you," she said. "All of you."

CHAPTER 51

Cassie left Charles and drove to her apartment. She sat in her truck a half block away, squinting into the mid-morning sun and watching her door for any sign of Charles's thugs or Stevens or whoever before she went into her apartment for maybe the last time. Get in, grab what she could, and get back to GENES before anyone could catch her. Then what? Die at GENES, once the bad guys found them? Go to jail? Leave Belva alone with no one to take care of her—if Belva comes out of this alive?

She tried to calm down and focus. A pair of joggers came around the corner and she slumped down so they couldn't see her while she studied them for gun bulges in their spandex outfits. As they got close, the girl chirped, "Hey, Cassie," and she recognized her neighbor and recognized how stupid it was for a six-two girl in a postal truck to try to go incognito.

Screw up.

Last Saturday, five days ago, she thought she had a miserable life and spent her time dreaming of a return to the fairy tale. Now, by trying to fight back against that shit-world, she had kicked herself into a hell a hundred times worse.

Screw up.

She got out of the truck and threw the back doors open and ran for her door. Even if she couldn't do stealth, she could do what she needed to do fast.

She unlocked the door, stepped inside, and locked the door behind her.

"You need a better lock."

Cassie jumped and slammed back into the door. Stevens was sitting in a chair against the wall, tucked back where the door hid him from view when she came in.

"I should have known," said Cassie. "My fairy godfather."

Enough light shone on the side of Stevens's face to see he was pissed.

"Yeah. Thank your lucky stars I'm here. If a black and white had found you, they'd have shot you on sight." He stood up, weary, lifting a bigger burden than his body.

"Cassandra Luna, you are under arrest . . ." He took two long steps to her, quick for a man his size, and grabbed her hand and tried to slap a handcuff on it.

"What the fuck?" He missed with the cuffs and the two of them pushed and shoved. Cassie fell away from him and the coffee table splintered under her and she snatched up a leg from the table and jumped up, shaking the leg in his face as he waved the cuffs. They stood three feet apart, huffing and puffing and red-faced.

"Cassie, this is the best way."

"Best for who? You? JPD? Every time someone does something bad to me, they tell me to 'play nice, it's good for you, this is the best way.' "

Stevens tried to say something but Cassie waved the leg again.

"You said I had till Friday. It's Wednesday afternoon. I still got time. Besides. I quit selling. You've got nothing on me."

She felt herself smiling, like she was bringing him a proud achievement and wanted his approval. She wiped the smile off and scowled at him.

Stevens said, "Maybe I'll ride around tonight, listen to every dope dealer and two-bit thief tell me they've changed their ways." He stared at her a long time. "Murderers, too."

They stood glaring at each other in the harsh half-light leaking out from the kitchen, looking like two dueling monsters in a black-and-white, Japanese horror movie.

"Murderer?" she said. "You going to arrest me for that killing this morning? What the fuck was Belva . . . we . . . I mean me . . . What the fuck was I supposed to do? Someone tries to kill you, you shoot them. Self-defense."

"So, you're confessing to murder?"

"Told you, scum like that deserved it."

"Scum. You think the victim was scum. But you did it?"

"Of course. Who else you think? It was me, by myself."

"Jesus, Cassie, you have literally descended to hell." He looked pale. "Cassandra Luna, I arrest you for the murder of Nancy Gurley Irvin. Anything you say . . ."

"Nancy Irvin? I'm talking about one of the Enforcer's thugs, tried to kill me and . . . just me. This morning. What the hell are you talking about? Nancy Irvin's not dead."

"A witness saw you kill Nancy Irvin this morning, and now I've got a confession. There's an APB out calling you armed and dangerous. Every cop in the city is looking for you, and they're not taking any chances." He paused. "You killed one of the Enforcer's men? Jesus, girl, you can't keep straight who you've killed and who you haven't."

"Shit," she said. "No, that's not—Why would anyone kill Nancy?"

"Cassie," he said. "I don't know what's going on. Maybe they're setting you up. Maybe they're right and you're out of control. In the last week, you've assaulted a cop—two cops, counting me. Now you've killed a man. Or maybe a woman. I've stood up for you, but, Cassie, you're too far gone."

"Me? You and your buddies are the ones who did these things, not me. Now you want me to take the fall? Frame me like you were doing with Ron?"

"That was different." He shook his head. "Cassie, I don't know what's going on. I got you into this. Maybe. Maybe you were one of them all along and I let you sucker me in. But all I can do now is make sure you get to jail safely, try to make sure you actually get a trial and maybe sort this out. The sheriff in the next county owes me a favor. He's going to let me put you in his jail where maybe you can stay alive. That's all I can do. Sorry. Maybe sorry. Maybe 'fuck you' if it turns out you're one of them."

She dropped her stick and put out her arms for the cuffs. Stevens stepped forward with more resignation than anger.

Cassie hit him in the stomach with her shoulder and drove him back into the wall. Kept her legs churning and punched a hole like Stevens's silhouette in the wall. She grabbed his cuffs and slapped one on his wrist and pulled the other cuff through the exposed pipe and on his other hand before he could resist.

"Cassie, what the fuck? You can't get away with this."

She reached past him and pulled his keys out of his pocket.

"Can, too," she said and started to walk away. Stevens rattled the cuffs against the pipes and she turned around.

"Listen to me." She had to say it twice before Stevens stopped cursing long enough to hear what she said.

"I. Did. Not. Kill. Nancy. Irvin. And I've got to have until Friday to catch whoever did."

"Yeah?" Stevens said. "Then who did you kill?"

She looked at him and wondered if he was really doing this good of a job of pretending not to know.

"One of yours. Y'all tried to burn me out, tried to shoot me. Now y'all are trying to arrest me. The only people who keep showing up are you and the bald man. I'm done playing nice with all of you."

"This is nice?" he said. "Cassie, don't do this. I'm the only chance for help you've got."

"Help? I've got to solve a murder and bring in the killers to . . . hell, I don't even know who to take them to when I catch them. And now I gotta do it before your buddies either arrest me or kill me themselves. What kind of damned help have you ever . . ." Cassie stopped and looked at Stevens.

"If I let you stay there like this," she said, "you're going to do nothing but cause a racket, aren't you? Get your precious JPD to rescue you so you can come after me."

She spun and threw open a closet door and came out with a big roll of duct tape.

Stevens looked at her. "You wouldn't."

She peeled off the end and wrapped his ankles together. Stevens squirmed and she sat on his hips and kept wrapping his legs, changed positions and moved up his body until he was a mummy covered from his ankles to his neck.

Stevens glared. "You will not get away with this."

Cassie snorted. "Your people are after me for two murders, one arson, an assault on an officer, and you think that the crime I can't get away with is misuse of duct tape?" She looked at him. She wrapped three layers around his mouth while he made muffled and furious noises.

She stood up and looked down at him and suddenly felt sorry.

"Mr. Stevens," she said, "I can't tell if you're on their side or not."

She went to the door and paused.

"But you sure as hell aren't on mine."

CHAPTER 52

What was that line from the poem from English Lit? thought Cassie. *Something about time's winged chariot snapping at your ass.* Not exactly the right words, but, God, that was how she felt right now. The old truck was struggling to hold sixty as she stood on the accelerator, darting glances in the mirror to see what was sneaking up on her.

Her phone chirped in her bag. She cursed and almost lost the truck as she fished out the phone.

"Yeah?"

"Hey, babe," Gene said. "You done at your place? Headed back here?"

" 'Done' might be exactly where I'm at now, like completely screwed. Oh, God, Gene, you won't believe what I—" She took a breath. "Never mind. OK, I'm better. We can talk later. But, no, I'm not heading back, not unless you've got something there that'll prove Ron's innocent or protect our asses or . . . hell, the to-do list I've got is too long to even run through—"

"We've got. You said it was a list 'you've got.' It's my list now, too."

She warmed and softened. "Yeah. We've got. Thanks, but, you know, it's not too late for you to bail, go somewhere and hide until this finishes, not matter what 'finishes' means."

"Way too late for me, in a couple of ways." He paused. "You know that."

"Yeah. Yeah, babe, I do. Thanks for that. If we can get out of this. Maybe even if we can't."

"We will. Now, I've been sitting here going over the stuff on that flash drive you took and listening to a police scanner. They've got an APB out for you and your truck."

"They're going to arrest the truck?"

"No, but they might drag the cute girl out of the truck and do uncute things to her."

" 'Cute'? Anyway, I already know they're looking for me. Just means I—we—have got to figure this thing out fast. But first, how's Belva?"

"Working on her computer, acting like nothing's happened. Look, I had an idea I wanted to run by you. Clearly, Belva can't just go back to school. With all the shit we've got going on, I'm not sure about her hanging around here."

"So, what, you're going to take her to the pound or something?"

"No, of course not. I've got a friend who graduated a couple of years ahead of me and hung out a shingle counseling kids. I talked to her. If you and Belva want, she'll let Belva hang out in her office for a couple of days, kind of like a young, unpaid intern—type stuff up and shit. It would let Belva hang out with Shirley, see other kids come in and work stuff out by talking about it. I gotta go out for an hour or so and pick up a couple of old mattresses for us to sleep on. I could drop Belva off at Shirley's then."

"Sounds like a winner." She laughed. "You're getting good at finding the Luna girls jobs that don't pay a dime."

"Hey, I'll raise your salary. Pay you double what I pay myself."

"How generous. Seriously, you take good care of Luna girls. And we are grateful."

"Then get home and be safe, help me take care of that beautiful, big Luna girl."

"Can't right now. Oh, just so you know, I left something

behind in my apartment."

"What's that?"

"Stevens."

"Shit. Thought you meant you left something like a shirt or some sexy lingerie or something."

"Please don't even make me imagine Stevens in sexy lingerie. No, he's wrapped up in duct tape. He came to arrest me and I didn't want to be arrested."

"So you wrapped him up like a Christmas present?"

"Short version, yes. But he won't stay like that for long. He'll figure some way to get loose, although that'll be tough, or somebody'll come along and find him. So the clock's running and I got to go somewhere and do something to wrap this thing up."

"Still think you ought to come back here and ditch your truck."

"Can't. Got places to go."

"Where?"

"That," she said, "I don't know."

CHAPTER 53

Cassie had been driving around trying to figure out where she was supposed to go and lost all track of where she was. Now she was driving through block after block of oversized houses that looked like castles, if the castles were all brand new and crammed together on two-acre lots with Mercedes parked in the driveways. Jericho wasn't that big and she had spent all but one of her twenty-two years here and yet she felt lost and overwhelmed and lost her train of thought and cruised slowly along the spotless streets.

Her phone rang.

"Hey," said Gene. "Just dropped Belva off."

"Good. Uh, do you know where I am? I'm kinda lost."

"What's that mean?"

"Well, totally lost. The nav app on my old phone's not working and I'm driving through all these shiny castles and shit."

"You make a wrong turn, drive to Disneyland?"

"Could be. Sure feels goofy. Ha."

Gene didn't laugh.

Cassie said, "Jericho is mostly either old Southern houses from before the tech boom, or ultra-modern after the money came in. Not very many castles."

"Give me a street sign."

"Give me a second. They're so tastefully small they're impossible to read. Oh, yeah. Funny. Intersection of Robin Hood and Sheriff's Way. Sounds like a dangerous place to be."

"Let me bring up my nav. Oh, I know where you are. New, rich neighborhood just across the mountain, on the other side of the gap. Called Nottingham, home to people who've struck it rich on Jericho's tech boom."

"Yeah, don't see a lot of homeless people."

Cassie strained and didn't see anybody on the streets. Just well-trimmed lawns and expensive cars. People probably didn't even walk to get their mail here; just drove the Hummer (or maybe the Mercedes convertible on sunny days) up the driveway to the mailbox and back.

"Walking is probably against the covenants," said Gene. "Would remind people there that they didn't exactly rob from the rich and give to the poor. The only good thing is that there's not a lot of cops out in the county, so maybe they won't spot you."

"If I can avoid having my truck towed away as a nuisance."

"OK, the nav says stay on Robin Hood East, away from the mountain. Take you to the highway back into town. Do you know where you're going when you get back?"

"Hell, no. But I've got to go somewhere. Wait."

She paused and focused on a car on the side of the road, the only car she had passed on the street.

"Hey," she said. "I just passed a red, white, and blue security car. Not a cop but—"

"But trouble. Rich neighborhoods like that sometimes have their own private security. Less concerned with crime than the police, but more concerned with watching for things that don't belong. Like beat-up old trucks. And if they get suspicious and call the cops, all hell's going to break loose."

"He's pulling in behind me."

"Make a turn or two. See if he stays with you."

Cassie took the next right at a small version of Buckingham palace.

"Still there."

"OK," said Gene. "I'm just on the other side of the mountain from you, heading your way. Be there in five, ten minutes."

Cassie snorted. "What do you think you're going to do when you get here—rescue the damsel in distress? Tell the guard to ignore me?"

"Damned if I know. Figure things out together as we go. Like we've been doing. Have faith."

Another snort. "Faith hasn't worked out so well for me so far. But, OK, I'm going out to the highway, see if he stays with me."

"You get there, don't turn left into town. Turn right, away from town and JPD."

"Gotcha."

Cassie made a couple of turns back onto Robin Hood. The All-American Dodge Charger stayed back at a respectful distance, but Cassie knew it could catch her in seconds. *Drag racing a muscle car with a junk heap,* she thought. *Feels like I keep bringing a knife to a gun fight.*

She turned onto the highway.

"He's still with me," she said.

"I'm getting close. Maybe two minutes."

"What are we going to do then? If you pick me up, he'll see us and get your plates. We'll be in the same mess with a little better truck."

"I'm thinking."

"Think faster."

"OK, try this, maybe. Slow down."

"Slow down? Let him catch me?"

"Think you can outrun him?"

"No."

"Use your strength instead of your weakness. Your truck is as good at going slow as he is."

246

"So my superpower is going slow? Comforting."

"You may have another one coming soon. Teleportation from one world to another."

Cassie snorted.

Gene said, "Have faith."

"I'd rather have an explanation."

"No time. Grab your bag."

Cassie reached down and grabbed the bag with her left hand. "You sure about this plan?"

"No."

"Now I've got a siren behind me, getting louder fast."

"Good."

"Good? Good for who?"

"You. Look ahead. Do you see a small bridge up ahead?"

"Yeah, low rock walls on both sides of the road, maybe an old stone bridge over a creek or something? About a quarter mile away. And I see flashing lights behind me, so JPD has joined the party."

"Good. Slow down more, like walking speed. Let the cop catch up."

"All-American is on my ass now, cop stacked up behind him."

"Good, that's where we want them. Slide your door open, now. They're driving in the left seat of their cars, you're driving on the right in that old postal truck. They won't see the door open. Get ready."

She slid the door open and felt the wind blow in.

"One hundred feet from the bridge. Gene, I'm not doing anything crazy without an explanation—"

"No time. As soon as you get to the stone wall, step out on it and leap as hard as you can."

"What? What?"

"Now! Now! Now!"

Shit! But she stepped out, planted her foot on the mossy

rocks of the rail, and flew away from the truck. There was nothing but Cassie and the air and the empty blue sky. She spun in the air and saw her empty truck coasting down the road. She tried to turn and see where she was falling but there was no time and the trees were rushing past and she braced herself for whatever came next.

Then she hit into something soft and thought *so this is dying* and then realized that she was alive and lying in a pile of mattresses in the back of Gene's truck and he was accelerating away. Just before the trees closed in overhead, she saw the two cars passing by overhead, focused on her truck and following it as they drifted down the road like a slow train that knew where it was going.

And she realized that she knew where she needed to go, too.

CHAPTER 54

Cassie said to Gene, "Left up here at the old Zesto's."

Gene turned his truck at a fancy restaurant with dark wood made to look old-fashioned, the name of the restaurant just "1898" in small, tasteful, brass letters. The kind of thing that would let you feel hip and smart because you knew what happened in 1898 (that was the year that Black Jack Pershing and the Buffalo Soldiers camped a couple of miles away). And let you feel intimidated if you didn't.

Gene cruised past a strip mall with a drug store and a grocery store and an antique shop.

"You're a real native," said Gene, "if you remember going to Zesto's for soft-serve ice cream and corndogs, before this whole block became yuppified."

"We used to walk down there on summer nights, when we lived in Old Town. You could still hear German spoken in the neighborhood from the original German rocket scientists who came here to start the U.S. rocket program."

"Jericho went from a small cotton town to Rocket City, USA, in about ten years."

"Yep. Make a right here."

Gene made the turn away from the yuppie district and into a block of old houses. The first house had a small historic marker and was carefully restored. Next door was an old frame house with white paint flaking off to show blue paint underneath.

"You don't know where you're going, do you?" he said.

"We've been all over this neighborhood."

"Of course I do," said Cassie. "You think I just make this shit up like you did back there, telling me to jump and hope I'd land on the mattresses?"

"Saved your ass," said Gene.

"Got lucky. Could have missed and broken my back on your truck. You ever see a roadrunner cartoon? See how many times Wily Coyote tried that same kind of stunt, wound up flat on the pavement somewhere?"

"Fine," said Gene. "I've saved your ass and won the coveted job as your chauffeur. Note the common element of you needing me to do something for you."

"Don't need you or anybody else." Cassie bent down and scanned the street. "Turn left up here."

"Yes, m'lady."

"You don't have much experience dealing with real women, do you? Left again."

"No experience at all in dealing with a woman like you."

"Left again."

"Left? Are we just going round and round the block to show me you can order me around?"

"Looking for my freedom. See that old house there? That's my apartment."

"We stopping?"

"Hell, no. Either there's somebody inside or there's not. Either way is bad. Left again."

"Jesus."

"There. Pull over."

Gene pulled into the curb. "What's here?"

Cassie unsnapped her seat belt and jumped out. Leaned back in and said, "My own ride, and freedom from your yammering. See, I knew Stevens didn't park at my house, but I knew he couldn't park far."

She walked over to Stevens's black sedan. Fished his keys out, got in, and pulled away, almost hitting Gene.

The big, black sedan felt like power. She came close to flipping all the switches for the lights and siren just to see what that would feel like but pulled her hand back. She turned the volume up on the police radio.

"Update on the Cassandra Luna APB," said the scratchy voice. "Suspect has abandoned her vehicle in the Nottingham area and may be on foot in vicinity. Suspect is still considered armed and dangerous. Take no chances."

Well, hell, thought Cassie. *I've never been officially dangerous before. Feels pretty damned good.*

The bravado faded and she realized that "dangerous" also meant something close to "shoot this mad dog on sight."

The radio continued. "Please be advised that Detective Arthur Stevens is missing at this time and may be involved with Cassandra Luna."

The shit has hit the fan, she thought. *Ain't going to be no ties in this game. Win or lose from now on.*

She found the house she was looking for. She parked Stevens's car a block away and walked back and knocked on the door.

No one answered. She saw a curtain pulled back, just a little, from a room two windows away. She turned to the window and the curtain closed.

She knocked on the door again.

"Dr. Morrison?" she called. "It's Cassie. Cassie Luna." She thought about it and wasn't sure she should be shouting her name right now. Too late. "I was a student of yours, two years ago. Came to your house once with a group. You helped us with a project. I'm kinda big. Some people say I'm kinda loud—"

A series of locks turned and the door opened. A middle-aged man, unshaven, in sweats and thick glasses, stood there.

251

"I know you are," he said.

"Can I talk to you?"

He stuck his head out and looked up and down the street.

"You know I'm not a teacher anymore?" he said.

"And I'm not a student anymore. But I think we've got a project to work on together."

He opened the door and said, "Come in," and looked both ways on the street again before closing it.

The lights were out and curtains closed. Cassie paused just inside the door, afraid of what she might step on.

Morrison stepped past her to a couch and motioned her to sit down.

"I'm sorry to bother you, sir," she said.

There was a noise in the back and Morrison said, "Excuse me" and hurried back. He returned in a minute and sat down in a chair across from Cassie.

"Sorry. That was my daughter. I've asked her to be quiet when other people are here."

Cassie said, "I understand," and Morrison laughed and said, "I doubt it."

She looked at him and said, "SYM."

His eyes flickered.

She said, "No, I'm not one of them. I'm one of the ones that want to put a stop to this. Want SYM to mean Stevens-Yakova-Morrison again."

"You got an army?"

"Not much."

"Got a plan?"

"Not much."

He stood up. "Then don't ask for much from me. We live quietly, now. I homeschool my daughter. We go out for only two things: we go to a store where people know us and protect us, and we go to a cemetery where there are people I could not

252

protect." He walked over and opened the door. "And we don't need any new friends bent on moving into the cemetery. Good day."

Cassie said, "And how long do you think this can work? How long do you think you can hide here until they come for your daughter, just to teach somebody else a lesson? Or—and this may be worse—how long before living like this breaks your daughter's spirit, and you wake up one day with the realization that you let them turn you into the instrument for destroying the one lovely thing they left in your life, knowing that those are the only memories she'll have of her family?"

"They say," he paused, hand on the door but eyes outside, "they say they'll leave us alone, as long as I keep quiet."

"You believe them?"

He closed the door.

"No. As long as I'm alive, and know what I know, there's a chance I can find someone who will listen. In the long run, they can't take that chance."

"So," said Cassie. "If you don't fight back, the best chance you've got is that, when they come for you, they'll leave your daughter alive to grow up an orphan. Or maybe raised by them."

Morrison slowly walked over and sat back down.

"So what chance are you offering?"

"Not much. A few people whose backs are so hard against the wall that they've got to fight back. A hiding place in the woods; maybe some place to fight a battle." She leaned forward. "Look, Dr. Morrison. I've got a niece they've drug into this. I'm going to find somebody to take her away from this, someplace she can hide and be safe. I can't go because they'd come after me. But I can get her out. And you and your daughter can go with them. But I need you to do something to help before you go."

He sat a long time before asking, "What's that?"

"There's an innocent man in jail they're putting the screws to."

He laughed, harsh and bitter. "Only one?"

"One in particular. He's sitting in jail. His bail is set low, but still too high for his mother to pay it. Frankly, they know nobody else is going to come forward. This guy's innocent. We've got proof. But the minute we come forward with the proof, they'll kill him."

"So, what—you want me to break him out of jail? I'm a professor—a former professor. Not James Bond."

"No. I want you to take the deed to your house down to the Public Safety Complex. With a deed in hand, you can bail him out in minutes, before they can react. Take him, his mother, your daughter and come to a place in the woods I'm going to tell you about. Pick up my niece and all of you can leave from there. I'll find someplace for you to go."

He thought. "I'm just supposed to load up my minivan with a bunch of people they've targeted, drive out of town, and hope they don't follow?"

"Those of us left behind are going to kick up such a shit-storm they won't have time to come after you. At least not for a while. Give you a fighting chance."

"More than I've got now." He sat and thought. "So where are we going?"

"LA. I've got friends there who will take care of you. New IDs, new lives."

"So Mandy will be safe?"

"No promises, but maybe."

He sat thinking some more.

"This guy in jail, is he a fighter? Somebody you have to have to stand up to these guys?"

"No."

"Good guy?"

"Hell, no. He's a worthless little weasel."

"So why am I risking my house and my daughter and myself for him?"

"He's innocent."

"That's enough for you? You—we—are going to risk our asses just because he's innocent?"

"Yes."

He sat some more. Finally, he said, "One more thing. Is there someone there in LA who can look after Mandy if she's alone? Someone you would trust?"

Cassie thought. "There's a woman out there I played ball with who I would trust. Let me call her."

"OK," he said. "If you get her on board, I'm sending Mandy out west and trust that she's taken care of. But I'm staying behind for the fight. You'll have to find someone else to make the trip west."

Cassie thought again, then pulled her phone out of her pocket. "Mr. Blackshear, this is Cassie. I need to talk to you. You and Kaitlin, and right now. Things with the Enforcer are about to get nasty. What do you think about getting Kait out of town for awhile?"

CHAPTER 55

The Sanker Counseling Center was a small, bright yellow, Victorian cottage nestled in begonias in the middle of a working-class neighborhood. Cassie sat at the curb and thought about how nice it would be to have Belva involved in something cheerful and clean like this after all the darkness she'd seen in the last few years. She wondered for the millionth time if she was doing the right thing in pulling her away from all this.

Belva rolled out smiling and Cassie helped her up onto the seat of Gene's pickup, loaded her wheelchair in the back, and climbed in.

"Ms. Sanker's cool," said Belva. "Every kind of kid you can imagine came in there to see her. Some of them hated her; some of them loved her. But they came.

"This one boy talked to me a long time. He said she was a goddess. He lost his mother; his father was off in the wind somewhere. They put him in a foster home where the old man was an asshole and he got into a lot of trouble. Said Ms. Sanker helped him see what was going on inside himself, showed him that that was more important than what those folks thought. Got him out of that home, too, into a better one where they loved him."

"Who knows?" said Cassie. "Maybe someday you'll end up helping people like that, hang around people like Ms. Sanker and learn how she does what she does."

Belva nodded furiously. "Maybe. I've got to tell you, seeing

Jeremy—that's his name—makes me glad of where I'm at now. I've got a home where they love me. You and me, Cassie. Nothing we can't do. Hey, you know, I know you don't like me talking street, but I've got one thing I want to do."

"What's that?"

"I'm going to get us a pair of tee shirts made up. Gonna say 'Amazing Crazy Bitches' in big flashing letters for the whole world to see."

"Yeah.

"Look," she said. "I think that'll be great. But, right now, I'm going to do a mom thing, even if I'm not your mom."

She turned in the seat and faced Belva.

"Belva, it's your life. No matter what anyone ever did to you, no matter what you do to yourself, no matter what's coming, it's your life, every day. Wasn't Jill's. Isn't mine."

"Hey, I know that."

"Good. Remember the intentions we talked about? I want you to promise me, no matter what happens, you'll take a minute to think of your intentions every day. No matter how bad the day starts, no matter who you're mad at, it's always your day, and you get to decide what you want to do with it. And I want you to think of something to be grateful for, no matter how bad things are. OK?"

"We talked about that. Sure, seems pretty easy."

"No, it's the toughest thing you'll ever do, make the here-and-now your life, not some faraway imagined place. Sometimes you've got to be tough with yourself, tell yourself when you need to change and when you need help."

She took a deep breath.

"Look, it's like that right now. You've got to know there's some bad sh—bad stuff going on. People might get hurt. People will get hurt. I want you away from it all. Early tomorrow morning, I'm putting you in a car and sending you to LA to some people who'll take care of you. For a while."

"Jesus, Cassie. I just got here with you and Gene. Can't this vacation or camp or whatever it is wait a little while?"

"No. In fact, I'm praying that even tomorrow morning might not be too late."

"Shit, Cassie—sorry. How long's this supposed to be?"

"I don't know. I'll get you back as soon as I think I can keep you safe here. But I don't know how long that will be."

Belva twisted and grabbed Cassie's arm.

"What's that supposed to mean? I am coming back, aren't I?"

Cassie bit her lip. "I don't know. But you've got to go. Belva, I'm sorry. I'm sorry. I'm—" She felt her voice cracking and her eyes watered and she knew she needed to stay as calm as she could. "I can't. This is the best I can do."

They sat there in almost silence, random curses from Belva but no real talking. Cassie pulled the truck away from the curb and headed home. As they turned onto the road to GENES, Cassie looked over at Belva. Belva's fists were balled up and hitting her lifeless legs.

"Belva, look, I wanted to give you so much and now I think I can't give you much of anything but maybe one thing to remember me by. Can you try? Give me an intention now? I know it's hard right now. But it's always going to be hard. Try."

Belva glared. "You want an intention? Here's one: I, Belva Luna, intend to kick some ass today. Starting with you."

"C'mon. Got to be something more."

The tears broke from Belva's eyes like a flood.

"Only intention I ever had was to be like you," she said. "Bitch."

CHAPTER 56

Four A.M., Cassie was parked under a bush at a dark edge of the QBot parking lot. She realized she had been holding her breath and her pulse was racing. She let it out with a whoosh and sat very still, bringing her yoga training back and focusing on her breathing: Inhale to a count of five, exhale for five. Calm. Centered.

There. She was relaxed and focused. Relaxed for about a second, until she felt the panic rising again and focused on her breathing and studied the building in front of her.

She touched the Bluetooth in her ear. "Gene, you sure about this?"

"No. If anything goes wrong, run."

"We're literally counting on a piece of gum. Several pieces of gum, actually—the gum I used to prop open Irving's private door. That was days ago. What if somebody found the gum . . . a cleaner or somebody?"

"And if it doesn't work, leave."

Across a hundred yards of asphalt was a steel cube of a building with a glass lobby off to her right. Behind the glass, there was probably some kind of real security guard behind a desk. Big companies like QBot tended to have better security than GENES. She had silence and invisibility (well, black clothes) and not much else.

She looked at it and looked back at the parking lot. The security lights dappled the lot with islands of bright light interspersed with darker areas and a few scattered cars. If she picked her spots, she could get to the side of the building by only crossing a couple of bright spots.

She pulled the black balaclava over her face, tapped the Bluetooth in her ear, and said "OK, I'm going in."

Gene said, "Watch your ass, babe. I'll keep listening to the scanner. Got a browser up with a floor plan of QBot."

"Thanks."

She cracked the door and stepped out of the Tesla. Crouched down in the darkness and crept to the edge of the first pool of light. Dashed across and hid behind a Toyota. Standing there, she realized that she was "behind" the car only to any cameras or people looking straight out from the building. Any camera looking in at the building from the edge of the lot was staring right at her ass. She cursed again, knew that she was hopped-up on caffeine and making mistakes. *If I ever get a decent night's sleep, I will never ever drink coffee again. If I get out of this alive.*

She sprinted across another pool, imagining red laser beams shooting out at her. She made it to some low bushes near the building, got on her stomach, and crawled to the side of the building.

She crept around to where she thought Irvin's private door would be. Found it. But the door had no handle and no obvious way of getting in. She picked up a small stick, wedged it into the gap and tried to pry the door open. It budged a little and she took her fingers and pulled.

The door sprang open and she jumped inside and pulled the door closed as fast as she could. She stood with her back pressed against the door until her breathing slowed.

"I'm in," she whispered. No alarm bells.

"Doesn't mean there's not an alarm going off at some guard's desk. Grab Irvin's computer and get out before they find you."

"OK. No, not OK. We're desperate. I'm in here. I want to see what else I can find."

"Bad idea, babe. I don't want to have to visit you in prison. Get out while you can."

"Look, if they check and find the only thing missing is Irvin's computer, they'll know somebody interested in his murder took it. Gonna take something else and make it look like just a robbery. I'll get out then as fast as I can."

"Hurry."

Cassie cracked the door open and held her breath as she looked out into the outer office. Nothing but a semi-dark desk and visitors' chairs. No sound but the hum of the air-conditioning.

She crept to the hallway and peered down one way and then the other. She realized she was crouching, as if that would keep someone from seeing her. The hallway to the right led to the front offices; she had come that way when she was here on her made-up interview. The other way had a big red-and-green tropical plant at the corner. That would give her a landmark in finding her way back. That's the way she went.

Cassie ducked into a bay filled with desks and low partitions. She felt like a peeping Tom here, looking at the minutiae of everyday lives: pictures of kids in soccer uniforms, coffee cups. There was an expensive mobile phone left out on a desk. Cassie thought of taking it, knew its owner would report the theft, but she couldn't bear the thought of the owner's personal pain when he found his phone gone.

There was a small step stool next to a solitary bookcase along the wall. She wondered why. Climbed up on the stool and felt around the top hoping for treasure. All she found was a two-year-old girly magazine. She shook her head and put it back.

She heard Gene in her ear.

"Get out. They've called the cops. Means QBot security is probably searching the building, too."

There was a flash from the front of the room.

She spun toward the flash. A QBot hovered in the doorway like a model helicopter with four rotors, one dull, red eye glowing red and a low hum from the rotors. The weapons pods were empty except for a camera pod that flashed again as Cassie stared.

Cassie jumped down and sprinted away. She heard a whoosh behind her, something sailed over her head and the QBot spun around in the air ten feet in front of her, hovering perfectly still like it had always been there.

She grabbed a book off a desk, threw it at the QBot, yelled, "Shit!" and blindly sprinted away. She made it to the opening and ran panicked down the hall, taking random lefts and rights at every turn.

The hall lights went from semi-darkness to bright light and alarm bells went off. She saw a double set of metal doors and ducked in them.

The room here was enormous. Facing Cassie were rows of QBots neatly folded and still. She caught her breath and waited for them to move.

They didn't. She ducked under a lab bench and tried to make herself small. Knew that she couldn't make herself small enough to hide from the mess she had got herself into this time.

"Gene," she hissed. "Get me out of here."

"Where are you?"

"In a big bay, filled with QBots. High ceiling . . ."

"Got it. Fastest way out is back through the president's office."

"Shit. I need a distraction."

She stood up. The lab bench had a tiny, ruggedized laptop painted in camo. She opened it. The screen glowed to life with a background of QBots and a single button in the middle marked "All Power." She hit it.

The room was filled with whirring noises. She turned and saw QBots rising from the floor like a swarm of angry bees, red eyes glowing. All of them turning toward her.

"Shit."

She grabbed a big, metal suitcase from the stack on the floor and smashed the laptop and crashed through the doors into the hall and turned to her right with the suitcase still in her hand. Saw the red-and-green plant and ran to it.

The QBot with the camera was hovering outside the president's office. Cassie spun around and saw another QBot hovering waist-high off the ground twenty feet behind her. This one had a dangling weapons pod.

A small red dot appeared on Cassie's leg and she jumped to one side as a gun fired and a bullet splattered into the wall behind her. Cassie charged the gun QBot and the QBot took aim.

She sprang at the last second, legs out like Michael Jordan going for a dunk, and sailed over the QBot as a bullet sailed between her legs. Grabbed the QBot and slung it hard into the other QBot on her way down.

She snatched Irvin's laptop in her free hand and burst out into the parking lot, running hard with the suitcase in one hand and the laptop in the other. Her breathing was not calm.

Chapter 57

Cassie said, "Thanks."

Randy Blackshear's daughter, Kaitlin said, "Not a big deal. Glad I can help."

Cassie released Kaitlin from a hug in the middle of GENES. "Yes, it is. I saw you at JU yesterday—was that just Saturday?— and I peeled out of there like my ass was on fire. I just couldn't face you because I . . . screwed up so big."

Kaitlin shrugged. "I always figured you were set up. Or had a good reason. And Dad never believed it."

"Lot of evidence splashed all over the TV news that said I was scum."

"I never believe what people say in the big, shiny TV world. I always had faith in the senior star who took care of us little freshman, for no reason other than she thought it was the right thing to do. You—well, your actions—stuck with me. Some mornings I get up discouraged, wonder what to do. Remember the old Gatorade ad with Michael Jordan that said, 'Be like Mike'? Well, I say, 'Be like Cassie' and get my ass going."

Cassie said, "Thanks for calling me after I blew you off."

"That's what Cassie would have done, if she saw somebody drive off crying."

Cassie shook her head but Kaitlin said, "You know you would."

Cassie said, "I sure as hell wouldn't volunteer to drive a van of kids and derelicts across country."

"No big deal. Class is over tomorrow. I'm good. You gave me a plane ticket home from LA, and a chance to talk to the coach of the Sparks while I'm out there. Not sure who's doing who a favor."

"I'm sure. And I'm grateful."

The Morrison minivan pulled into GENES and Kaitlin hoisted her backpack on her shoulder. Dr. Morrison stepped out of the driver's side, looking heavier and older than he had a few hours ago. He went around to the passenger's side and a teen-aged girl got out. They hugged, cried, and said things that nobody else could hear.

Cassie saw movement in the third row of seats, squinted, and saw Ron and his mother. The Morrison girl climbed into the middle row; Kaitlin climbed into the driver's seat and adjusted the mirror. Cassie kept watching the minivan and knew she was putting off what she had to do. It was time.

She turned around to get Belva and found Belva sitting in her wheelchair behind her.

"Let's get this done," said Belva.

"Belva," said Cassie. "You'll be all right."

"Hell, yeah. I already put up with worse than what's waiting for me in that minivan. Don't need nothing from nobody to be all right." She looked up at Cassie. "Except you. I want something from you, one little thing that's just Cassie to hold onto until I get back."

"Oh, God, I don't know. I don't have any kind of precious family ring or anything, but—"

"Gimme a promise. Gimme your word that I'm coming back."

Cassie hesitated. "I want to give you that more than anything else in the world. All I can promise is that I'll do my best to make it happen and that there is nothing my heart wants more."

Belva glared. "I'm coming back. You know it, I know it. Nothing going to stop me."

Cassie could feel her eyes getting wet but she smiled. "Hell, yeah. Nothing's ever going to stop you at anything."

"Fuckin' A. So what are you going to give me?"

"I know it's weird, but how about an intention?"

"Oh, shit." Belva rolled her eyes. "Ain't we past that new-age crap here?"

"I don't know. It feels like it's me. I mean, my old yoga teacher Malisa taught it to me, but it's always felt like me, you know. And I want you to think of it when you think of us, what we are and want to be."

Belva smiled. "Told you what I want for us. 'Amazing Crazy Bitches.' "

"Yeah," said Cassie. "That's a good one, too. Think of the intention as the long version of 'Amazing Crazy Bitches.' "

"All right," said Belva. "That's our bond. My tee shirt and your intention. Give me an intention I'll say every day and you meet me at the door wearing your tee shirt, holding mine out for me."

"Deal."

"OK. What're these magic words, make me feel like a Luna girl every day from now on?"

"What . . ." Cassie's voice broke and she pulled her hands up into a prayer position and calmed herself.

"What can I do with these hands, this heart, this body, today?" Belva repeated them.

"That's a Cassie thing," she said. "A Cassie and Belva thing."

They loaded Belva in the van and she was gone.

CHAPTER 58

Cassie felt like she was watching her life drive out the door from GENES. Dr. Morrison walked over and closed the door behind them.

"First time in a long time," he said, "I've felt like my daughter's got a future. First time I've felt like I was doing the best thing for my family. Thanks."

Cassie's face was wet and she was staring at the closed door.

"Yeah," she said. "I guess. Maybe."

"In any case, they're safe. Or, at least, they have a chance to be safe somewhere. If we want them to come back here someday and be safe here with us, we better get to work."

Cassie wiped her face. "Hell, yeah."

Something pulled at her hair like a bird pecking on the top of her head and she jumped and slapped at it. She looked up and saw a QBot whirring quietly above her with a metal claw dangling from its body and pinching at her hair.

"What the hell?"

Gene giggled, standing behind them with a militarized laptop in his hands.

"Meet Spot," he said. "Turns out, you picked up our own personal QBot last night. Pretty easy to use."

"If I picked him up, he's mine."

"I named him and trained him. Look at this."

Gene threw a ruler past the QBot and said into the laptop, "Spot, fetch." The QBot spun and chased the ruler, plucked it out of the air, and returned it to Gene.

Cassie said, "Spot?"

"I always wanted a dog."

"This toy qualifies?"

"He's not a toy. Give him general parameters and he'll execute. Kinda semi-intelligent. Here. Let me show you. Spot, drop. Spot, come to me."

Spot dropped the ruler and flew up and stopped in front of Gene. Gene held up a broomstick.

"Spot, lance."

Spot grabbed the broomstick like a lance and charged imaginary foes in the air.

"Well, tell Sir Spot-a-lot if he touches me he'll be scrap metal."

Dr. Morrison said, "Glad to meet you, Spot. Can you come over here and let me have a look at you?"

Gene wiggled a joystick and Spot settled between Cassie and Dr. Morrison, hovering motionless five feet off the ground in front of them. Cassie and Dr. Morrison circled Spot.

Dr. Morrison said, "We worked on these. What else have you got for the pod?"

"Yeah," said Cassie. "Gun, rocket launcher? Something useful."

"What you see is what you got," said Gene. "Claw and camera." He reached up and took the broomstick. "And lance. Maybe, in time, we can come up with something else."

"We don't have time," said Cassie. "Put your toy up and let's see if we can come up with something useful ourselves." She turned and walked over to the picnic table in the computer section.

Gene and Dr. Morrison sat down at the table with Cassie.

"All right, Gene," said Cassie. "You've been working with Irvin's computer—when you weren't playing with your new toy.

What have you got?"

"Not much. But, let me show you something else first." He reached over and wiggled the mouse on Cassie's computer. There was a video from a news station, frozen with Cassie in her black outfit and mask in the QBot offices last night, looking like a dark shadow with glowing, blue eyes. Gene pressed the play icon and muted the sound.

"I'll spare you the breathless audio. JPD put this out to the media. They're calling him—her, but they think it's a him—the 'Shadow Giant,' warning people that he's a monster over seven feet tall who broke into QBot and stole dangerous military weapons. Be on the lookout, all that."

"He?" said Cassie. "Seven feet tall? You do know who we're talking about here? Oh, wait, I was standing on that box when they took that picture. Maybe I was seven feet tall." She laughed. "Wish I'd been a seven-footer when I played ball."

"Keep watching. Their video cameras in the parking lot must be set to a long shutter time in the darkness, blurry at the distance you parked the Tesla."

They watched a black blur as the Tesla streaked across the back of the lot.

"Police said whatever that was made no sound. People are speculating that the Giant can fly or at least run superfast."

"Damn I'm good," said Cassie. "Why are they publicizing this? You'd think they'd want to keep this quiet."

Dr. Morrison said, "Bullies get scared shitless when they think there's somebody bigger than them around."

"Yeah, but—"

"There may be something more. The mayor's got a press conference scheduled for Friday—tomorrow—morning about a major public safety issue. Maybe they broke the story because they want people scared now."

"I don't know if this is good news or bad news for us," said Cassie.

Gene shrugged.

She said, "But it just means we've got to get this thing wrapped up. And we've run out of places to even look for answers. What'd you find on Irvin's laptop?"

Gene shrugged again. "Really, not much. Just looks like the kind of business stuff you'd expect. Most of the technical or classified stuff is probably held on a server somewhere and not kept on local laptops anyway."

"So nothing?" said Cassie.

"Well, not much. But here's the one thing that was odd. You remember that thumb drive you picked up on your first trip there, labelled 'Fueltown'?"

"Yeah."

"Well, Fueltown's a diesel fuel station for trucks over in River City. If you look at the books on Irvin's laptop, QBot makes payments to Fueltown."

"Makes sense," said Morrison. "QBot makes the bodies of their drones in Mexico, then trucks them to Jericho for final assembly. They've got a small fleet of their own trucks for the job. Gotta pay for fuel somewhere."

"Yeah. Like I said, Irvin's computer—the official reports—shows payments from QBot to Fueltown. But the thumb drives show payments from Fueltown to Irvin."

"Kickbacks?" said Cassie.

"Maybe," said Gene. "But the payments from Fueltown to QBot are bigger than the payments from QBot to Fueltown."

Morrison said, "Maybe that's what got Irvin killed. But, if all we've got are small-time kickbacks, that's not going to be big enough for us to take down the whole Raiders organization. Or stop them from killing us."

Gene said, "There's something else odd about this. I looked

at Fueltown. Their security is for shit; wasn't hard to look at their books. They've only got a few customers: QBot and a couple of Huntsville furniture stores."

"So?"

"So Fueltown's in River City. Why would QBot trucks stop in the River City, when they're only twenty miles from home? And why would Jericho furniture stores send their trucks twenty miles out of their way to get fuel?"

Cassie stood up.

"Don't know. But I do know someone who says she knows everything that goes on in River City."

CHAPTER 59

Cassie parked Gene's pickup in front of Ann's house and marched up the steps and past Ann standing on the veranda.

Ann said, "Work trucks go around the back."

Cassie yanked the front door open. "You said you know everything there is to know about River City. We need to talk."

She walked into the house and Ann scampered to catch up. Cassie realized that the house was quiet and she stopped.

"No servants? I expected you to have a house full of people bowing and scraping."

"I gave them all today off," said Ann. "And tomorrow, too, because I am a fine Christian woman who cares for people."

Cassie stared at her.

"And I've got some business stuff I need to do from home today and tomorrow and didn't want to be disturbed. If it's any of your business, missy."

Cassie walked into a kitchen bigger than most houses, with bright, tasteful colors and a big bay window opening to the river. Next to the bay there was an opening for French doors covered now with a sheet of plastic looking out on a massive deck under construction.

Cassie gestured at the plastic.

"Remodeling," said Ann. "Going to have a deck bigger than most stadiums—"

"Aren't you worried about security?"

Ann snorted. "I am Ann Gurley. No one messes with me.

Now, what can I do for you—other than teach you manners—before I throw you out and get back to my business?"

Cassie walked through a door open to a study off the kitchen. There was a clean, mahogany desk facing the door. Behind the door, the corner was taken up with a computer center with a 60-inch video screen hanging on the wall, equipment and papers scattered across, and a laptop open on it.

"That's your work?" Cassie pointed at the screen filled with an app full of sliders and click boxes. "Looks more like a video game." Cassie read the title. " 'Morph VOX'? Never heard of that one. Never picked you for a gamer."

Ann quick-stepped past Cassie and shut the laptop and the screen went dark.

"All right, missy, you caught me. I'm a video-game junkie. Bad as any of those nerds in your Jericho. Happy? Now get to your point or get out."

"You're right; I need to stick to the point. Something's rotten over here in your precious River City." She paused and stared down at Ann. "And you say you've got a finger in every pie over here."

"Watch your tone. One phone call and I can have the kind of security in here that you don't want to deal with."

"What do you know about a connection between QBot and River City?"

"There isn't one."

"Well, yeah, but what if I told you that QBot and some other Jericho businesses are using something called Fueltown—"

"Then I would say I don't deal with gas stations. And I told Jim Irvin to keep his dirty Jericho business over in Jericho. Don't crap in my home, I told him. Did you know he was tied up in that mess over there? Up to his neck with Stevens and his boys."

"Stevens and Irvin had a connection?"

"Of course they did. Stevens is the one that runs all that Raider organization over there. Everybody but you knows it. But you just keep on listening to Stevens, swallowing his crap like it was gospel."

Cassie laughed. "Well, not exactly. Last night I—"

"Yeah, yeah," said Ann. "Bet you didn't know this, did you? Stevens burned another business down last night. Except, this time, there was a witness that saw him do it. JPD's looking for him even as we speak. If that doesn't prove he's behind this to you and everybody else, I don't know what will."

"Last night?"

"Two A.M. If you'd turn on your TV, you'd see this for yourself."

"JPD has a witness?"

"A reliable witness."

They both studied each other's face for a long time.

"Yeah," said Cassie, finally. "Nothing like a reliable JPD witness."

"That prove something to you?"

"Yeah," said Cassie.

"Good," said Ann. "Now go put Stevens in jail and leave me alone."

Cassie walked to the door and turned around.

"You know, Ann, you once said that what we both had in common was that we were good sisters. Your sister died yesterday. JPD says I killed her. But you haven't even mentioned that. Like you don't care about Nancy dying, like you know I didn't kill her."

Ann's mouth turned into a tight line and she picked up the phone. "I'm calling the police."

Cassie got lost on the way back and drove past River City High School. She looked up at the big sign above the stadium: Home of the Raiders.

Chapter 60

Cassie was wrestling with the duct tape around Stevens's mouth. He was grunting and moaning, probably trying to say things she didn't want to hear.

"I'm sorry," she said for the second time. "I'm trying to find some easy way to get this tape off. I don't want to hurt you." She paused. "Any more than I have."

Stevens glared, wiggled, and made more muffled noises. It was all he could do, but still, Cassie got the point.

"No easy way to do this." Cassie grabbed the tape and ripped straight up.

Stevens screamed a long, formless noise followed by every swear word Cassie had ever heard.

"I know, I know, it hurts," she said. "And I know you didn't burn down that business last night."

"What? What? You tie me up like a pig, leave me here overnight, and all you've got to say for yourself is that I didn't burn down a business? Wait, what business?"

"Look, I said I was sorry. I didn't know what else to do. You sure looked guilty to me. Eww, Stevens, you pissed yourself. You're a mess."

"Of course I pissed myself. You try going all night, wrapped up in duct tape like a project from a crazy-girl home-improvement show. Get me out of this, now, or I'm going to start screaming for the police. And I don't care what they do to you when they get here. I might even shoot you myself."

"No, you won't. We need each other. I didn't see that until just a few minutes ago over in River City, but we do."

Stevens wiggled his arms.

"All right," said Cassie. "I'll do your arms. But I'm not coming near those pants."

She unwound the tape from his hands and arms. Stevens stretched his arms and wiggled his fingers and moaned from the effort.

"I ought to use these hands to strangle you," he said. He bent down and started peeling tape.

"Not when you hear what's gone on while you were napping here. We've got someplace to go. I'll tell you everything while we're driving."

She wrinkled her nose. "After you clean yourself up."

CHAPTER 61

They were sitting around the picnic table at GENES: Cassie and Gene, Stevens and Morrison. Nearly empty coffee pot in the center of the raw, wooden table, Gene and Morrison each with blank legal pads and pens, Stevens with his hands laced over his belly, Cassie drumming her fingers on the table.

Cassie said, "So we're hiding out here and hoping they don't find us. We know it can't last. Knowing if we take one step back into the city we're dead. I don't like it. I remember summer nights outside on my family's patio in Jericho, my dad and the other rocket scientists checking their watches and then pointing up at the sky when the International Space Station went over. Their station. They built it, here in their city. My city now. I was born here and grew up here. I'm not giving up even one little barbeque stand or broken-down arts center."

Stevens smiled, proud, but said nothing.

"Fine," said Gene. "But we've got to find a way to stay alive."

"And we can't just sit here, anyway," said Stevens. "We've got one day." He looked at his watch. "Less than a day."

"Oh, give me a break," said Cassie. "You've been shooting off your mouth about 'Friday' all week long. I've got news for you. Around here, bad things happen on Mondays and Tuesdays and Wednesdays and . . . Friday just another shitty day."

"Yeah," said Stevens. "Just another day raining fire all over the city. You remember how your house exploded?" He pointed at Morrison. "Your business?" He turned to Cassie. "You think

277

some human being firebombed your house? No. QBots."

Cassie looked surprised but Morrison just nodded.

"Right now," Stevens said, "the police have a few unarmed QBots on traffic watch, and the Raiders have one or two QBots with God knows what kind of armament. Friday morning, Mayor O'Brien's going to announce that, thanks to a generous grant from the Good Government Group, the city's going to purchase enough armed QBots to replace half the police officers in Jericho. The honest half. We don't break this group up tonight, before that money gets transferred tomorrow at ten o'clock and the mayor makes his announcement, you'll have invisible eyes in the sky all the time, on everybody, with the power to rain fire and bullets whenever they want."

He pointed a finger at Cassie. "Remember when that cop got out of hand with you at the Haunted Castle? Gave you a black eye? Next time, that cop'll be a machine hovering over your head, deciding whether to fry you or fill you with holes. And deciding whether to keep a video record and blame you as a criminal, or delete the record and pretend it never happened. Try kicking that thing's butt. Or getting anybody to fight the organization that controls these things. We either fight this thing now, or we get on a bus and follow the children."

"We ain't leaving," said Cassie.

"I'll tell you another reason to strike now," said Dr. Morrison. "We've got support right now, if we can make something happen. Maybe an ally, too. I don't know if that Shadow Giant is real or just a stunt, but business owners are convinced he's real. They saw him on TV, and a bar owner's spreading stories about talking to him. Owners are ready to back him up, but they can't if the Enforcer's going to keep killing them or burning them out."

"They're not the only ones," said Stevens. "The mayor and the police commissioner have had it with these guys. Give them half a chance, and they'll turn this into a clean city again. Well, cleaner than it is now, anyway. But they can't do it with a gun to their heads." He nodded at Cassie. "They'd listen to your evidence exonerating Ron Lyle, if it wouldn't get them killed." He laughed. "Hell, they might even let you off the hook for your crime rampage the last few days."

"Big talk," said Cassie. "So what do we do? We don't know who these guys are, at least not all of them. We sure don't know where to go find them."

Gene said, "I don't want to fight them on their own turf. I want them out here, where we can plan the surprises."

Stevens said, "I can do that."

Stevens stood up, still stiff from a night in duct tape, and hobbled over to his squad car with the other three behind him. He slid into the driver's seat and took out his keys.

"Last chance. Once I make this call, they're coming." He swept their faces. "Sure?"

"Sure," said Gene.

"Sure," said Dr. Morrison.

Cassie said, "Hell, yeah."

Stevens switched the key and pulled the mic up.

"This is Stevens. I've got Cassandra Luna holed up out in the county in the old Gateways building on Tri-Forks road. Requesting backup to bring her in."

He put down the mic and ignored the squawking coming back at him.

"The Raiders listen in on everything. Unless I miss my guess, they'll come and the police will pretend they never heard the call."

Gene said, "We need to get busy. We've got a lot to get ready."

CHAPTER 62

"They'll wait until dusk," said Stevens. "Maybe."

Gene was sitting next to him, studying the QBot laptop. "Nothing on Spot's screen yet. I've got him hovering at a thousand feet, scanning the sky and the road with radar and IR. He'll beep anytime he sees something."

Cassie came out of the back dressed in her black outfit. "I'm getting into position," she said.

Stevens looked at her. "So that's the giant?"

Cassie said, "Let's hope so."

"Don't look seven feet tall. Gonna put on some heels or something?"

"Running around in the woods? Hell, no. Maybe I can stand on a little hill or something. If I can't scare them enough like that, we'll have to come up with Plan B. Or maybe C, D . . ."

"Think we're already on Z. This is it, sister."

"Yeah."

Gene looked up from the laptop.

"Look," he said. "Be careful out there."

Cassie laughed. "Wasn't that from some old TV show?"

Gene glanced at Morrison and Stevens, uncomfortable with their presence.

"Cassie, this isn't TV: please take care of yourself. For me. I know that's selfish of me, and I don't care. I really like having you in my life. I'd like to keep it that way. For a lot longer than just tonight."

"Let's do that," said Cassie. "Stay alive beyond tonight. Together. Try to build something good and real and intentional together. Something based on what we want, and not on the fairy tale that people have told us we're supposed to want. With you. With me."

Gene nodded.

Stevens said, "Then let's try to keep everybody alive. Cassie, you got your gun?"

She nodded, reached into the back of her pants, and pulled out the Glock she'd taken off of the Enforcer. Stevens took it out of her hand.

"If you have to use this, something's gone wrong. The plan is for you to scare them and me to shoot them. You come out of the woods when they get here." He paused. "*If* they get here. Maybe they'll just send a QBot. Maybe they won't come at all. Then we'll have to start all over. But—if they get here, you step out of the woods and get their attention. I'll come around the corner of the building and get the drop on them. Whatever happens after that is between them and me. You get back behind a tree. But I'm counting on you coming out from behind that giant oak tree when I need you. Don't be anywhere else or I might shoot you by accident."

He stared at Cassie, demanding a nod, and got nothing. He looked down at the gun and popped the magazine.

"Ten shots," he said. "If you've got to use this thing, that's all you've got."

He slapped the magazine back in. Took the gun in two hands and pointed it away from the others.

"If you've got to shoot, hold it like this. Point, don't try to aim. Don't try to hit anything more than ten yards away; anything you hit beyond that is luck. When you squeeze the trigger, the gun will kick up. Like this." He pulled the gun up. "Let it. Don't fight it. Bring it back down, point it, and fire again. Keep shooting until whatever you're shooting at goes down and stays down."

He handed it back to Cassie.

"Don't shoot unless you have to. But if you have to, don't hesitate. Got it?"

She looked down at the gun in her hand. "Yes, boss." It sounded more sarcastic than she meant.

Stevens made a sour face. "I ain't anybody's boss. Sorry I tried to be your boss, fucked up your life. I hope we can get it back."

"I'm the one who fucked up my life. And I'm the one who's got to get it back." She popped the magazine out and checked it for herself. Snapped it back in place.

The laptop beeped.

Gene said, "Two targets, inbound, flying at five hundred feet, about a mile away."

CHAPTER 63

The shapes on the laptop were blurry in the twilight sky, coming into focus slowly on Spot's IR camera. The QBots looked like expensive toys painted in camouflage, something that you might imagine a twelve-year-old boy piloting from the ground while his mother calls him to dinner.

Dr. Morrison pointed to the blobs hanging under each of them. "They're coming with everything they've got. Last I heard, they've only got two of these things. See this one? That's the rocket. Heavy enough that they can only carry one. Even with that, they have to get in fairly close to fire because their range is limited. So we've got time while they maneuver. And they won't be expecting us. They'll probably just think Spot's a bird."

"Bird with a big stick." Gene pointed on the screen to the broomstick Spot was carrying.

Cassie snorted. "Wasn't there a movie line about bringing a knife to a gunfight? We're bringing a stick to a rocket battle."

"Not just a rocket battle," said Dr. Morrison. "See that second pod? That's a lightweight machine gun, basically a stripped down AR-15. Only holds thirty rounds, but each one can kill."

"Spot's tough," said Gene. "They're going to wish he was playing fetch with that stick instead of medieval warrior."

"We'll see," said Dr. Morrison. "Maneuver off to the side, come at them with a few random movements like a bird might.

283

Don't raise their suspicions."

Cassie said, "While you're doing that, keep Spot glancing at the road every few seconds. Don't want the Enforcer sneaking up on us while you're playing birdman."

"You really think he's coming, too?" said Dr. Morrison.

Cassie said, "I hope so."

Stevens looked at her.

Dr. Morrison pointed at the screen. "The good news is that the QBots aren't reacting to Spot. So they're still not expecting anything. QBots—and their operators—aren't trained for defense. They're kind of disposable bullies, at least in the battle planning. The idea is to have a lot of them in the field, have them survive by being almost invisible from the ground. So they haven't even considered the possibility that someone's going to attack them."

"Gene," said Morrison, "put Spot below them, maybe a little off to the side. Let them lose him in the ground clutter."

Gene spoke into the laptop. "Spot, juke down. Juke down. Juke left."

It took Spot a moment to execute and then refocus. Now the screen had the two QBots against a darkening sky. The QBots were bigger now, the weapons pods clearly visible on the screen.

"Designate the rocket QBot as a target," said Dr. Morrison. He leaned over Gene's shoulder and looked at the numbers on the screen. "Thirty seconds to contact. I'm guessing the QBot is still more than a minute away from firing. Should be close. Keep Spot moving towards the QBots but twist him around to scan the road."

"Just a motorcycle and a delivery van between here and the Interstate," said Gene after a second.

"Good," said Cassie.

"Still might be them," said Stevens. "Doesn't sound like the way they would travel, but I'm going out front and keep some eyes on the road. Cassie, if I call on your cell, you take off running out the back door and don't stop until you get into position."

"Yes, sir."

"Ten seconds," said Gene.

The QBots looked big now, with nothing in the frame but them and the tip of Spot's broomstick lance bouncing on the screen between them.

Spot's lance hit the body of the rocket QBot like a jousting knight catching his opponent square in the shield. Gene twisted the joystick on the laptop and Spot drove the skewered QBot into the second QBot and all three of them fell apart. The screen spun crazily for a second: black sky, a quick flash of one QBot, and then the other. Spot stabilized and focused on the QBot with the gun. One of his rotors was frozen but the QBot was adjusting.

"That one's going to be trouble," said Dr. Morrison.

Spot found the rocket QBot. It was falling, spinning slowly and fighting for control.

"Stay with him, Gene. As long as he's alive, he's dangerous."

Spot dove and speared the rocket QBot from the top and the QBot flipped as it spun, losing more control as it fell.

"Stay with it until it's dead," said Dr. Morrison. "When they figure out what's going on, they can still get a shot off."

Spot hit the QBot again and shoved it toward the rising ground. The QBot fell faster, but, as they watched, the flipping stopped and the spinning slowed to a wobble.

"They've figured out what we're doing," said Morrison. He pointed at the screen. "The safety clamp is off the rocket. They're about to take a shot."

Gene twisted the joystick and Spot fell full-speed into the QBot just as the screen flashed orange as the rocket fired.

Cassie looked at Morrison.

He shrugged. "We'll know in about five seconds, whether Spot messed up their shot or not. Gene," he said. "Go back to the gunner. The rocket QBot can't hurt us." He paused. "Anymore."

The gunner QBot filled the screen as Cassie's count hit three. It was pointed at Spot and there were flashes from the gun. The picture jerked as something hit Spot.

"Juke right," yelled Gene.

There was an explosion outside. Cassie looked out through the open garage door as the giant oak she was supposed to hide behind burst into flame.

"Missed the building," she said.

"Barely," said Dr. Morrison. "Gene," he said. "Keep Spot moving. QBots are built to track slow-moving targets like trucks and tanks." The screen jerked again.

The status screen flashed red.

"Lost one rotor. We can fly with three, but two gets dicey."

"The gunner's down to three rotors, too," said Gene.

The gunner QBot on the screen kept twisting and firing, but Spot kept getting closer. The gun flashed so bright as Spot hit him that the screen washed out for a second. When it cleared they could see the gunner QBot hovering with Spot's broomstick stuck in its frame, pulled loose from Spot.

"Shit," said Dr. Morrison. "The stick won't do any damage where it's at. We better get out of here and hope that thing doesn't have enough bullets left to hit us."

"Spot doesn't run away," said Gene. "Spot, fetch."

Spot dove and clamped the broomstick. The gunner QBot shuddered as Spot grabbed the broomstick in mid-air.

"Spot, juke left. Juke right. Juke up."

Spot shook the stick and the gunner like a dog with a bone. Parts fell off of the gunner.

"Spot, spin."

The sky behind the gunner started flashing bits of sky and ground as Spot swung him round and round. As a bit of ground showed, Gene yelled, "Spot, release."

The QBot fell toward the ground, spinning and falling end over end with the broomstick jutting out of its body and flailing at the sky. Parts were raining off the gunner in bunches and his rotors were dead.

Cassie's earpiece buzzed.

"Cassie, get your ass outside, now," yelled Stevens.

Cassie ran for the garage door and the fire outside.

CHAPTER 64

Cassie ran for the fire. Stevens wanted her at the oak tree and she was by-God done disappointing people.

"Black SUV just drove by," she heard Stevens say in the Bluetooth in her ear. "If it's them, they're going to turn around and be back in a minute. I want you where you can come out of nowhere at their backs if they're facing me."

Cassie got as close to the oak as the flames would let her, and found a hidey-hole on a stump between two bushes. She could see light coming out from the lobby and Dr. Morrison moving in the shadows inside. On the far side of the building, Stevens stepped out from the corner just for a moment to show his position to her, then faded back around the corner.

She stood and waited, feeling the heat on her back and the night air on her face. The heat felt like hell and she wondered if the fire could set off the bullets in her gun. She decided the sweat she was feeling wasn't from the fire. Her right hand was trembling and she realized she was holding it out from her body like a gunfighter in an old movie, except that her hand was shaking too much to aim a gun. She touched the gun in her waistband and pressed her hand against her side to still the shaking.

She glanced down at her hand. *Will my hand do what it needs to do? Make me a killer, but maybe protect people and get Belva back here safe?*

She waited. *Maybe Stevens won't need me.*

The waiting didn't last. A black SUV pulled into the lot and stopped beside the door. Came in with its lights on like it was just pulling into a convenience store.

"They don't even think they have to watch out for us," Cassie said into her Bluetooth.

Stevens whispered, "They are afraid of neither God nor man. Just here to clean up the trash that their toys missed."

Cassie said, "But we have the biggest and the baddest, Stevens. Remember that."

The interior lights of the SUV flashed and the doors opened and the Enforcer got out of the passenger side and the driver got out of his side and the two of them joined up at the back of the SUV.

The parking lot lights came on and the driver threw up his hand to shield his eyes. The Enforcer scanned the edges of the lot.

Stevens stepped around the corner with his gun out.

"Police. Freeze."

The Enforcer smiled and stepped away from the driver casually.

"Detective Stevens?" he said. "Heard a lot about you. Heard you were the last stupid cop in Jericho. You're on the list to be replaced tomorrow, you know? We got a piece of tin that can do your job better than you."

"That's tomorrow," said Stevens. "Tonight, you and your friend are going to take your guns out and put them on the pavement real careful. Then we're going to get back in that car and drive up to Nashville. I've got a federal marshal up there that will listen to what I have to say. Got some other people with things to tell him, too."

"I don't see all those people you say you have, Detective. All I see is one big-ass target that a blind man couldn't miss. There's two of us here and one of you. Maybe you'll get lucky and hit one of us, but the other will get you. And life will go on in Jericho just as it always has."

"But I can get you," said Stevens. "With no QBots and no Enforcer, a lot of people will come out of the woodwork on our side."

"Don't see them here now."

"That's because you're not looking in the right direction. Behind you."

The Enforcer stayed focused on Stevens but the driver turned as Cassie, with her mask down and her gun up, waved from the woods toward them with the fire at her back.

"Shit," said the driver. "It's that giant thing."

He threw up his hands but the Enforcer drew and fired at Stevens and dove for the SUV. Stevens fired back and they both missed.

The Enforcer was behind the SUV now, hidden from Stevens but right in front of Cassie with the driver still standing in the parking lot with his arms frozen.

Stevens yelled, "Take the shot."

She pointed the gun at the Enforcer and hesitated as he spun and fired at her and something set fire in her left shoulder. Stevens was running across the lot, fast for his size. The Enforcer took aim at Cassie again as Stevens cleared the rear of the SUV. The Enforcer turned back to Stevens and they both got a shot off.

The Enforcer fell on the pavement with blood spurting out of his head. Stevens stood up, panting. The driver put his hands on his head and said to Cassie, "Please."

CHAPTER 65

Cassie was lying on the picnic table with her black shirt pulled off and the three guys hovering over her bloody shoulder.

"I'm the one with 'doctor' in his name," said Dr. Morrison.

"If her shoulder were software, that might matter," said Gene. "But it's flesh and blood. And I take care of her flesh and blood."

"Flesh and blood with a bullet wound," said Stevens. "I'm the only one here who's even *seen* bullet wounds."

"Stop it, you bunch of children," said Cassie. "Gene takes care of me. Stevens, you look at the wound and see what you think. I never thought sitting around in my underwear with three guys staring at me would be such a pain."

Gene bent over Cassie and opened the first-aid kit. When the wound was washed, he leaned back so Stevens could see.

"Aw, you don't even have anything to brag about. Missed bone and arteries. Not even bleeding now."

"Still hurts like hell when I raise my arm."

"Just trauma," said Stevens. "Be OK in a day or two."

Gene swabbed the shoulder with antiseptic. "We're still taking you to a hospital and get you checked out." He glared at Dr. Morrison. "By a real doctor."

"Later," said Cassie. "We've still got to finish this thing up."

Gene said, "Babe, you can barely use this arm."

"Got one good hand. Stevens, what about the Enforcer and his pal?"

Stevens said, "I've got the driver handcuffed in the SUV,

Enforcer's body next to him. There's a place in the woods near here where we found the body of the first victim killed by the Enforcer, back before 'SYM' and all that shit. I caught the case, worked it until I got close and the powers that be suddenly decided it was suicide. I remember the look on the Chief's face when he called me in and told me. The Chief was an honest cop, knew I was right when I was screaming at him all the reasons it couldn't be suicide. But he just sat there, pale as a ghost, tight-lipped, repeating, 'The coroner's verdict is suicide.' Now that the Chief has a chance with his hands untied, he's going to give these guys some payback."

"Long as we aren't the ones that get the payback, from either the cops or what's left of the Raiders," said Cassie.

"I've done what I could. I've wiped everything down, dug my bullets out of the pavement. Made sure the driver fired his weapon—a Glock, like mine—so he'd test positive for gunshot residue, if the cops get involved. Made sure he touched everything I could think of. We'll turn him loose in the woods next to the SUV with the Enforcer in it, let him wander back home and tell any pals he's got left. We never let him get a good look at you, Cassie, so he'll tell them about the giant that came out of the fire. Without the Enforcer, I'm betting they'll be running by morning."

"Maybe," said Cassie. "But don't let him go, just yet. As long as the head of that organization's still alive, I'm betting she'll just hire more troops. And still get the mayor to replace the cops with her QBots."

"She?" said Stevens.

"Sure seems that way to me. I need something to be sure before I bring her here."

Gene taped some gauze over her shoulder. Cassie picked up her black top.

"You want something clean?" said Gene.

"No, I need this one more time. Gene, you play video games. Ever hear of one called 'Morph VOX'?"

"No." He reached over and opened the laptop. After a couple of seconds he said, "It's not a game. Voice scrambling software."

"Could you use that to make a phone call?"

"Sure. Route the output over IP. Make it next to impossible to trace."

"Yeah," said Cassie. "Could come from anywhere and be anyone."

Stevens said, "Is that the proof you need?"

"Maybe." She pulled the shirt on and picked up her gun and checked the magazine. The men watched her.

"I need the Tesla," she said.

Gene nodded.

"You want any backup?" said Stevens. "Want them arrested?"

She shoved the gun in the back of her waistband and said, "No. This is mine. Wait half an hour to release your guy. You take care of your obligations, I'll take care of mine."

CHAPTER 66

Cassie tucked the Tesla into a stand of trees in the woods behind Ann's house. She pulled the mask down, checked her Glock, and crept along the riverbank until she could see the back of Ann's house. Every light in the place was on, the house fairly glowing like a fairy-tale palace. She sat on a tree root and tapped her Bluetooth to call Gene.

"Yeah?" Stevens answered.

"Who—Jesus, I think I liked you better when I thought you were evil. I want to talk to Gene."

"Well, I'm answering this phone until we get the call that you're alive and driving away. Still think I should be there."

"This is my job. Something a cop can't do. Besides, it's hard to see you lumbering through the woods without stampeding wildlife."

"So you're in the woods now?"

"Yeah. I'm in the back of Ann's house, watching. She's sitting in her office, behind a big desk with her laptop on."

"Anybody else there?"

"Not that I can see. The place is huge, but all lit up and I don't see anything else moving."

"Give it ten minutes before you move. Then get in, grab Gurley, and bring her back here. We'll get her back and take her to Nashville."

"Yeah. Then explain to the feds that she's an obnoxiously aggressive real-estate agent? We still don't have any real evidence."

"Let me worry about that. You just do what I tell you and get yourself back here safe and—"

"Sure." Cassie snapped the phone shut.

She watched Ann yelling at the computer loud enough that she could hear screeches out here in the woods. Ann launched a final stream at the top of her lungs, punched a key, and stood up and marched out of the room. Even here, Cassie could hear the furious tack-tack-tack of Ann's heels. Ann reappeared in the kitchen, stepped through it, and disappeared into the house.

Cassie saw an opportunity and ran for the bushes fronting the new deck. She ducked as she ran and then wondered if there was any point in hiding. Anybody watching would see her anyway. She prayed there were no watchers or monitored cameras or . . .

She slipped under a railing onto the new deck construction and ducked under the plastic sheeting. She heard nothing and went in through the kitchen to the office.

Ann's desk was a wide, expensive, mahogany slab, clean except for the open laptop and a small sheet of paper with numbers and phrases. She took a picture of the page and the screen of the computer and cursed when her cell phone flashed.

She heard Ann's heels clicking across the tile, fast even for Ann. Cassie drew her gun and backed into a corner.

Ann stepped into the room and turned to Cassie like she'd known she was there all along. "Put that thing away. I knew that was you when I saw something flash. Sometimes I think you are the biggest, clumsiest, most predictable thing on God's green earth. And I've already called my security. They'll be here before you can pull that trigger, and you won't like them. Land sakes, child, what is that smell on you? Blood?"

"It came from retiring your security team. Right now, there's two flying toys of yours crashed in the woods and a bald man's body rotting beside them. The only one standing is telling the rest of your team to run because a giant is coming after them."

Ann paused with her mouth open. Then she said, "I don't know what you're talking about. But I do know that you are the so-called giant terrorizing Jericho. I figured out who you are."

"Yeah," said Cassie. "And I figured out who you are. My mentor is the one trying to kill me and destroy my family and my city."

Cassie edged to the desk until her left hand could reach the laptop. She snatched it away and pain shot through her shoulder. "This is mine. Going to keep all those financial windows open, see that this money doesn't make it to Jericho tomorrow."

Ann lunged across the desk and snatched up the sheet with the passwords.

"The computer's yours. This is mine. I can buy another computer. You—" She waved the sheet. "Can't do anything without this."

Cassie waved the gun and stepped toward Ann. "Gimme."

Ann stuffed the sheet in her mouth and started chewing. "Make me." Came out more like "ace che" but Cassie got the idea.

Ann swallowed. "God, I need a glass of merlot with that."

"So what? Are you going to read passwords from inside your stomach?"

"You think I'm stupid? There's a copy in my safe upstairs. I only copy these down when I need them. I can get into the safe. You can't."

Ann walked around the desk and joined Cassie.

"Look, you're going to find out my security team doesn't scare as easily as you think—even if you're telling the truth about some of them being dead and some scared. Some of them going to be here any minute."

Cassie said, "Lot of money from a real-estate empire."

"You know better. Every dime of drug money in this area flows through here. Drugs come up from Mexico in QBot trucks. Who's going to search a high-tech government contractor? Drop the drugs off at Fueltown, ship them to Jericho in furniture trucks." She sighed. "Like you, it started with my sister. I had to have more money than selling houses would bring. One thing led to another." She nodded at Cassie. "We're two peas in a pod."

"Jim Irvin?"

"Jim got tired of it. Hinted one too many times that he was going to stop. He wasn't real keen on the next step either."

"QBot policemen?"

Ann snorted and Cassie thought it sounded like her.

"Yeah. All those QBot policemen will have JPD logos, but they're going to be controlled by me. Us. Cassie, I still think I can use you. And I am a good Christian woman who is willing to let bygones be bygones with you."

"A good Christian woman who has her own sister killed."

Ann shrugged again. "You saw her. Nobody could trust her to keep her mouth shut. But I can forgive you for your betrayals."

"You sent people to burn down my family home and try to kill me and my niece."

"I am your friend, the only one who wants to put you back in the land of the powerful. But you've got to learn, in this world, everybody's got to be your friend or they've got to be dead."

Ann was still leaning on the desk. She smiled a big smile at Cassie as her hand slid under the middle of the desk.

"Which will it be, Cassie, dear? Fairy-tale castle or hell?"

"In between. Staying in the real world, where I can do some good. Don't want your fairy tale."

"Then go to hell." Ann pulled her hand out with a gun in it and fired fast at Cassie. Cassie dove for the door and felt the heat from the bullet as it went by her head. Ann fired again but Cassie was moving too fast.

Cassie smashed into a bookcase with her bad arm, the pain searing as she dropped the laptop and fell with the heavy bookcase crashing on top of her. Her good hand and the gun were trapped underneath, hidden in the space where the books had been.

Ann took her time walking over. She kicked the laptop away.

"Told you this was mine," she said. "I can recover. Too bad that you," she took aim at Cassie's head, "can't say the same."

Cassie fired through the case and Ann's head exploded and she went down.

Cassie wiggled out. Her left arm—and hand—were throbbing. She stood over Ann for a long time, looking down at the mess she had made of what she had thought she admired and envied.

She heard a car door slam and ran out the back.

CHAPTER 67

Cassie and Stevens sat across from each other at the picnic table in front of the Haunted Castle. The early summer sun made their faces shine and the breeze was blowing fresh-cut grass sweet.

"I talked to the Chief," said Stevens. "The charges against Ron are being dropped. The Red Rock owner came through and gave them a statement. They want you to bring the hatchet wrapping in when you get a chance."

"No problem."

Her hair was pulled back in a loose ponytail, tied with a little-girl ribbon with Disney princesses on it. She had on a soft, cotton sweater, turquoise, and white linen slacks. She leaned over at Stevens and her ponytail fell across her shoulder and she enjoyed the fresh shampoo smell her hair gave off today.

"Ann? The Enforcer?"

"Those deaths are being blamed on the Shadow Giant. Video outside of Gurley's house showed the Giant leaving."

"Hope they don't catch him," said Cassie.

"Yeah."

"QBots?" said Cassie.

"Cancelled when the money didn't show up. Speaking of which, you've still got the laptop with the connections to the accounts."

"And the passwords."

"Yeah. So what you going to do with it?"

"Don't know. Can't spend it on myself; it's not mine." She stretched, lazy in the sun. "Some use will turn up."

She yawned and apologized.

"I can't wake up. Feel like I need to sleep for a week."

"Want some coffee?"

"God, no. No more of those drugs. Clean living."

Stevens laughed. "Yeah."

"What I need is a nap. I've got a couple of hours before Belva and the rest of them get back. Got one errand I've got to run first, but I'm going to find someplace and get an hour's nap first."

"How far did they get before you turned them around?"

"Albuquerque."

"Be good to have them all back."

"Yes."

Stevens stood up. "C'mon. Let me show you what I called you down here for. May have a place for that nap of yours, too."

They went in past the artists' kiosks and the used-book store to a partitioned-off area in the back corner. There was a hand-painted sign by the door.

Saturn Rocket Services.

Cassie laughed. "You?"

Stevens said, "Maybe both of us. We both know another shit storm's coming. Don't know who or how, but when you kill a hundred cockroaches, two hundred more come out of the woodwork."

"Yeah."

"So, next time," said Stevens, "I don't want my hands tied by JPD rules. I took retirement and opened my own detective shop." He paused. "Raymond Chandler wrote some of the great early stories about detectives. Talked about a guy going down mean streets but keeping his innocence."

Cassie laughed. "You?" She thought a minute and said, "I

think Chandler got it wrong. It's not about innocence and fairy tale. It's about what you do after you're guilty."

Stevens said, "Room on the sign to add a rocket-ess."

"Good grammar. No, let me be informal, kind of help you when you need me sometimes. I've got my own job. And life."

He nodded. "Any way you want to do this." Paused and said, "You know, you asked me one time why I picked you. I told you it was because I owned you. Not true. I own a lot of people. Owned, past tense. But I saw you play one time, back when you were just a sophomore, playing against a girl two inches taller and twenty pounds heavier."

"Yeah. Glover. She was tough."

"Had you beat and outclassed every way possible. But every time she shoved you a foot, you shoved her two feet. You left that game with a bloody lip and a black eye." He stopped and looked at her face. "Same eye. But you left pointing up at a W on the scoreboard."

"I don't quit." Cassie paused, then smiled. "Even as an informal partner, there's a price."

"What?"

"Every morning, Saturn Rocket Services will do this." She folded her hands in a prayer and said, "What can I do with these hands, this heart, this body today?"

Stevens cocked his head. "That is the single dumbest thing I've ever heard. I think my intention is to have no fucking intention."

Cassie locked eyes with him and held it until he broke.

"All right. I'm not chanting any New Age prayers, but I'll know you're saying it."

"Fair enough. Now, can I borrow that beat-up couch of yours?"

"Sure."

"Wake me in an hour, OK? Got places to be."

"Sure."

Cassie snuggled down into the couch and grunted when something stabbed her back. She reached back and pulled her Glock out of the holster in the back of her slacks and set it next to her head. She was snoring before Stevens had a chance to move.

He looked at Cassie, sleeping little-girl pretty and helpless in her soft clothes, trusting him.

Little-girl pretty, with a gun in her hand.

"Child," he said softly. "I'm scared for you." Laughed a little. "Scared of you."

Two hours later, Gene rolled open the garage door to the lab and the Morrison minivan rolled into the opening. Cassie stood beside him, in her home, wearing her pink ACB tee shirt and holding Belva's shirt in her hand.

ABOUT THE AUTHOR

Michael Guillebeau is the author of *Josh Whoever,* which was named a Mystery Debut of the Month by *Library Journal* and was a finalist for the Silver Falchion Award for Best First Novel in Literary Suspense, and *A Study in Detail.* He has published more than twenty short stories, including three in *Ellery Queen's Mystery Magazine.* Mike splits his time between Huntsville, Alabama, and Panama City Beach, Florida. He is a member of the Mystery Writers of America and the Sisters in Crime Guppies. You can find Mike online at www.michaelguillebeau.com.